the wedding beat

devan sipher

NEW AMERICAN LIBRARY

NEW AMERICAN LIBRARY
Published by New American Library, a division of
Penguin Group (USA) Inc., 375 Hudson Street,
New York, New York 10014, USA
Penguin Group (Canada), 90 Eglinton Avenue East, Suite 700, Toronto,
Ontario M4P 2Y3, Canada (a division of Pearson Penguin Canada Inc.)
Penguin Books Ltd., 80 Strand, London WC2R 0RL, England
Penguin Ireland, 25 St. Stephen's Green, Dublin 2,
Ireland (a division of Penguin Books Ltd.)
Penguin Group (Australia), 250 Camberwell Road, Camberwell, Victoria 3124,
Australia (a division of Pearson Australia Group Pty. Ltd.)
Penguin Books India Pvt. Ltd., 11 Community Centre, Panchsheel Park,
New Delhi - 110 017, India
Penguin Group (NZ), 67 Apollo Drive, Rosedale, Auckland 0632,
New Zealand (a division of Pearson New Zealand Ltd.)
Penguin Books (South Africa) (Pty.) Ltd., 24 Sturdee Avenue,
Rosebank, Johannesburg 2196, South Africa

Penguin Books Ltd., Registered Offices:
80 Strand, London WC2R 0RL, England

First published by New American Library,
a division of Penguin Group (USA) Inc.

First Printing, April 2012
10 9 8 7 6 5 4 3 2 1

 REGISTERED TRADEMARK—MARCA REGISTRADA

LIBRARY OF CONGRESS CATALOGING-IN-PUBLICATION DATA:
Sipher, Devan.
    The wedding beat/Devan Sipher.
       p. cm.
    ISBN 978-0-451-23579-4
    1. Journalists—Fiction.   2. Man-woman relationships—Fiction.   I. Title.
    PS3619.I5763W43 2012
    813'.6—dc23   2011045426

Set in Bauer Bodoni
Designed by Ginger Legato

Printed in the United States of America

*To all the brides and grooms
who shared their stories—and inspired mine*

the wedding beat

Prologue

Help! I'm being held hostage at a black-tie wedding on New Year's Eve. Well, not so much a hostage as an indentured servant for a Pulitzer Prize–winning newspaper that cannot be named.

Fifty-seven minutes and counting, and the ceremony hasn't even started. The chamber quartet is playing "Endless Love" for the third time. Shoot me now.

I'm scribbling in my pad and trying to forget I'm a thirty-seven-year-old single guy alone on New Year's. No, not alone. Surrounded by married couples. The only single woman is the bride's grandmother, who is eighty-five and a humpback. And even she has a date.

I don't want to be here. I don't want to be writing about a wedding at the Angel Orensanz Foundation for the Arts, a nineteenth-century former synagogue on the Lower East Side, where uptown brides look for downtown panache. I want to be with Jill. I want to be kissing the back of her neck and wrapping my arms around her as we sway to the gentle beat of samba music at the Blue Iguana.

A bridesmaid is finally walking down the aisle. Slowly. I've never heard Pachelbel's *Canon* played so slowly. A flower girl floats by on a cloud of white taffeta. All big eyes and brown ringlets.

I see the bride stand in the amber glow of candlelight, and something inside me surrenders. I can't help thinking of all the brides that came before her, linked together by a white dress, a band of gold and a first kiss. It's a moment of transcendent hope.

And it makes me feel unbearably alone.

Chapter One

A Dead Fish at the Head Table and Other Celebration Snafus

"**D**id you know that Sarah Jessica Parker was married here?" Barbara babbled.

The party planner was trying to distract me. And with good reason. Sarah Jessica Parker never killed a koi. I glanced toward a golden-hued, imported fish floating listlessly in the bridal table's centerpiece.

"You know, Mimi and Sarah Jessica go to the same massage therapist," Barbara informed me, speaking reverently of both the bride and the trendsetting actress. "They have a very similar aesthetic."

The only aesthetic I could detect was unmitigated extravagance. Tuxedoed waiters were serving Dom Pérignon and beluga blini appetizers beneath hanging gardens of white hydrangeas, suspended from the vaulted ceiling of the Angel Orensanz. The sanctuary-turned–art and event space was decked out for the holiday nuptials with seven-foot silver candelabra and curtains of crystal beads surrounding twenty-five tables draped in shimmering white silk and French lace that matched the bride's gown. From the center of each table rose a cylindrical glass aquarium of iridescent koi swimming among submerged orchids.

Except for the bridal table, where the drowned flowers were not the only casualty.

"Get me the fish wrangler," Barbara barked into her headset. Her shapeless black suit was all shoulders and elbows as she shooed away Eddie Wong, the Annie Leibovitz of wedding photographers, who was snapping pictures of the kamikaze koi.

"Promise me you won't write about this in The Paper," Barbara implored, grasping hold of my arm as if it were a personal flotation device. "It would destroy the bride. She's a vegetarian."

I smiled as if I understood the connection. Bad choice. Smiling just encourages people to keep talking.

"Mimi wanted this day to be perfect. Just like her love for Mylo. You know, she would love him even if he was a ditchdigger."

But Mylo was not a ditchdigger. He was a partner in a real estate hedge fund that didn't like having its name in a newspaper. Or so I was told a half dozen times by their communications director.

"Mimi knew she was destined to be with Mylo from the night they met," Barbara continued. "They're like Romeo and Juliet. Without the suicide."

The couple's apothecary-free saga began last summer at a surprise birthday party on a 210-foot yacht anchored in Sag Harbor. The yacht was his. The surprise was hers. And the attraction was immediate. The party ended at about four in the morning, and she stayed on board—for the next six weeks. Then she moved into his Park Avenue duplex penthouse. That was the end of act one. Act two began when she found out there already was a Mrs. Mylo, who was giving up the honorific very reluctantly. There were tears. There was packing. And there were canceled reservations in St. Barts.

"Gavin." Barbara purred my name. "No one but you could capture the magic of their story. Are you staying for the midnight balloon drop?" She had already asked me six times. "There's going to be a virtual fireworks display designed by Stephano Spanetto."

I didn't care if it was designed by Steven Spielberg. The only fireworks I was interested in were the kind I experienced when I was with Jill, and my goal was to be by her side when the clock struck midnight. I had snagged a reservation at the Blue Iguana for eleven thirty in the hope I'd be done in time, and Jill had been a trouper about playing things by ear. The problem was that it was already after ten.

"I'll see," I answered evasively.

"But, Gavin, it's New Year's Eve."

Precisely. I didn't want to spend it watching real estate developers party like it was 2006. I was not going to let work be my only priority. Not this year. I was no longer the thirty-two-year-old who had landed a job at the number-one newspaper in the country. Five years had gone by in the blink of an eye, or, more accurately, in a state of sleep deprivation, since I was working more than eighty hours a week. Gray hairs were sneaking in among my sandy brown ones, and I had made a resolution that things were going to change. This was the year I was going to find someone smart and savvy. Someone with a quick wit, a kind heart and a great smile. Someone like Jill.

An advertising account executive with an unlikely predilection for Fellini films, she caught my attention the previous month during a 5k race in Central Park. I ran beside her for the last lap and made a point of letting her beat me. She was charmed. I was stoked. We'd squeezed in only a few dates since then, so spending New Year's together was a leap. Not for mankind. But the reporter in me prefers to look before I leap—and line up corroborating sources.

"The balloon drop is a symbolic representation of the bride's emotional journey on her wedding day," Barbara persisted without irony. "It's imperative that you see it."

Barbara had gone from fawning fan to fascist in training. I'd been at the Angel Orensanz for hours and had interviewed everyone but the restroom attendants. Though the wedding had been called for seven, it was well past eight when the Episcopal priest started the mysteriously delayed ceremony—"an act of God" according to Barbara. Translation: The bride had a wardrobe malfunction (solved by a strategically placed small diamond brooch that the bridegroom acquisitioned on a search-and-rescue mission at Bergdorf).

The cocktail "hour" was approaching the ninety-minute mark. I calculated that if I snuck out after the bridal dance, I'd have just enough time to pick up Jill and make our reservation, assuming the taxi gods were on my side.

But what if there really was something extraordinary about the balloon drop? What if the couple said or did something at midnight that exquisitely expressed the essence of their relationship?

As I checked my watch, I reminded myself of the half dozen prewedding interviews I'd already done with the bride and groom. I had a computer file with more than forty typed pages, or roughly ten thousand words of notes for a thousand-word piece. But there was always more I could do, and I'm someone who perpetually fears I'm going to miss something essential.

"Mimi will be so disappointed if you're not here," Barbara

stage-whispered as the couple finally made their grand entrance. They swept into the room, her slender mermaid silhouette preceding his wide-shouldered frame snugly buttoned into a narrow-lapelled tux. The metallic silver color of his tie matched the glittering hairpins in her updo. As they made their way through the crowd, they smiled and waved and clasped and kissed. And, yes, they glowed.

"You would never guess what she's been through." Barbara sighed before scurrying away toward an unshaved man in shirtsleeves carrying a fish net. And a bucket.

Mimi was hardly the tragic heroine Barbara intimated, but at fourteen she was diagnosed with scoliosis and spent three years wearing a back brace. During one of our conversations, she showed me a picture of herself as a teenager with a freakish-looking contraption of metal rods covering half her body. Her sister described her as an outgoing, athletic young girl whose world changed overnight. At an unforgivingly status-conscious high school, she was taunted daily by her former tennis teammates about her inevitable weight gain and frumpy, loose-fitting outfits. Relegated to radioactive status at cotillions, she swore one day she would be able to stand tall in a strapless dress. And there she was, less than a decade later, wrapped in ethereal beaded lace.

Something in me melted. No, she didn't want to find a cure for cancer or make the world a better place for an endangered owl species. She just wanted to be pretty. And have good posture. And she was. And she did. She was so proud of how she looked and how he looked at her. You could see how much he wanted her beside him. How lonely his right arm looked without her encircled by it. In that moment, I truly believed she would have loved him even if he were a ditchdigger. Hell, even if he were a newspaper columnist.

When they reached the dance floor, the twelve-piece swing band launched into a lush arrangement of Justin Timberlake's "SexyBack," and my eyes misted. Then I pulled out my cell phone to call Jill.

"I'm on my way," I said, eager to see where the evening could lead us.

"Gavin, I'm not feeling great," Jill said weakly, sounding farther away than a mile uptown. "I ran a half marathon this morning, and it wiped me out."

I didn't ask why she ran a half marathon on New Year's Eve, because that would have sounded judgmental. But it had crossed my mind more than once that Jill was a little obsessed with the whole marathon thing. I enjoyed the runner's high, but there's something a bit too punishing about a twenty-six-mile race. However, I liked that she was passionate and feisty. And who was I kidding? I also liked what great shape she was in.

"I'm sorry. If you prefer, we could stay in tonight." I was already picturing a quiet evening in her cozy West Village walk-up, with just the two of us and a bottle of champagne. Truth be told, I've never been a fan of fancy New Year's celebrations. Too many people too desperate to be happy.

"I don't want to ruin your holiday," she said. Red warning signs flashed in my brain. But I ignored them.

"I can pick up something from that Italian place you like," I offered.

"You're at a great party. Why would you want to leave?"

"Because I'd prefer to be with you," I said, hoping I sounded charming and not needy. "How about sushi?" No response. "I can be at your place in a half hour."

"That's not a good idea." Sirens blared inside my head. "I have company," she stated, sounding vaguely apologetic.

I swallowed hard. Be cool, I told myself. Be strong. Be confident.

"Does this mean you don't want to date anymore?" I asked.

NOOOOOOOOOOOOO!!!! How could I have said that? This is why I'm a writer. This is why I write words down on paper. So I can edit myself. So I don't say the first idiotic thing that pops into my head.

There was silence. Painful, awkward silence. And there was nothing I could do but wait it out as the Don Diamond Orchestra segued into a disco version of "Can't Buy Me Love."

"It's nothing personal," Jill finally said before clicking off.

Giddy couples glided by me on their way to the dance floor. A waiter passed out color-coordinated noisemakers and party hats.

Barbara rushed by. "Jonathan Adler designed the hats and signed each one. They're collectibles. Are you staying for the balloon drop? Tell me you're staying."

"Sure," I said dully as a drunk groomsman honked on a designer party favor, welcoming the new year.

Chapter Two

Never Have Parents

"We're concerned about your ex-wife," said my father. It was the first thing he said when he phoned me at eight a.m. the next morning, proving that it was never too early for delusional behavior.

"I don't have an ex-wife," I said.

"But you may one day," he said.

I had bolted out of my sofa bed, thinking it was my editor calling, so I was relieved it was just my father wishing me a happy New Year. Or at least I assumed that was why Saul Greene was calling his firstborn. Good tidings and random assaults were often interchangeable in my family.

"You need to be prepared for the worst-case scenario," my father declared.

"We went to an estate-planning seminar," my mother chimed in after picking up another line at their Floridian compound in Boca Raton, on the wrong side of the interstate. Their new hobby was obsessing about their wills. From what I could tell, the purpose was to find new and unusual ways to torment my younger brother and me.

"Gavin, do you know the divorce rate in New York?" my mother asked before proceeding to tell me it was very high.

"We have to think about the future," my father said. "We have to think about our grandchildren." Except they didn't have any, which was a frequent subject of discussion.

"What if she remarries?" my mother said.

"Who?" I asked groggily.

"Your ex-wife!" she cried out.

"You're jumping to conclusions, Lorraine," my father chastised, becoming the voice of reason on the topic of my future ex-spouse. "We don't know that she'll remarry. Sometimes couples get back together. Look at Elizabeth Taylor and Richard Burton."

"That's different!" my mother protested. "She converted for him."

"She converted for Eddie Fisher!"

"Didn't she convert back?"

I put down the phone and reached for a box of Raisin Bran, then decided it was more of a Frosted Flakes day. There was an open bottle of Absolut vodka on the cluttered kitchen counter. I remembered taking it out when I got home from the wedding, intending to drink myself into oblivion. But I don't really like the taste of straight vodka. I had looked in the fridge for something to mix with it, but there was only an empty jug of milk, three bottles of Sam Adams, and a couple desiccated chili peppers. The freezer was better stocked, and I had taken out a bag of frozen berries to make myself a vodka slush. But then I concluded that drinking a fruity frozen drink by myself on New Year's was not the way to improve my self-image.

Looking at the bottle in the morning, I thought again about taking a swig. I would never be the next Ernest Hemingway if my tastes ran to berry coladas. Of course, in Hemingway's journalist days, he wrote about the Spanish Civil War, not society weddings.

Does the man make the beat or the beat make the man? I put the vodka back in the freezer alongside the berries and several cartons of Ben & Jerry's, then sat down in my office/dining nook, box of Frosted reinforcement in hand. Eyeing the stack of reporter's notebooks by my laptop, I found myself dreading the long hours of writing about Mimi and Mylo that were awaiting me. The story was due in a little more than twenty-four hours, since the holiday had fallen on a Monday rather than on a weekend. If I started immediately, there was a small chance I'd finish without having to stay up all night. I picked up the phone. My mother's high-pitched voice was unmistakably audible before the handset reached my ear.

"What if your ex-wife has children with her second husband? Do you want them to inherit your money?" My mother missed her calling. She should have been working for the IRS. "Your life will be over before you know it. And all you can do is hope that your children will succeed where you failed. But you don't have any children. And it just kills me, thinking of you dead and your ex-wife off spending your money on children that aren't even related to you. Do you see why I worry so?"

I knew better than to respond. Another one of my resolutions was minimizing altercations with my parents. Emotionally drained, I just said, "Happy New Year." The small nicety threw my mother off balance. She paused, possibly to consider what passes for holiday interaction in less colorful families.

"Were you with Janice last night?" my mother asked.

"Who's Janice?" I replied before considering whether I wanted to know.

"The girl you're dating," my father said. By my father's definition, a girl was any unmarried woman under eighty.

"Her name is Jill," I said, choking on her name as a corn flake went down the wrong pipe. I had forgotten that my parents had met her briefly while they were in town for a weekend in December. It was a drive-by introduction. Literally. I was putting them in a taxi to go see a matinee of *Mamma Mia!* when Jill showed up early for a running date.

"She said her name was Janice," my father insisted.

"Why would she say it was Janice when it's Jill?" I said through clenched teeth.

"Maybe her sister's name is Janice," my mother offered unhelpfully.

"Her name is Jill!"

"Does her family call her Janice?" my dad persisted.

"HER NAME IS JILL! ONLY JILL!"

I do not want to yell at my parents. I do not want to yell at my parents. I repeated the words in my mind like Bart Simpson scrawling on a chalkboard.

"Bernie's in the hospital," my mother announced while I was still stabilizing my heart rate. Bernie Perlstein was my grandmother's husband. Her fourth, but who was counting? I was dizzy from the abrupt change in topics. A conversation with my parents was like living out a Dada manifesto.

I tried to remember how recently I had spoken with Bernie. A World War II veteran and former airline pilot, he was a proud but generous man and devoted to my grandmother. He'd seemed fine at Thanksgiving, but I recalled that he was being treated for a blood-protein problem.

"He had an accident," my father said nonchalantly. My father never said anything nonchalantly. My parents don't do understated. This was not about blood proteins. Something was terribly wrong.

"I told Grandma not to let him drive," my mother said, hinting at the potential peril I risked whenever I ignored her advice.

"Was Grandma with him?" I asked as a hundred other questions came to mind. My chest constricted, imagining my grandmother amid broken glass and twisted metal. She was eighty-two and still ran three miles every morning. (She wore bikinis until she was eighty.) She was dauntless and irrepressible—and the only person in the world who loved me unconditionally.

"They should be releasing her from the hospital soon," my father said.

"Don't worry," my mother fluttered. "The car is fine."

Chapter Three

Let Dead Fish Lie

*M*imi Martin is not crying over popped balloons.

Ugh. I backspaced and tried again. I was still on the first line of my column after hours of typing and deleting but mostly worrying about my grandmother, whom I hadn't been able to reach despite numerous attempts. I sat hunched over my laptop, which was going to do wonders for my posture if I was lucky enough to also make it to eighty-two.

Tears weren't the only thing falling at Mimi Martin's wedding on New Year's Eve.

Worse.

When Mimi Martin met Mylo Nikolaidis on his private yacht, she thought he was a catch. And after their wedding last week, there was one less fish in the sea.

Barbara's stricken face flashed before me.

My brain refused to function. On a good day, my writing process was more pain than pleasure. This was not a good day.

Thomas Mann once said, "A writer is somebody for whom writing is more difficult than it is for other people." I tried not to think about Thomas Mann. I tried not to think about Jill. I wanted to call her, but I knew that I shouldn't. Couldn't. Shouldn't.

So I called Hope instead. Hope was my in-case-of-emergency person, and this was an emotional emergency. But her voice mail was full. Probably because I had been leaving messages all day. I returned to staring at my computer screen.

Inadequate.

Not just my lede paragraph. My life. Who was I to expound on marriage? I was a fraud. It was only a matter of time before people figured it out. There would be a write-in campaign from outraged readers. My editor would purge my columns from the database. And who was going to want to go out with an unemployed journalist who lived in a studio apartment and had a fourteen-inch neck? My cell phone rang.

"Are you spiraling?" asked my brother, Gary.

"No," I lied.

"Well, stop," he said, then laughed. I had e-mailed him after my parents' news flash and also detailed my New Year's debacle. Deferring to the three-hour time difference in Los Angeles, I had refrained from calling, but it turned out that my father had no such hesitation. Gary's girlfriend was less than thrilled.

"I kept asking him, 'What time is it, Dad?'" Gary said. "'What time do you think it is in LA?' He said, 'Why are you asking me about the time? Do you need a new clock?'"

Gary and I had a habit of indulging each other's rants about our parents' infractions, though we'd usually conclude the other was overreacting.

"They called me too," I pointed out.

Gary didn't appreciate my lack of sympathy. "Last week I

listened to you carry on for an hour after Mom suggested you get a mail-order bride."

I changed the topic. "I talked to a nurse on Grandma's floor at Delray Medical Center. She said she'd have a doctor get back to me."

"Way ahead of you, Reporter Boy," Gary said. Only two years younger and five inches taller, he liked to tweak my ego whenever possible. "I e-mailed the ER doctor who admitted her. He said they only kept her overnight for observation." I was relieved to hear that. "Also found out that Bernie is in the ICU."

So did I, I almost responded, momentarily feeling more competitive than compassionate.

"So can you go down to Florida?" he asked, just casually enough to convince me it was the main reason for his call.

"I'm on deadline," I said. My first instinct had been to go to Florida immediately. I had already checked out airfares, but I wasn't about to tell Gary that. When it came to family obligations, he was very generous with volunteering my time.

"Grandma shouldn't be alone," he said, knowing full well that she wasn't, since our parents lived less than a half hour away. Close enough to torment her in good times and assist in bad. "You know how much it would mean to her to have one of us there." Yes, I did, and it was clear which one of us he had in mind. "It seems the least we can do."

"No, it's the least *you* can do," I shot back, feeling guilty I wasn't already on a plane but knowing there was little I could do there.

"Leslie and I have been up since six. We tracked down this Dr. Stein, who, by the way, is one of more than a dozen Dr. Steins in Delray Beach. And Leslie already sent a basket of brownies and a bouquet of flowers, both of which she signed your name to."

Leslie was his latest in a long string of live-in girlfriends, and her effort was more predictable than praiseworthy. They had been together about six months, which was usually when his girlfriends began thinking he was interested in a long-term commitment. Unlike me, he never hesitated about opening his heart, his wallet, and his home. He just refused to close off the option of moving on if someone better came along. My parents had given up on him ever marrying. "Maybe he'll get one of his girlfriends pregnant by mistake," my mother had said to me. "A mother can only hope."

"Leslie was sorry to hear about Jill," Gary said in a way that seemed as much about flattering Leslie as consoling me.

"I'm thinking of calling her," I said.

"Leslie?"

"Jill!"

"Don't," he snapped. There was often a hint of coldness beneath Gary's concern. Something his girlfriends inevitably learned too late. "You got dumped on New Year's, and that sucks. But there's no point in dwelling on it."

I wasn't dwelling. I was regretting. Not just the evening but everything I had hoped would happen afterward.

"You romanticize things too much," Gary said. "You keep looking for the one woman who's going to rock your world, and she doesn't exist."

But she did exist. In my head. She was smart. Extraordinarily smart. I imagined she went to Harvard (where I was only wait-listed). And she was curious about the world. Not just curious. Passionate and adventurous. She had backpacked through South America. Or taught English in Estonia. Or she was the kind of person who would consider doing so. What was so wrong with wanting Jill to be that person?

"You need to stop searching for a soul mate and just find a date," Gary said. "Is Hope still single?" he asked with the subtlety of a B-1 Bomber.

Gary and Hope had gone out one time, five years back. Ever since, he'd been trying to convince me to date her. I suspected it was to score one for the team.

"We're friends," I said for the umpteenth time. "Very good friends."

"Very good place to start a relationship. You're like Patrick Dempsey in *Made of Honor*. You're going to figure out you want her when it's too late." Conversations with Gary inevitably included movie references. Sometimes classics like *Casablanca*, but usually something of a more dubious vintage that his PR firm was promoting. "I can feel your sperm dying inside of you, one at a time," he said, quoting from the cinematic gem about a male bridesmaid.

Fortunately, my call waiting beeped. It was Hope.

"Ask her out," Gary said.

"I don't want to ask her out."

"You have nothing to lose but your bar privileges," he said. "*Eight Men Out*. Great flick."

I swapped calls.

"I'm going to end up spending the rest of my life alone," said Hope.

She was stealing my opening line. But empathy got the better of me.

"What happened to Number Two?" I asked. Hope had stopped referring to the men she dated by name. Instead she assigned them leader-board rankings. It was to help her keep from getting emotionally attached to them. It wasn't really working. She yearned to date with reckless abandon, but Hope's idea of recklessness was eating a chocolate cupcake before dinner. The perennial number one on her list was Conrad Eberhart III, her once and future ex-boyfriend with whom she compared every other man she met. Number two at the moment was a Japanese chef from Seattle.

"Number Two has been eighty-sixed," she said. His name was Sebastian. They met in October at St. Vincent's emergency room when she stitched his thumb back together after an unfortunate *Iron Chef* episode that won't be airing any time soon. As she was suturing the wound, he asked if a patient had ever kissed her. Then he did. She had been to Seattle every other weekend since then, but he had made the cross-country trip for the holiday.

"He broke my bed," she said. "Which sounds much more fun than it was."

"Still seems like you had a better night than I did," I said.

"That was early. Then we went to my chief of staff's annual bash." A deadly affair I had been coerced to attend the previous year. Dr. Aldridge lived in a large, overstuffed apartment on Park Avenue with his wife and children (also large and overstuffed). The evening's entertainment consisted of ER doctors trying to outdrink the surgeons, while the radiologists and anesthesiologists compared malpractice rates, and the psychiatrists smoked compulsively. "I had warned him it would be boring," Hope said defensively. "He said he would amuse himself. I guess he did, because at midnight I couldn't find him. Do you know what it's like to be in a room full of drunk couples and you're the only one not being kissed?"

She was describing my life. I flashed back on the cascade of silver and black balloons the night before. I had focused on the balloons to avert my gaze from the lithe women in low-cut gowns, welcoming the open mouths of strong-jawed men. Barbara had pecked me on the cheek, which only made me feel worse.

I shook free of the memory to realize Hope was near the end of her story. "I finally found Number Two in the kitchen, with his tongue down the caterer's throat."

"What did he say?"

"He asked if we could bring her back to my apartment." I could hear Hope munching on something. "You have to stop me before I OD on chocolate," she said.

"Stop eating chocolate," I commanded.

"Telling me doesn't do any good. I have to be physically restrained. And it would help if you ply me with nonfat meringue cookies that we can pick up at Trader Joe's on the way to the open house." I had completely forgotten she had invited me to a party.

"I can't go. I'm working."

"If you're working, why did you call me seventeen times?" She sounded displeased I had commandeered her voice mail.

"In between calls I was working," I said unconvincingly.

"If you come to my aid, you will be rewarded with good karma, and your column will get done sooner." I was usually susceptible to such logic, but it was going to take a lot more than karma to get this piece done in the number of hours remaining.

"It's a holiday," Hope reminded me.

"I work on holidays. I work on weekends. Which is why I have no social life and I'm going to spend the rest of my life alone." There. I had said it. Hope wasn't the only one suffering. It had been almost three years since I had sustained a relationship for more than a month. Since Laurel. I wasn't going to think about Laurel. The rule was that I never thought about Laurel.

Hope tried to say something comforting. But I didn't want to be comforted. I wanted to be in love.

"Forty-eight hours ago you were worried you were making a mistake going out with Jill on New Year's. You said she was superficial and you had almost nothing in common but running."

If I didn't want to be comforted, I sure as hell didn't want to be logical. "What if she was the best I'm going to find? I'm an almost-forty-year-old guy who lives in a studio apartment and has a—"

"Are you going to start in about your neck size again?"

"I have a small neck," I said, somewhat wounded.

"Women don't go around looking at guys' necks. It's just not something we do. If we're going to look at something, we'll look at their pecs, and you have very nice pecs. Okay?"

I was rather proud of my pecs. And my abs. At an age when my friends were getting love handles, I had developed a six-pack. Sometimes even an eight-pack, as long as I didn't inhale.

"Gavin, I don't want to go to this party by myself," Hope said softly. "I had a really awful night. Please don't make me go alone."

I had come to realize that being alone isn't just a feeling. It's a scarlet letter. It's the first thing other people see. No matter what else you've accomplished, it brands you as a failure in their eyes—and, worse, in your own.

"I'll meet you there at five," I said, "but I can only stay an hour." I hung up and started typing again.

When it came to love, Mimi Martin thought she had missed the boat.

Last summer, she was on the cusp of thirty and self-consciously solo, when she found herself running late to a friend's birthday party aboard the Venus de Mylo. *Tripping on the gangway, she was afraid her entrance was about to make the wrong kind of splash. But a handsome stranger helped her regain her balance just in time.*

With his arm around her waist, Mylo Nikolaidis said, "It's a good thing we have life preservers on board."

"Is that what they call you?" she asked.

It was a start. Sometimes that's all you need.

Chapter Four

What a Fool Believes

I regretted being at the party before I even arrived.

I barely got past the front door of the Chelsea building. It was one of those new luxury constructions crammed into a narrow lot between two stodgy, prewar edifices. The gleaming glass facade seemed to scream out, "Don't hate me because I'm beautiful. Hate yourself because you can't afford me."

The penthouse apartment wasn't the largest I'd ever seen, and, topping only a seven-story building, it wasn't the loftiest. But it might have been the most crowded. I had anticipated a low-key gathering of a dozen or so physicians, jazz music and white wine. Instead, it was rum punch and kamikaze shots with nearly two hundred inebriated people wedged between the transparent walls and teetering amid the retro sixties furniture and shag rugs. Loud talk and louder music predominated. Mostly eighties tunes, for some reason. Lots of Michael Jackson, Cyndi Lauper and Spandau Ballet. The fact that I recognized

Spandau Ballet songs depressed me immeasurably. I looked for Hope, but couldn't spot her in the density of revelers.

What happened to spending New Year's Day in bed or hung-over or both? There was something desperate in the air. As if everyone there was trying to make up for missed opportunities the night before.

A blowsy blonde careened into me, eyeing me like prime beef. "What kind of medicine do you practice?" she screeched directly into my ear canal. It was the third time I'd been asked. Not everyone in the room was a doctor. Some were there to meet doctors. I burrowed deeper into the throng, just wanting to find Hope and get out.

But she was nowhere in sight, and I was trapped. To my right, a dermatologically challenged cardiologist was regaling a pediatrician with tales of his surgical prowess. To my left, the party's host seemed to be examining the tonsils of a buxom ophthalmologist. I unsuccessfully tried to squeeze around them, brushing against the backside of the eye doctor. She gave me a nasty look, and the host shot me a nastier one. I could feel the space around me contracting, and I was only moments away from becoming party roadkill.

That's when I saw her. Not Hope. A young Sandra Bullock with a tangle of loose brown curls obscuring her eyes but not her wide cheekbones and glossy, plum-colored lips. I could see only her face through the crowd, but that was enough. She was leaning back against a bedroom doorway, and when she smiled, she seemed to be channeling deep reservoirs of joy. I realized I was staring and quickly looked away. When I looked back, I saw she was talking to a thick-necked, young blond guy with arms the size of my thighs.

I pumped up my pecs. But my five-foot-nine swimmer's build was no match for a six-foot-three Matthew McConaughey in training. Especially one who probably had an "MD" after his name. I had every reason to turn my attention elsewhere, but there was something irresistible about the way she sipped the fluorescent-colored punch from her nearly empty glass. She tilted toward the McConaughey wannabe, and I strained to hear her voice. She was only a few yards away, but it was bumper-to-bumper people in between.

Then a half dozen rowdy partygoers emerged from the kitchen, unsettling the tectonic balance of the room. As the sea of bodies shifted, I edged forward six inches, but then I found myself being inexorably pulled in the opposite direction. Like an undertow, the more I fought it, the farther away I drifted. Until I was pushed up against the sliding glass door leading to the rooftop terrace, and she had disappeared into the bedroom, as had the buff blond twentysomething.

"Do you work at St. Luke's?" asked a flush-faced man jammed against my left side. "I think I recognize you from my gastroenterology residency."

In fact, I had gone to medical school once upon a lifetime, but I hadn't made it to residency. I had attended Columbia, which is where I met Hope. But after three semesters, I took a leave of absence for a year. Then a year became two. I decided that if you leave a door open for too long, you start to feel a draft. So I officially disenrolled. More than a decade later, my Jewish parents were still recovering.

I told the GI guy what I did for a living, but it was his wife, pressed against his other side, who responded. "Oh, my God, I love your articles!" she squealed with delight. "Can I take your picture?"

I squirmed as she wrested her camera phone out of her purse. It was an odd perk of my job that strangers sometimes wanted my picture or autograph.

"You're so cute!" she said. "You look just like James Franco. I bet you get that a lot." I had to admit I'd heard it once or twice.

"But older," said her husband.

"My brother's getting married in two weeks," she said, "and he would be perfect for your column." The trouble with receiving adulation was the inevitable request to give something in return.

"It's a great story," she said, which was what people always said before proceeding to tell me a really bad story. "You see, my brother goes to the Laundromat every Monday night. Like clockwork. But one week, and only one week, mind you, he went on a *Tuesday* night and—"

I cut her off. "I'm sorry. I already have my assignments for the rest of the month, but I hope your brother has a great wedding."

"She took your friggin' picture," said her husband. "The least you can do is listen to her stupid story."

Did James Franco have this problem?

I was spared further interaction with the couple when a husky man backed into the small pocket of space between us. There were bodies smashed against me from all sides, and I was conscious of the increasing moistness under my arms and across my brow. There was still no sign of Hope, so I pulled open the sliding door and escaped into the crisp winter air.

Seven floors were not enough to have an unobstructed city view, but a pink and purple, Disney-colored sunset was visible between the buildings. It felt good to have some breathing room. I stepped over to the railing and looked down.

"Did you bring a bungee cord?" a female voice asked.

I turned around. And there she was. The girl with the brown curls.

"It would be a much faster exit than fighting a way back to

the front door," she said with a dimpled smile. She had a heart-shaped face and tiny laugh lines in the corners of her chocolate brown eyes, suggesting both merriment and age appropriateness. She looked to be around thirty and much more petite than she had seemed from a distance, only about five foot three in her suede boots. She was wearing snug-fitting jeans and a cream-colored cashmere sweater with a V-neck that provided a modest glimpse of her surprisingly robust cleavage.

"Left my bungee at home," I said, wondering if I could have come up with something lamer to say. It turned out I could. "Are you into bungee jumping?" I asked.

"Never done it," she said. "I'm afraid of heights." I noticed she was pressed against the glass wall, holding the banister of a white spiral staircase beside her.

"Good thing you're not standing on an open terrace."

"I like to challenge myself." She took a swallow from a bottle of Corona she was now nursing. "Just don't ask me to stand next to the ledge." She smiled again, and I wanted to live inside her smile.

"I'm Gavin," I remembered to say.

"Melinda."

"I've never met a Melinda before." Yet something about her seemed familiar. "So what kind of medicine do you practice?"

She laughed. "The closest I got to medical school was walking by the campus once at Harvard." The word "Harvard" bounced around my head like a loose pinball. "I'm a journalist. Well, travel writer. If that's a real job. I travel to exotic places and pretend it's work. Or I used to. Until last year. Now I'm working on a book." Her words tumbled out at an impetuous velocity. "What I really want to be is a photojournalist. But I'm too short. Or too shy. Not that I'm shy. But photojournalists need pretty sharp elbows."

"I think you have excellent elbows," I said.

Her dimples made a reappearance. I noticed they were slightly asymmetrical, which somehow made her even more appealing.

"Is that your professional medical opinion?" she teased.

"I'm not a doctor."

"I'm so sorry," she quickly said. "I think it's great that more men are going into nursing."

I had gone from pigeonholer to pigeonholee. But before I could correct the situation, a certain blond freak of nature poked his tree trunk–like neck out of the bedroom door.

"There you are," the McConinator boomed while flexing his trapezius muscles. He bounded toward us despite my best don't-mess-with-a-trained-reporter scowl. "I almost lost an arm scoring these," he said, holding up two Coronas in his oversized paw.

Melinda held up her own. "Sorry. Already snagged one." She turned to me. "Do you want a beer?"

There was a long, awkward pause before I said, "Sure," and an even longer one before he handed me a bottle. We eyed each other suspiciously, standing our ground, shoulder to solar plexus.

Melinda kick-started a conversation. "So, Gavin, how did you decide to become a nurse?"

"I didn't," I started to say.

"I know exactly what you mean, dude," he said, interrupting me. "I don't feel I decided to become an orthopedic surgeon. It's just something I was compelled to do. I think it's a calling. Like being an artist, and it's an incredible responsibility. To hold someone's broken bones in your hands and know you have the ability to mend them." There was no way I could compete with a sensitive surgeon in a size thirteen shoe.

"That's odd," Melinda said. "I've always thought of surgeons as being more technicians than artists." The McConatron flinched.

"It's cold out here," he said.

"Maybe you should go inside and warm up," she said with a sympathetic smile, not at all the same as her dazzling one. It seemed to knock the wind out of his surgical scrubs. He saluted me with his Corona and retreated indoors. It was like slaying Goliath. With someone else's arrows.

"Some people just don't take a hint," Melinda said, furrowing her brow. She wasn't relishing the conquest as much as I was. A pained expression crossed her face as she nibbled on a fingernail. She turned away from me, and I wondered if I was also supposed to be taking a hint.

"What do you think's up there?" She was pointing to the top of the spiral staircase, not far above our heads.

"The roof," I offered unhelpfully.

"What do you think's *on* the roof?" She was already heading up the narrow steel steps, and I was right behind her.

"My guess would be air ducts, a water tank and maybe a satellite dish," I said, just trying to keep the conversation going while hustling up the last stairs.

"Your guess would be wrong," she said softly.

A wooden boardwalk meandered through waist-high, straw-colored grass. Small lanterns dotted the landscape, like fireflies suspended in the darkening sky. We drifted along the winding path until reaching a cul-de-sac around a shallow, pond-shaped whirlpool with steam rising like mist from its rippling surface. I felt like Heathcliff on the moors.

With little but vapor between us, we started circling the pool. Her long curls danced in the light wind, backlit by the city skyscape. I needed to say something. Anything. "So, where did you last travel?"

"I lived for six months in Katmandu." She could have said Kansas City and I would still have been mesmerized. But she didn't say Kansas City. "I volunteered at a girls' orphanage while working as a stringer for Lonely Planet. Then spent a month teaching English in a rural village and writing freelance articles about the cultural impact of the adventure-travel industry."

She made me feel deficient as a journalist—and a human.

"I might be the only person who ever went to Nepal without going mountain climbing," she said. "The vertigo thing is a drag."

"You did pretty well getting up here," I said, moving closer to her as we continued our slow orbit of the burbling water.

"Eleanor Roosevelt said to do one thing every day that scares you," she said, "but one flight on a staircase with handrails is about as much hiking as I do at high elevations." Unless I was imagining things, she seemed to be moving closer to me as well. "Even at lower altitudes I can get myself in trouble. I remember being at the edge of a Himalayan lake at sunset with the fog rolling in through the banyan trees. I must have taken a hundred pictures and lost track of time. The trail seemed to vanish in the darkness. I was convinced I was never going to find my way back to civilization."

"You weren't traveling by yourself, were you?"

"That's what my grandfather asked when I told him." *Ouch.* "I adore my grandfather," she added.

"It's impressive for a woman to go to those places alone." I hoped I didn't sound like a misogynist as well as an octogenarian.

"It's insane," she said. "I was terrified, but I'm terrified just getting out of bed in the morning. I'm not joking. I used to have these dreams when I was a kid that a plane was going to come crashing through my window. This was way before nine-eleven, so it was just me being morbid. Oh, God. Now you're going to think I'm one of those neurotic women you meet at parties in New York."

"I don't think you're neurotic."

She bestowed another smile. It was the perfect opportunity to say something devastatingly clever. Instead, I said, "I'm not a nurse."

"Let me guess," she said, stopping and turning to me with an impish look. "You're a magician."

"I am," I said, matching her flirtatious tone while still racking my brain for a clever remark. It was much easier at my computer. I considered going downstairs and texting her.

"What's your favorite magic trick?" she asked.

"Making a beautiful woman feel like she's bungee jumping while she's standing still." I was still figuring out what I meant when I noticed she was blushing, which I took as a good sign.

"Did you go to magician school to learn that?"

"I guess you could say that," I said, leaning toward her. "I spent two years in grad school, which made thirty thousand dollars of my savings magically disappear." She was close enough for me to kiss her.

"I'm starting a master's program in writing at NYU to help with my book. So I'll see your thirty and raise you ten." Before I could up the ante, a lanky guy in a leather coat appeared behind her and slipped his arms around her waist.

"Hey, sexy," he cooed.

She lit up as she embraced him enthusiastically. And extendedly. I metamorphosed into a pillar of chopped liver. After what felt like the longest fifteen seconds of my life, I loudly cleared my throat.

"Gavin," she said, disentangling herself. "This is Jamie." He nodded in my direction, though he might have just been flipping his dark, wavy hair. "Jamie's roommate knows someone who works with the guy throwing the party. We're interlopers."

Well, *he* certainly was. And he seemed to be in a hurry to get to the next stop on their party hop. The walkway wasn't wide enough for all three of us, so I was awkwardly shadowing them as we retraced our steps. He whispered something in her ear, and she briefly giggled. His skin was pale and pockmarked, and he was only a couple inches taller than me. I wasn't intimidated.

"We met at a Vishnu shrine in Katmandu," Melinda said, "and Jamie gave me a ride on his motorbike to the Bandipur hills." Maybe I was a little intimidated. "We've been pals ever since." Not lovers. Pals. But if they were pals, why was his hand still glued to her waist?

He leaned into her. Again with the whispering. "It wasn't Bandipur," she laughed. "It was Gorkha."

I had very little to offer in the way of romantic memories of Nepal. I needed to switch subjects fast.

"What's your book about?" I asked.

"Nepal," she said. I wanted to shoot myself. "It's not going as well as I want. Someone once said a writer is a person for whom writing is more difficult than it is for other people."

"It was Thomas Mann," I said, convinced I had found my soul mate.

Her eyes widened and she seemed to look at me with new appreciation. "The problem is, I want the book to be about more than just my experiences. I want it to be about what it means to travel someplace as a person, both internally and externally."

We had arrived back at the staircase, and Jamie headed down first. I still couldn't figure out whether they were a couple. His willingness to leave her alone with me suggested supreme confidence—or disinterest.

"You may not know this," Melinda said, "but the word 'travel' comes from the word 'travail.' And 'travail' comes from the Latin word 'tripalium,' which, surprisingly, is the name of a three-pronged instrument of torture."

Speaking of torture, Jamie rapped impatiently on the metal banister at the bottom of the stairs. Melinda seemed reluctant to end our conversation, yet she moved toward the lip of the roof. The terrace was beneath us, and beyond that a patchwork of illuminated windows and gray slivers of the Hudson River.

"So travel," she continued, "was initially conceived of as a painful and arduous experience."

"And that was before Homeland Security," I quipped, wanting to make a move and finding it hard to believe anything could be more painful or arduous.

She laughed as she tentatively took hold of the banisters. She was trembling. "Going down's the hard part."

"Turn around," I said impulsively, and she did, gripping the handrails tightly. "Keep your eyes on me." She did that as well, lifting her chin until it was parallel to my own. I held her gaze as she haltingly descended one step. Then another. I lowered myself in tandem, stair by stair, synchronizing my movement. Even my breath.

"Don't look down," I kept saying, as if I'd done this a hundred times. Her hand grazed mine, and my heart stopped. Or it felt like it did. It felt like everything stopped.

Then Jamie swooped in and lifted her off the stairs.

"Thanks, mate," he said as he carried her away. The Australian accent was the clincher.

The Doobie Brothers were blasting from the stereo when I finally dragged myself inside. As I closed the glass door behind me, I felt depleted. It wasn't possible that this year had 364 more days to go. I saw Hope eagerly waving at me from the kitchen, and the party had thinned out enough for me to weave my way over. She was wearing an emerald green knit dress that showed off her athletic frame, and she seemed rather cheerful for someone supposedly in the depths of depression.

"I'm sorry I'm late," she said with a big hug. "Conrad called." Whenever she felt weak, she went running back to her commitment-phobe ex, who bore a more than passing resemblance to her estranged father. But we had a pact. She never mentioned Laurel. I never mentioned her father.

"Conrad called?" I asked suspiciously.

"Okay, I called him," she said. "What's important is I feel good about myself."

"Just how good do you feel?"

"Good enough to see him Friday night?" she squeaked, anticipating my disapproval.

"One phone call and leader board be damned?"

"It seems to work better in theory than in practice," she said.

I had grown fond of the leader-board system, but who was I to judge? I was now measuring relationships in quarter hours. Hope picked up on my morose mood.

"You're going to meet someone perfect for you," she said soothingly. Now that she had a date lined up, she had transformed into Our Lady of Tranquillity. "Someone who makes you entirely forget about Laurel."

Hope knew better than to use the L word, and I knew better than to go out when I had an article due. I was irritated with Hope for pressuring me to come to the party. Mostly, I was irritated with myself about falling so quickly for Melinda.

"I met someone perfect for me, but I wasn't perfect for her. I wasn't anything for her."

"Do you want to tell me about her?"

"No," I said, before launching into a monologue about

Melinda's travels and quirky charm. "AND she went to Harvard. AND she's a journalist."

"She must have been impressed when you told her where you worked," Hope said. That shut me up. "You told her, didn't you?"

"I was asking her questions," I said in my defense. "You always tell me that women like to be asked questions."

"How could you not tell a journalist that you work for one of the top newspapers on the planet?" I was better at asking questions than answering them. "Your problem isn't meeting women. Your problem is you get insecure and sabotage yourself."

"If I were insecure, I wouldn't have lasted one day at my job."

"You're confident when it comes to work," Hope said, "but when you're around a woman you like, you regress to the age of twelve."

"I don't do that, and if I ever did do that, I didn't do it this time," I said, sounding at least fourteen.

Someone tapped me on the shoulder. I turned around, and it was Melinda. She was wearing a gray pea coat and a sweet expression. I saw the Aussie waiting for her by the front door, and a pubescent pang of jealousy burned beneath my rib cage.

"I just wanted to say that it was nice meeting you," she said, tilting her head up at me, her curly bangs spilling across her forehead. I wanted to take her in my arms and tell her how breathtakingly adorable she was. I settled for holding her slender hand.

"Same here," I said, wishing there was no Aussie.

"Good. I mean, thank you. I mean, happy New Year."

I let her fingers go and watched her walk away. Then I turned back to Hope, mouthing, "That was her!"

"She's cute," Hope said. "Did you get her number?"

"I told you—she has a boyfriend."

"Then why did she come say good-bye to you?"

"She was just being nice. Which makes her that much more amazing. She went out of her way to find me just so she could say—" I stopped myself midsentence as I had a horrifyingly delayed realization about why she would have made that effort. I whipped myself around just in time to see the door closing.

"Gavin, you're a fool," Hope said in the kindest way possible.

I bolted through the crowd, dodging and ducking and tackling one unfortunate couple that was standing between me and the door. I threw it open, hoping to see Melinda in the vestibule, but she wasn't there.

I banged on the elevator call button. The electronic display showed the single elevator was already down to the third floor. I couldn't wait for it to make it back to the seventh. I flew down the stairwell, taking the steps two at a time and jumping over the last few before each landing. As soon as I caught up to her I would explain that I hadn't been thinking. That of course I wanted her number. No, I didn't just want her number; I wanted to kiss her. I wouldn't say I wanted to kiss her; I would just kiss her. I couldn't wait to kiss her. I stumbled into the lobby and out of the building, breathing hard. The dark avenue was deserted. But she couldn't have gotten far. I raced north a block to Twenty-sixth Street and looked up and down the cross street. No one. I must have gone the wrong way. I sprinted back the other direction to Twenty-fifth. Then Twenty-fourth. Searching for a sign of her coat or her curls. I spun round. Still no one.

She was gone.

Chapter Five

If Cinderella Were on Facebook, Would Jiminy Cricket Tweet?

I didn't have her number. I didn't have her last name. And the host of the party said he didn't know any Melindas or Australians. My only lead was Lonely Planet, but the odds of them having record of a stringer in Nepal were minimal. The odds of them sharing it were even less. So I did what any self-respecting journalist would do. I Googled.

I got 2,340,000 results when I searched for "Melinda" and "travel." I added "Nepal," reducing it to a relatively low 10,700.

Melinda Shapiro posted a review of a hotel in Katmandu.

Bob and Melinda Blanchard wrote a book called *Live What You Love.*

Melinda Windsor was the Playmate of the Month in February 1966. Wasn't sure what the Nepal connection was, but I was briefly diverted. The eBay listing for the *Playboy* issue didn't show any pictures, but there was an extracted quote: "I never go out with married men, so won't you please come in?" I wondered if someone had fact-checked that.

I had promised myself that I would take only a ten-minute break before finishing my column. After an hour of clicking on unpromising links, I had my first lead when I came across an article about low-cost flights to Nepal by Melinda Adams on the Travel Channel Web site. There were also blog entries. But no picture.

It was a long shot, but I tried Google Image search. I typed in "Melinda Adams" and "Nepal." And there she was in a photo on AdventureTraveler.com. A blue-eyed redhead who looked about nineteen.

I was at a dead end. I pictured Melinda's face tilting up toward mine as her fingers slipped through my grasp. There were nearly ten thousand remaining results from my initial Google search and no guarantee that any of them would be the right Melinda. Just thinking about reading through all of them was enervating. So I didn't think.

Melinda Lopez was looking for a bi-curious Buddhist woman for travel and other explorations.

Melinda Davis was protesting Chinese policies in Tibet with a Himalayan-themed sorority party at Tulane.

And Melinda Finn wrote an article about trekking with a Nepalese Gurkha for the *New York Observer*. More than one article. My pulse quickened as I perused the articles. The *Observer* described her as a writer in New York. Nothing came up when I did an image search, but I wasn't going to let that stop me. More perplexing was the fact that there weren't any Melinda Finns in New York registered on Facebook, and Yahoo's People Search didn't show any living in New York under the age of fifty-three. However, there were phone numbers listed for twenty-seven M. Finns.

As I began dialing, it occurred to me that I was potentially becoming a stalker, but I preferred to see it in more chivalrous terms. There is a long literary tradition of enterprising gestures by romantic heroes, and compared to going door-to-door with a glass slipper, I was behaving quite rationally. I didn't really see a problem until I found myself explaining to Sheldon Finn why I was calling his ten-year-old daughter, Madelyn.

Afraid I might trigger an AMBER Alert, I reconsidered my approach. I read the *Observer* articles in more detail, looking for clues to assist me. In one of the pieces, she mentioned a boyfriend hiking with her. I pictured Jamie standing in silhouette on a granite outcropping, and then I saw him turning and sneering at me. I shuddered and kept reading. In a more recent story, she specifically referred to traveling alone. Other than that, there were no identifying characteristics. Nothing about her height or hair color or a predilection for Australian imports.

Then I noticed something that made my stomach do a somersault. There was an e-mail address printed at the bottom of one of the articles. It was an address at the *Observer*. But it was still an address, and it was hers. She was just a click away.

I boldly typed my business e-mail into the sender field. It was a subtle but effective way of letting her know where I worked. Hope would be proud of me. Plus it would look professional— just one journalist contacting another—in case someone else at the newspaper had access to her e-mail. I figured I would keep the message professional as well.

It was a pleasure conversing with you.

There was professional, and then there was stiff.

I really enjoyed our conversation, and I sincerely hope I have the opportunity to continue it.

Sounding awkward and insecure was not the way to get her to give me a second chance.

Your incandescent smile short-circuited my brain. I can't stop thinking about you, and I will be eternally grateful if you agree to have dinner with me.

I hit SEND before I had time to change my mind.

Chapter Six

The News Zoo Revue

By morning light, my impetuousness seemed more self-destructive than seductive.

As I hurried to work, I realized I had no way of knowing if the Melinda I e-mailed was the Melinda I was seeking. Even if she was, she might not appreciate an amorous missive sent to her workplace. And if she was a freelancer, which was likely, the odds were good that she wouldn't even receive the e-mail. My message was going to end up in some general-delivery account read by an overambitious, undercompensated peon. My best hope was that said peon would then forward it to Melinda. As opposed to reading it aloud for his coworkers' amusement before deleting it. Or, worse, he might notice the sender's address, which would not be good. Well, not for me.

If I had used my Hotmail address, I would have remained anonymous. Instead, I had chosen to broadcast that I worked at The Paper. I might as well have sent naked photos of myself to the *National Enquirer*. Actually, that would have been a safer choice. The *Enquirer* wouldn't have much interest in a mere journalist. The *Observer* would. I could see the next day's headline: WEDDING COLUMNIST IN WOEFUL NEED OF ROMANCE TUTORIAL.

If it's possible to cringe and run at the same time, I was doing it. I wanted to get to The Paper as soon as possible. Or, more specifically, to my message in-box.

The state-of-the-art, glass-and-steel headquarters towered over the eastern edge of Midtown. Draped in a gray, gridlike sheath, its facade resembled soaring pages of colossal newsprint with The Paper's name spelled out like a fifty-foot-high banner headline along the top floors. Even in my rush, I experienced a surge of pride. At a time when the Internet was threatening The Paper's existence, the newly completed, sixty-one-story building thrust itself onto the city's skyline, defying gravity and globalization in a physical declaration of relevance. Newspapers were not going anywhere, the edifice seemed to attest. Or at least not this iconic newspaper.

It wasn't a place of work so much as a system of beliefs. When people talk of the press as a fourth estate, the implication is that journalism rivals the three branches of government—and at The Paper, you were expected to act as if democracy itself were at stake with each deadline. You didn't take a job there to punch a time clock but to devote your life to a larger purpose: the pursuit of truth and excellence. I dodged the remaining construction crews and breezed into the vast lobby. My back instinctively straightened at the security check as I brandished my identification card, my proof of membership in an exclusive fraternity.

My pride diminished somewhat when I hit the crowd of people waiting at the elevator bank. Unlike the neo-Gothic building we'd recently vacated, there was no stairway access from the lobby, yet there was increased demand for elevators, since employees were now spread over forty floors rather than twenty. It could have been worse. The company had planned to inhabit additional floors of the new building, but as revenue forecasts trended groundward, so did real estate aspirations.

The high-tech, "smart" conveyor system eschewed standard up and down buttons, replacing them with a computerized panel. I punched in my desired floor, 5, and endured the requisite delay for the screen to display my assigned car. Except it didn't. It said ERROR. I quickly tried again and received the same message. Frustrated, I stabbed at the panel a third time, and I was directed to elevator F, where I joined a dozen type-A journalists queued up like passengers on a Disney theme-park ride. Like our tourist counterparts, we relinquished all control upon finally entering one of the transport vehicles. Woe be he who changed his mind about his destination, because there were no floor buttons. Apparently, real reporters don't have senior moments.

I tapped my foot restlessly. The waiting was making me agitated. I pictured a flashing red light on my desk phone and anticipated a voice mail from the ethics and standards editor, asking me to meet with him. I could hear his gravelly baritone stating, "I have some questions about a call I received this morning from the *Observer*." I wondered what, precisely, constituted sexual harassment.

The elevator doors opened. "What floor are we on?" asked a woman in the back, since floor numbers were not displayed. (Real reporters trust their instincts.) Someone near the doors said, "Five," and I darted out.

The terrariumlike two-story newsroom buzzed with countless hushed conversations as I briskly traversed the football-field-sized space. Managers huddled with senior editors in small, glass-walled offices, while reporters hunkered down at their desktop computers with phone cords dangling from their less-than-cutting-edge headsets. There were poker-faced clerks pecking away at their keyboards and art directors fixated on their oversized monitors. Though the newsroom was the nerve center of The Paper's output, what went on there didn't look that different from an advertising agency. Or an accounting firm. Sunlight flooded the cherrywood-paneled cubicles as I turned left at a hallway on the far side and made a beeline for my desk.

There was no red light. I was safe. For the moment.

"This is a newspaper, not the Good Ship Lollipop!" my editor bellowed from over my shoulder. I whipped around, worried what that portended. Renée Brodsky, a five-foot dynamo, was standing in the cubicle behind me with her headset in place over short, spiky, gray hair. Her steel blue eyes had narrowed behind her chunky black frames. She was gazing directly at me, but, thankfully, she was focused on a phone conversation.

"The wedding pages are the same as any other pages. We don't candy-coat the news," she said, her throaty voice curdling with disdain. A flinty reporter-turned-editor with a fondness for rugelach and racy jokes, Renée had little tolerance for anyone who impugned her judgment—or The Paper's.

"We deal with facts, Ms. Murphy," she continued as her head bobbed over tall stacks of wedding submissions. "And the fact is that this is going to be your *third* marriage. If we are going to publish an article about it, we are obligated to include the facts of the story."

Renée had worked at The Paper for almost fifty years, and as far as she was concerned, there was no difference between a wedding announcement and a Page One feature. As many a hapless bride had learned. I was simply relieved that her ire wasn't directed at me. This time.

My phone rang. It was Tony Fontana, who was sitting three feet away in the cubicle to my right. "Another bride bites the dust," he whispered.

"Did the tirade wake you up?" I asked as I booted up my computer. The question was facetious, since Tony was a workhorse, in the office by six a.m. He wrote for three different sections and coached hockey teams for all four of his kids. Somehow he also found time to be president of the Trekkie club in Great Neck.

"Oh, you'll get your wake-up call soon as Brunhilda sets her sights on your column," he said with a chuckle. Renée was born in Germany, which is why Tony teased her with the Brunhilda moniker when she was in a bad mood. But jokes aside, it was clear she was not in the best frame of mind for editing my piece, which I had filed electronically before I went to bed.

"Go harass a bridegroom," I responded while double-clicking on my e-mail program.

"Keeping the world safe for democracy, one wedding at a time," he said before hanging up.

With trepidation, I scanned the multitude of new e-mails I had received, scrolling down through far too many offers for penile enlargement. There were several messages from a nervous bride confirming and then reconfirming our scheduled interview on Friday morning, but there didn't seem to be anything from the *Observer*—or from Melinda. I was relieved. And disappointed. I reminded myself I was lucky if I simply managed to avert destroying my career. Yet there was a soft ache in my chest as I envisioned Melinda's dimples.

"Brides!" Renée exclaimed as she disengaged from her diatribe and sat back down.

"Is it really so terrible to want to leave previous marriages out of your wedding announcement?" asked Alison Dolan. Tony and I simultaneously popped our heads up above our cubicles with morbid anticipation. Alison was two years out of Barnard and confused why she wasn't managing editor of The Paper yet. We were confused how she kept her job.

"We all want things," Renée snapped as she shot back upright. "I want to be living in the south of France." That wasn't really true. Renée was convinced she would shrivel up and die if she spent more than a week away from The Paper. No one knew her exact age, but she had to be nearing seventy, and retirement was a nonissue.

"If we quote someone in an election article about who they're voting for, we don't say how many times they were married," Alison persisted in her languid whine.

"And when we quote someone in a wedding article, we don't say who they're voting for," Renée said a little defensively. "If a story's about marriage, then a previous marriage is relevant. Everything is about context." Renée sat back down, then sprung up again. "In 1977, Lana Fogerty and I were the only two female reporters on the Washington desk. Then Lana was fired because she had an affair with a congressman. Not while she was working here, but *previously*." Renée hammered home the "previously" before continuing her reminiscence. "I thought it reeked of sexism and I went straight to J. D. Rosenberg. J.D. said, 'I don't care if my reporters are sleeping with elephants, as long as they aren't covering the circus.'"

The bestiality metaphor was troubling, but it was the reference to a reporter being fired for sexual misconduct that made me blanch. I knew all too well that moral integrity was not an expectation at The Paper so much as a sacrosanct demand.

My phone rang again, and I flinched. I didn't recognize the number. Not particularly unusual. But what if it was the *Observer*? Best choice was to let it go to voice mail. Just in case.

But what if they then called the standards editor? I needed to get a grip.

I went back to reading my e-mails and found one from my grandmother buried amid the spam:

> *I'm out of the hospital. I just needed a few*
> *stitches. You'll have to wait a little longer for*
> *your inheritance.*
>
> *Love,*
> *Gramma*

I immediately started dialing.

"Gavin!" my grandmother exclaimed delightedly upon answering her cell phone. "I'm at the Winn-Dixie. How did you know where to find me?" Her embrace of technology didn't include entirely understanding it. "Did you go running this morning?"

"Not this morning, Grandma."

"Why not? When I got home from the hospital, first thing I did was go running."

"Why didn't you call me afterward?" I asked. "I left you a dozen messages."

"I didn't want to bother you while you were working."

"I'm always working," I said, "but I'm thinking about taking time off to come visit you."

"You shouldn't take off of work," she said. "Nine thousand people lost their jobs at Verizon." My grandmother followed unemployment reports the way baseball fans track batting averages.

"I'm not going to lose my job," I assured her before asking for details about her health. She insisted she was just bruised and tired. It was Bernie she was concerned about. He was still in the ICU.

"Last night was the first time we slept apart since we were married," she said. There was a tremor in her voice. "I don't want you visiting now. Save your money for taking a nice girl to dinner." She abruptly said she had to go, and I was still holding the receiver when Renée rapped on my cubicle.

"Your column's at the copy desk," she told me.

Renée didn't send a story to the copy editors until she was finished with her edit, which was usually a grueling ordeal over several hours or even days.

"You don't have any questions for me?" I asked, somewhat disbelieving. And rather proud of myself.

"I'm sure I could come up with some," she said with a hint of menace. "However, Al said he has a query for you."

"Captain Al!" Tony's voice boomed. "Must be a whale of a tale."

Al Macallister led the copy desk with the kind of detailed attention that helped earn The Paper its acclaimed reputation. He was also a monomaniac.

"It's about your lede," Al said when I called him. *Oh, God,* I thought. *Please don't change my lede after all the hours I spent coming up with it.*

Al read the opening sentence robotically, with no inflection in his nasal voice: "'When it came to love, Mimi Martin thought she had missed the boat.'" He paused before citing my linguistic crime.

"*Which* boat?" he asked. "Which particular boat did Ms. Martin miss?"

There's a thin line between editorial accuracy and anal-retentiveness.

"I wasn't really referring to one particular boat," I said,

trying not to reveal my inner John McEnroe ("You cannot be serious!").

"But you used the word 'the,' which, in fact, implies one specific boat," he countered. "If you don't have a specific boat in mind, you should change it to '*a* boat.' Otherwise our readers are going to wonder what boat you're referring to."

The only thing our readers were going to wonder was what planet we were on.

"It's supposed to be funny," I said, feebly attempting to reason with him, but if you have to explain that something's funny, it's not. "It's a colloquialism: 'I missed the boat.'"

"You didn't write that YOU missed a boat. You wrote that Miss Martin missed a boat," Captain Al pointed out, always on the alert for a factual error.

"The point is, it's a turn of phrase that doesn't make sense with the word 'a,'" I insisted.

"I don't know," he said. *What doesn't he know?* I wondered. *How people talk in real life?* "I think it's best to be accurate."

I hung up the phone, grumbling, "Al is killing my lede."

Renée's head popped up again over her cubicle. "In 1968, Archie Donovan was the copy editor when I wrote a story about John Wayne's Oscar win. My lede was, 'Better late than never. John Wayne showed *True Grit*, winning an Academy Award for his one hundred and thirty-ninth film.' Donovan, who believed there was no such thing as too few words, changed it to 'John Wayne was *the late winner* of the Academy Award for his one hundred and thirty-ninth film.' That's how you literally kill a lede." She let loose a raspy guffaw, then plopped back down into her chair. From behind the wall she said, "I'll talk to Al."

I was grateful for one fewer thing to worry about. Then an e-mail alert appeared on my screen. I had a new message, and it was from Melinda.

Chapter Seven

Dream Date

I was deliberating between roses and tulips at a Midtown deli before meeting Melinda for a late dinner. Roses made a strong statement. Possibly too strong. I was overthinking it. Or, more likely, I was overdoing it. It was just a first date. I wondered if I had been too eager on my first date with Jill. I had brought her a miniature box of Belgian truffles. Maybe that's what had turned her off. I wished I could ask her. There should be exit interviews for dating. Just a brief evaluation of the highlights and challenges of the relationship, and maybe a few questions like "So what exactly was it that motivated you to dump me?"

I decided against the flowers. But picked up a package of breath mints. I wasn't nervous. Or I wasn't as nervous as I was when I received Melinda's e-mail two days prior. I had stared at my computer monitor for about ten minutes before opening the message, half expecting her to tell me to cease and desist.

Instead, she enthusiastically accepted my invitation. Not only wasn't she offended, but she also said she was flattered by my boldness. Only problem was maintaining it. I asked Hope to recommend a bold restaurant.

"Bold food or bold design?" she asked. I didn't really have an opinion, but that didn't seem like a very bold thing to admit. "How about a bold location?" she said.

"Like a foreign country?" I asked.

"I was thinking more like the Bronx."

"New parameters," I said. "Bold without crossing a major body of water."

"How about *in* the water?"

There is something to be said for being bland, I thought as I climbed the narrow vertical ladder on the port side of *The Lightship*, an eighty-year-old boat that had been salvaged from the bottom of the Chesapeake Bay and was now docked at a pier on the Hudson River.

When Hope recommended the place, I imagined myself following in the footsteps of Mimi and Mylo's marina-kindled romance. But that was summer in the Hamptons, and this was winter along the West Side Highway.

A frigid wind blew off the Hudson, and the dark waves sloshing against *The Lightship* seemed more threatening than buoyant. As I hoisted myself aboard, I reminded myself that Melinda enjoyed adventures.

A metal stairway led into the belly of the boat, where R&B emanated from the barnacle-clad engine room that housed an intimate lounge. With candlelit catwalks cutting through the rusting hull, it was a cross between a swanky bar and Davy Jones's locker.

There was no sign of Melinda among the twenty- and thir-tysomething fashionistas in their all-black ensembles. I was wearing a dark gray jacket and jeans, my standard uniform, but I had tucked in my shirt.

I positioned myself on a bar stool. After a couple minutes I realized I was slouching, so I stood instead. I checked my watch. It was five after nine. I had an eight a.m. interview I hadn't finished preparing for. I promised myself I wouldn't think about it.

My cell phone vibrated, and I worried Melinda was cancel-ing. But it was my parents calling. They'd been updating me regularly about my grandmother's health. There was nothing to update, since I'd been calling her every morning on my way to work; however, that had negligible impact on the frequency of my parents' bulletins.

"Just wanted to let you know that there's no change in your grandmother's condition," my father said.

"She doesn't have a condition," I said. "She has stitches."

"Well, she didn't get any more stitches today," my mother clarified.

"She's not going to get any more stitches," I said.

"Suddenly you're a doctor," my father commented.

"It's not too late for you to go back to medical school," my mother said. "My Zumba instructor's nephew didn't go until he was thirty-eight, and by the time he graduated he was married."

"I'm not going back to medical school," I assured her.

"Have you reconsidered looking into mail-order brides?"

Before I could reply, my father said, "Bernie was moved out of the ICU."

As usual, my parents had buried the lede.

"That's great news," I said.

"Make sure to say that to your grandmother."

"I will," I said before asking the obvious question. "Why wouldn't I?"

"Bernie's still unconscious," my mother said. "The doctor said he wasn't optimistic."

"That's not what the doctor said," my father objected.

"He said that Bernie may never gain consciousness."

"But he didn't use the word 'optimistic'!"

"Because he wasn't!"

I looked around the dark room. A shellacked lobster seemed to be eyeing me. Melinda was late. Bernie was dying. My parents were dysfunctional. And I was alone. Figuratively. There were about twenty people sprawled on the sofas and shimmying in the shadows as Mary J. Blige insisted things were "Just Fine."

My phone beeped. It was Melinda.

"I need to put you on hold," I told my parents, interrupting them midsquabble. I clicked through to Melinda, fearing bad news and hoping she was merely delayed by the subway or Somalian pirates.

"Where are you?" she asked.

"Where are *you*?" I replied.

"I'm sitting at a lovely table for two, minus my plus-one," she said, before I realized I was hearing Mary J. Blige in stereo through my handset.

"I am so there," I said, bounding up the steps. I could have sworn I had suggested meeting in the bar, but it didn't matter. Nothing mattered but seeing her.

The dining room was deck side. Rows of red-and-white-checker-clothed tables were arranged under a tent amid torch-like heater lamps wrapped in strings of colored Christmas lights.

"I'm on the deck," I said, still holding my phone to my ear.

"I'm toward the stern on the starboard side," she said.

"Is this a test?" I tried to remember if stern was front or back.

"Yes," she said with a laugh. "If you fail we'll never meet." I liked her challenging but flirtatious tone.

"Aren't you going to help me?" I asked as I strode between the tables, my head swiveling from side to side.

"What kind of romantic hero seeks navigational assistance?"

"The kind who might be doomed by a lack of nautical knowledge," I said, psyched that she thought of me as a romantic hero.

"Fear not, Braveheart, and veer not from your path, as I will be your beacon."

"Huh?"

"I'm waving at you," she said, and I could detect someone waving an arm. But in the dim light I couldn't see her. "Do not tarry," she said before hanging up. *Fat chance*, I thought, pocketing my phone and hurrying toward her.

She stood to greet me. All six feet of her. She enveloped me as I hesitantly embraced her. We sat down and she smoothed a few strands of salt-and-pepper hair.

"I have to confess, when I got your e-mail, I wasn't sure who you were," she said. "But now of course I remember we met at a party last summer in Southampton."

I didn't know what to say. "I've never seen you before in my life" seemed inappropriate. But accurate.

Or better yet: "Who are you and what have you done with Melinda?" Though, as Captain Al would undoubtedly have pointed out, she was in fact "a" Melinda. Just not the one I was looking for.

Why did she respond to my e-mail if she didn't know who I

was? Why didn't she realize she wasn't the intended recipient? On the other hand, I was grateful she assumed I was a legitimate suitor rather than an incompetent stalker.

Looking at her across the candlelit table, there was no reason she couldn't be the object of a man's obsession. Though I was guessing that she was in her mid-fifties, she was curvy in the right places with robust lips and doelike eyes.

"You picked a great place," she said, bobbing her head to the music. "I feel ten years younger just being among all these fabulous kids."

I instantly felt ten years older. I became uncomfortably aware that I was probably the second-oldest person on board.

"My ex-husband would hate this place," she said.

I must have done something terrible in a previous life, I thought as she chronicled twenty-five years of her former spouse's foibles. "When I met him, he thought the Himalayas were a sexual position." She also spoke of her two grandchildren— and shared pictures.

All I wanted was to extricate myself as quickly as possible.

My phone buzzed. It was my parents again, and I realized that I had inadvertently hung up on them. I was about to say I needed to take the call and use it as an excuse to escape, but I remembered that I had invited her to dinner. She hadn't sought out the invitation. She hadn't been the one prowling the Internet for a date. She simply consented to accompany me for a meal, and the least I could do was provide one.

"Have you looked at the menu?" I asked.

"I was too busy admiring the view," she said. I stiffened, and not in a good way. But then I humbly noticed she was looking out a plastic window embedded in the tent wall beside us. The lights of Midtown twinkled beneath a clear sky.

"This is a perfect romantic spot," she said. It was. We both gazed out the window that gently billowed in the night breeze, while the candles flickered and nearby couples caressed. The moment was everything I had imagined. Except I was with the wrong Melinda.

Chapter Eight

Arrested Development

"If it was up to me, we would elope," said Amy Wu the next morning, sucking down her second grande latte at a Starbucks in Union Square.

She wasn't the only one who needed perking up.

I hadn't slept well, having spent most of the night mourning the loss of a relationship I never had. The last thing I wanted was to hear someone talk about finding her soul mate, and I hoped Amy wouldn't use the words "soul mate." I had also hoped she would be an easy interview, but the pixieish brunette was less enthusiastic about our meeting than I had expected. A fashion editor at *Elle* magazine, she was used to staying behind the scenes and was becoming increasingly agitated being the focus of attention.

"I spent an hour on the phone yesterday with a vendor for color-coordinated confetti," said the twenty-eight-year-old as she tugged at the hem of her body-hugging gray sweater. "Six months ago I didn't even know there was such a thing. I still don't know why I need it. Or why I need an article in The Paper. No offense, but I'm not a winner of the Nobel Peace Prize."

"If you were, I would have paid for your coffee," I said, trying to calm the caffeinated bride-to-be.

A nervous smile played across her angular face as she licked foam from the edge of her cup. She was rather adorable, I noted with a modicum of despair. Somewhere in the city, Melinda might also be enjoying a morning coffee. I banished the thought and concentrated on my near-empty notepad while nursing my Caramel Macchiato.

"Most people who want to elope don't invite two hundred people to the Rainbow Room," I said, changing tacks.

"Mike wanted a big wedding," she said. "Sometimes, I swear—he's such a girl. Don't quote that. Mike will cry. I mean, freak. He'll freak out. In a manly way."

Mike Russo was a professional dating coach who had appeared on *Oprah*. Possibly in need of his own services, he had taken a month to get a first date with Amy. The question was why. The answer was not forthcoming.

"You must get tired asking people how they met," she said, deflecting my query. "Doesn't every bride's story start to sound the same?"

I was tempted to say yes. However, I needed to salvage the interview. "I don't write about *every* bride," I said, "but I do want to write about an Ohio native climbing the ladder at *Elle* who gets her future husband arrested for asking her out."

"You're not going to include that, are you?" she asked, her brown eyes widening.

Of course I was including it. It was how I had pitched the piece to Renée. "Is it not true?" I said, hoping I could coax her into revealing more.

"I didn't get him arrested," was all she said.

"That's not what *he* said." Sometimes my job was a lot like playing Bob Eubanks on *The Newlywed Game.*

"I didn't know I was marrying Chatty Cathy," she said. "Did he also tell you about harassing me on the subway?" All I recalled was they had met on a crowded R train after work. He stood up to give her his seat, and there was a spark. According to him, it was mutual.

"I thought he was cute," she admitted, blushing. "Handsome. Say *very* handsome."

A six-foot former competitive skier, Mike's attractiveness was not in doubt, but she seemed protective of him. I imagined what it would feel like to have someone be that way about me.

"When I got up at my stop, he asked for my phone number." *Of course he did*, I thought, *because that's what normal people do.* If only I had done the same, I could be dating the right Melinda.

"I wouldn't give it to him," Amy said flatly. I didn't think I heard right. "He looked about as confused as you do now," she said with a laugh.

I prided myself on not being so transparent, but I *was* confused. "You said you thought he was attractive."

"I don't give my number to random guys on the subway," she said.

"But you had a spark," I sputtered. "He gave you his seat." If a guy like Mike Russo couldn't seal the deal, I had no chance whatsoever.

"So he was a polite, random guy. Do you know how many freaks there are in this city? And speaking of freaks, the next morning he was waiting for me on the uptown subway platform. Right here at Union Square."

"How did he know what time you left for work?"

"How did he even know where I lived?" she said, pushing a

loose strand of straight, dark hair behind her ear. It was the same shoulder length as Melinda's. "When he saw me get off the train, I could have been going to dinner or visiting a friend. It's crazy. He's crazy. He got to the station at six in the morning and waited until I showed up at eight thirty." I was impressed that he made such an effort. Especially since there was no guarantee he would even see her.

"He came over and said, 'Good morning,' like it was the most natural thing in the world, shooting me this big toothy smile. I asked him what he was smiling about, and he said, 'I can't help but smile when I see you,' which is the corniest line ever. Which I told him. He told me he could come up with cornier ones, and after three years together I can tell you he wasn't lying. So I asked him if he lived in the area, and he said, 'No. I'm just here to invite you to dinner.' I couldn't believe his audacity." Neither could I, but he was a camera-ready dating professional. Mere mortals couldn't be expected to be that ballsy.

"I told him I had plans," she said.

"How did that go over?" I was very curious how a guy like Mike handled being turned down.

"The next morning he was there again." He had just become my hero. "This time with Starbucks coffee and mini cupcakes from Crumbs Bake Shop. He asked me out again, and I said no again."

"Why?" I found myself taking the rejection personally. This wasn't just an interview anymore; it was an education. After my missteps of the past week, this was my chance to penetrate the labyrinth of the female mind. "What did he do wrong?"

She bit her lip and seemed to be deliberating about sharing more. "I just didn't feel like going out," she finally said. "I had a bad breakup a month beforehand. The guy I had dated since college dumped me at my sister's big, fat Chinese wedding. I was the maid of honor, so I was wearing this cheesy fuchsia brides-maid dress and my hair was all in ringlets. Which took hours. Before the ceremony we were posing for pictures in a vintage convertible, and he told me he had fallen in love with someone else. So let's just say that I wasn't keen on romance when I met Mike. As my Grandma Jade used to say, if you let someone sweep you off your feet, you better be prepared to land on your ass."

"So what changed things?" It was a standard question in my repertoire, but I really wanted to know. I was no longer a jour-nalist. I was a lonely guy seeking vital knowledge. Something fundamental I was supposed to have learned years ago. I feared that my academic honors at Cornell had come at the expense of an incomplete grade in Relationships 101.

"He kept showing up with coffee and cupcakes, and I kept turning him down."

"You turned down the cupcakes?"

"No. The dinner invitation. I love cupcakes." She smiled, and for a moment she looked about twelve. "Then a week later, there was a power outage on the subway. No trains were run-ning. But we didn't know that. We were just standing there waiting. And waiting. Until we finally gave up and tried to get a taxi. Except there were no taxis to get. Which is when I started freaking, because I had a nine fifteen presentation scheduled at work. So Mike ran into the middle of the street, zigzagging through the traffic and flagging down drivers until he con-vinced someone to give us a ride uptown. We were smushed together in the back of this Honda Fit, and as I climbed over him to get out, he asked for my number again."

"That's when you gave it to him."

"No." She laughed, shaking her head. "That's when I called the cops. Well, actually, I called my roommate's brother, who works as a PI and had offered to do a background check. He's the one who contacted the police. How was I supposed to know Mike had a dozen unpaid parking tickets?"

If incarceration was a form of foreplay, I had more to learn than I thought.

"The background check somehow triggered him getting sent a bench warrant for the tickets," she said. "He had to appear in court and pay a fine, but the way he carries on, you'd think troopers showed up at his door and handcuffed him."

I needed to know how these two people ended up together. Because it wasn't inevitable. When I interviewed couples it was easy to believe that their relationships were predestined, but I knew that wasn't true. Something happened between dodging motor vehicles and picking confetti colors, and I needed to understand what it was. More to the point, I needed to understand love. I was like a scientist studying the components of a foreign substance, and for the first time I realized that my job offered the ideal laboratory. I'd been so focused on the irony of being a single man writing about weddings that I'd overlooked the serendipity. I'd been going about my articles with blinders on, fixated on deadlines and word counts and not appreciating that each of the couples I met had something crucial to teach me. If I could just figure out what it was.

"Did Mike stop showing up in the morning?" I asked, wondering if he pulled back.

"Are you kidding?" She looked amused. "He insisted that after all the trouble I caused, the least I could do was go out with him." Seemed logical to me.

"And I considered it," she said.

He was asking for a measly date, not a bank rescue, I almost shouted in frustration. What was there to think about?

"I debated the pros and cons in my head. Was I ready to start dating again? Was I not ready? Should I go on a diet first? I have a crazy brain. I ponder all the possible combinations and per-mutations. When we go to sleep at night, he says to me, 'I can hear your thoughts. They're very loud.'"

Okay, she was a little neurotic. In a Zooey Deschanel kind of way. I got it. So what won her over? That was what I wanted to know. She had skipped over that one crucial detail. "Why did you finally agree to go on a date?"

"I didn't," she said. "He showed up at my office at lunchtime one day with white calla lilies, a bottle of Moët, and takeout from Nobu. We had a picnic in the conference room. Who can say no to Nobu?" It all came down to expensive sushi and cham-pagne? He must have spent two hundred dollars. I couldn't afford that. At least not on a first date, and it wasn't even a first date. It was a pitch for a first date.

"You didn't at any point encourage him?" I asked, dumb-founded. It was a new concept for me, and I was having trouble fully grasping it.

"Well, I didn't *discourage* him," she said. Was he supposed to comprehend the difference? Was I? "It's not like I didn't talk to him. Even the first day he showed up on the subway platform. We got into a stupid conversation about *Harold & Kumar Go To White Castle.* I remember calling him a doofus, and he called me a movie snob. Which is completely untrue. My all-time favorite movie is *Shrek.* Which I told him. And he started jump-ing up and down like he needed Ritalin or something, and shrieking that it was also his favorite. Total BS, right? But then he showed me he was wearing a Shrek watch. Who wears a Shrek watch?" No one I knew. But no one I knew would pursue a woman who continually turned him down.

"He was so sure of himself and so sure of wanting me," Amy said, growing pensive. "The way I look at it, Mike found me. He found me over and over. Even though I didn't know that I was lost."

Chapter Nine

Fire, Aim, Ready

"I need to find Melinda," I said to Gary, whom I called while heading downtown from Starbucks.

"You need to have sex," he told me. "Let me clarify that. You need to have sex with someone you can physically touch."

I had phoned to get an update on Bernie, but Gary was more interested in critiquing my love life. Or lack thereof.

"You need to meet people," he said. "Have you thought about taking a class?"

"In dating?"

"No," he groaned, "in something like wine tasting, where you might meet someone."

"I did meet someone," I said as I crossed Waverly Street. "I met Melinda." I just wasn't making much headway in locating her. I had contacted Lonely Planet, and, as I suspected, they didn't give out personal or personnel information.

"You're never going to see that girl again."

"Thanks for the vote of confidence." I noticed I was passing NYU's school of the arts, and I remembered that Melinda had said she was starting a master's program there. I had about thirty mintues to kill before my next interview. Possibly forty-five if I took a taxi.

" 'Why do you suppose it is we only feel compelled to chase the ones that run away?' That's *Dangerous Liaisons.*" He emphasized the word "dangerous."

"I'm going to find her," I said with new resolve.

"As Julia Roberts once said, 'You're a restraining order waiting to happen.' "

"Have you talked to Bernie's doctor?" I changed topics as I turned about-face and dashed toward the school.

"Not yet," Gary said, "but I noticed that flights from New York to Fort Lauderdale are on sale. Not that I want to pressure you. Just trying to keep you out of trouble."

It was too late for that.

"You're asking me to do something in violation of school policy," said the work-study student manning the desk in the writing department. I had hoped the romantic nature of my mission would convince her to let me peek at the list of first-year master's students so that I could learn Melinda's last name, but the grad student's eyes flared with indignity behind her circular wire-framed glasses.

"How about if you just confirm there is someone named Melinda currently enrolled?" I asked.

"That would also be a violation," she said, tilting her computer screen toward her in a way that seemed intended to guard both its contents and her maidenhood.

The office was a cramped space with unwieldy furniture,

which I suspected had a psychological impact on those who worked there. I kept looking toward the open doorway in the hope of seeing Melinda appear.

"Could I just get a schedule of classes while I'm here? That's available online anyway." I was bluffing.

"That information is absolutely *not* available online," she said. She was either a darn good poker player or had a potential future career as a medical-claims adjuster.

"I'm sure I could find it if I tried," I said in a friendly, light-hearted way.

"I doubt it."

I wanted to point out that I was a reporter for The Paper, but if I mentioned that, I'd be breaching all kinds of ethical lines. As I considered my options, two undergraduate bohemians in training wearing clashing plaid shirts squeezed their way around me.

"Do you have any more drop/add slips?" one asked.

My adversary efficiently distributed Xeroxed forms, and the teenage boys slumped out of the office as a dark-skinned man with dreadlocks darted in. He declared that he had a manuscript for Professor Rubin, which he handed over before promptly leaving.

"Busy day?" I asked. She glared. "Listen," I said, "you're absolutely right to not give out private information. I think the best thing for me to do is to just hang out. Here."

"Here?" she said, her eyebrows furrowing.

"Seems like anyone in the department would come through at some point. So I'll just stay here between classes and during lunch. I've got time right now." About eight minutes, but she didn't know that. "I can keep you company for the next week. Or two. Or however long it takes until Melinda shows up. And we don't have to worry about breaking any rules."

"Loitering is also against the rules," she said. "We have a strict policy about nonstudents."

"But I *am* a student." I flashed the same NYU identification card I had used at the security desk. It was from a French class I'd taken a couple years back (*Je parle mauvais français*). I doubted it would stand up to much scrutiny, but Bride of Cerberus didn't know that. "In fact, I was thinking about enrolling in one of your graduate writing workshops," I added for good measure.

"You'd need to get approval from the director of the department."

"Thanks for the heads-up," I said, plopping myself down on the vinyl love seat.

"There's a reading tonight by Joan Didion that all students are expected to attend," she said with a hint of nervous desperation. "Information about the reading is available online."

The reading was at the NYU student center on the south side of Washington Square Park. I arrived an hour early and positioned myself just inside the front doors of the building.

This was it. In less than an hour I would see Melinda again. It occurred to me that I had no idea what to say to her. "I just happened to be in the neighborhood" wasn't going to work. "I haven't been able to stop thinking about you" would be the most sincere approach, if it didn't make me sound borderline psychotic. Then I thought of Mike Russo, and decided I would simply tell Melinda I was there to ask her out to dinner. It was direct, truthful and flattering. I was ready.

I was also nauseous.

I noticed my reflection in the glass doors. The unflattering lighting made my skin look sallow and splotchy, and standing alone in the lobby was like being in a fishbowl. An overly bright fishbowl with no plastic sea galleon to hide behind. I repositioned myself outside the doors as a woman approached from the park. She had a knit hat pulled down over her ears and was clutching her pea coat tight around her. Melinda's coat! I took a couple steps instinctively toward her, but as she passed beneath a streetlight I could see red hair springing from beneath her hat, where there should have been brown curls. She looked at me suspiciously, and I quickly turned away. When I turned back, she was standing a few feet away, lighting a cigarette. I smiled nervously, and she shot me another suspicious look.

I called Hope.

"If a guy you met only once showed up out of the blue, would you think he was stalking you?"

"It would depend on how cute he was," she said.

"I'm serious," I said.

"It would seriously depend on how cute he was." I filled her in on my plan, and to her credit, she didn't question my sanity, only my odds of success. "I'm just saying you're operating with a suboptimal hazard ratio," she said, regressing into doctor-speak. I suspected she wasn't fully focused on me, because, well, she said, "I can't really focus on you at the moment, since I'm backed up with trauma patients and need to get out of here BECAUSE . . . tonight's my date with Conrad!"

She was dismayed that I had forgotten.

"I'm meeting him at the Modern," she said, referring to the restaurant at the Museum of Modern Art known for sleek design and steep prices.

"He's dragging you all the way uptown?"

"It's a great place, and he's making a statement." The statement being that money was no object. For all of Hope's savvy, sometimes she was still the girl from Ohio, easily dazzled by

New York glitterati. Something Conrad was well aware of. "I think everything's going to be different this time." That's what she said the last time, but I wasn't going to voice that. People standing by glass doors shouldn't throw stones.

She wished me luck and clicked off as a couple entered the building, hand in hand. What if Melinda came to the reading with another guy? Didn't matter. I was going to do what I was there to do. I was a man on a mission—the James Bond of dysfunctional dating habits.

I relentlessly scrutinized the faces of all incoming females. A freckled woman approaching from the west. Black-clad poet type with dark bangs from the east. A group of four women passed by too quickly for me to see them clearly, so I followed them inside, circling round until I was sure Melinda was not among them. As I returned to my sentry post outside, I held the door for a porcelain-skinned undergrad with long eyelashes. I suddenly felt like an aging lothario. It didn't help that the red-head smoker was scowling at me.

When guys did this kind of thing in movies, it seemed less lecherous. Usually there was romantic music playing. Maybe my iPod would help. With earphones in place, I continued my search for Melinda as Cee Lo Green crowed about being "Crazy."

The crowd thickened, and my head was pivoting from side to side when I saw a petite figure with a windblown mop of dark ringlets waving at someone to my right. I hurried in that direction. Then scurried back when I saw my least-favorite redhead waving in response.

The two women embraced. In a nonsexual way, I noted with some relief. Then they hurried inside before I could glimpse anything but curls and coat. I trailed behind them (at a non-threatening distance). The lights in the lobby flickered on and off, and so did my faith in my quest.

Making a quick change in tactics, I entered the auditorium and strode purposefully to the front row. Then I turned around and scoured the audience as if I was looking for someone—and, of course, I was.

There were close to two hundred people seated or wrestling with their coats. I slowly walked up the aisle, scanning each and every row. Melinda was somewhere in the room, and I was going to find her.

Or so I believed for the first ten rows. By the thirteenth row, I was having a bad feeling. But there in the last row was a familiar flash of scarlet frizz and scowl, and one seat over I could see bounteous brunet tresses. She was bent over, looking for something in her bag. Though I couldn't see her face, I knew it was Melinda. I knew it ten feet away. I knew it three feet away. I knew it as she looked up at me with a mystical expression on her tawny, African-American face.

I was doomed to keep pursuing the wrong Melindas.

Two hours later, I was sitting on a park bench, facing the brightly lit lobby of the student center as the last of the lecture's attendees filed out of the auditorium. I watched a rail-thin guy with shaggy dark hair hold the door for a winsome blonde. There was something effortless about the way he put his arm around her. They stood together at the street corner, leaning against each other, her mittened hand stroking his cheek.

"Stop feeling sorry for yourself," said Hope, who magically appeared at my side. Actually, it wasn't that magical, because I had left her a message telling her exactly where I was, in case her date ended early.

"You didn't have to come," I said, very grateful that she had. Her warm green eyes were wet from the cold. Though I'd never admit it to Gary, there were moments I imagined Hope was the woman I belonged with. She was compassionate and insightful and made kick-ass ravioli from scratch. She was also taller than me without heels. She said dating shorter men made her feel like a circus freak. And it was hard for me to picture being with a woman whose neck was bigger than mine.

"Why are you sitting outside?" she asked as she sat down beside me. It was in the thirties, but there was no wind. I found the cool temperature made it easier to think. Not that thinking was helping.

"The important thing is you did something," Hope said. I looked at her glumly. "Or you tried to do something. That's all any of us can do."

"There's another lecture here next week," I said.

"Do you really want to do this again?"

"Mike Russo showed up at a subway station every day for weeks."

"You're not Mike Russo," she pointed out. "You can show up here every single day for the rest of the semester, if that will make you happy. You may eventually find Melinda, and she may remember you. It's possible."

The way she said "possible" suggested she firmly believed it wasn't. I suddenly felt very tired. I could feel my motivation dissipating out of my arteries and into the brisk night air.

"How was your date?" I remembered to ask her.

"Conrad proposed," she said softly.

I was shocked. He had done everything to convince her (and me) that he was not interested in any form of cohabitation. Then after five years of noncommittal bullshit, presto change-o, he dove into the deep end of the pool. I had underestimated him, and I felt like an idiot. Especially since Hope had let me carry on about Melinda before telling me her great news. "Congratulations!" I said, embracing her.

She started crying. "He didn't propose to *me*. He proposed to a girl he met five months ago in the Hamptons." She pulled a used Kleenex out of her coat pocket and dabbed at her eyes.

"Why would he take you out on a date if he's engaged to someone else?" I was incensed on her behalf.

"He didn't take me on a date. He had a glass of wine with me before meeting *her* for dinner. He said he wanted to let me know in person. But what he really wanted was for me to let you know, so that you would write about their wedding. Promise me you will not write about their wedding."

"Of course not."

"It's going to be some over-the-top event at a château in Provence. The scumbag promised to take me to Provence last summer, but then he said he was too busy."

"You've been to Provence," I said, trying to console her. "Twice."

"That's not the point!" she snapped. "He said she's everything he's ever wanted. Meaning a Parisian size-two former model with a PhD in art history and an aristocratic title. And don't ask where he met her." I wasn't going to, but I was curious.

"I'm sorry," was all I could say. I suspected losing Conrad wasn't the hardest part for Hope. It was having it happen in the same way her mother lost her father. But Hope wasn't married to Conrad. And they didn't have a seven-year-old daughter.

"I'm better off," she said. "I had no business dating a guy who waxes his eyebrows." She stood up and took a deep breath, gazing sadly across the street at the now-empty lobby. "Are you ready to go?"

"No," I said, also getting up. I couldn't tell Hope that the thought of her ex marrying a French model with a doctorate made me even more queasy than I felt at the start of the evening. Instead, I took her hand in mine.

"It's going to be a long weekend," she said, still focused somewhere in the distance.

"At least you don't have to go to a wedding tomorrow," I said, realizing how much I was dreading it.

"The love coach?"

"That's next week. This week I've got a Secret Service agent who met his fiancée at a firearms convention."

Hope's eyes were watering.

"Everything's going to be okay," I said, wanting to believe it. She hugged me tightly, and I thought my life would be so much easier if I were in love with her.

"I'm thinking of trying online dating again," she said, resting her forehead against my own. "Do you think that's a good idea?"

I didn't, but I nodded anyway.

Chapter Ten

Dating for Dummies

"You gotta make your own luck," said Mike Russo. I was in the SoHo office of the buff dating guru and star of the new syndicated series *Don't Think Twice: Russo's Rules of Romance*. He looked unnaturally tan for mid-January as he proselytized to his audience of one. "That's what I tell my clients. When you see someone you're attracted to, you talk to her. Anytime. Anywhere."

"In a doctor's office?" I was skeptical.

"In a freaking ambulance," he said. It was our last interview before Mike's wedding, and as we veered off topic, he was loosening up. "I'm also a big fan of anyplace you have to stand in line. People waiting in line are miserable, and misery loves company. I particularly like banks, grocery stores, and the Department of Motor Vehicles."

"How often are people at the Department of Motor Vehicles?"

"There are worse ways to spend an afternoon," he said with the dreamy look of a man remembering a weekend in Ibiza—and not remembering Ibiza.

"So you advise your clients to just go up to women they don't know?" I was still holding to the pretense that my questions were exclusively related to the wedding article.

"Ask for the time. That's a standard icebreaker."

"Women often ask me for the time, but I don't assume they're coming on to me."

"You *should*," he admonished. "You're an attractive guy with an impressive job. You shouldn't have any problem meeting women."

Then why was he assuming that I did?

"First thing out of your mouth should be where you work. I know a guy at the *Wall Street Journal* who's dating a Versace model, and he's a total dog. You've got that whole sensitive-wedding-columnist thing going for you. Chicks eat that up."

It was almost a week since the reading at NYU, and I had stopped looking for Melinda. Well, other than in a random kind of way, when walking to work or riding the subway. I hadn't met anyone new, but I didn't think there was anything wrong with that. I had a feeling Mike would disagree.

"Gavin, when's the last time you approached a woman on the street?" he asked. I was trying to remember if I ever had, but he had already moved on. "I want you to tell me what you do when you see someone on the street you're attracted to."

We had gone from interview to intervention.

"I look," I said. Mike's silence told me he was waiting for more. "Sometimes I stop and turn around."

"Good. That's the first step."

"The first step toward what?" I asked. "Being a horndog?"

"No, the first step toward knowing what you want and acting on it."

My training was more along the line of not jumping to conclusions before having all the facts.

"I knew I wanted Amy the first moment I saw her on Fifty-seventh Street," Mike said.

"I thought you met on a train."

"That's the G-rated version. She walked by while I was bent over buying a newspaper by Carnegie Hall. She was checking out my ass. She won't admit it, but she was. She turned and looked back over her shoulder with those big brown eyes, and I was a goner. I ran after her into the subway station, but I lost her in the rush-hour crowd. I got on a train and was totally bumming, when I looked up and there she was. Gavin, you can't imagine how bad I wanted her, and I'm not talking about wanting to have sex with her. That goes without saying. I mean, I wanted her in my life. It was a gut reaction."

"You didn't know anything about her," I said. That was my gut reaction.

"You have to trust what you feel. It's when you start second-guessing yourself that you get in trouble."

What some call second-guessing is what others call making rational decisions. "A lot of mental-health professionals would disagree," I said. "Successful relationships aren't based solely on instant physical chemistry."

"That's not what I'm talking about at all. I get so frustrated when people use their physical connection as an excuse to stay or go. Gavin, I can't tell you how many times I hear, 'We had great sex, so why won't she return my calls?' Or 'The sex wasn't great, so what's the point of another date?' That's all bullshit, Monday-morning quarterbacking. I'm talking about being present in the moment and knowing what you feel. It may not be what you feel a day or a month later, but you need to respect what you're feeling when you're feeling it."

He spouted therapy talk with the enthusiasm of a car salesman, matching the empathy and lingo with direct eye contact and open body language. Even his furniture was purposefully transparent. Glass desk, glass coffee table and glass shelving. Outside the oversized picture windows, moody gray clouds were gathering.

"No regrets," he said, pointing an index finger at me. *Was that dating advice or a quote from a Vin Diesel movie?*

"This is going to sound Neanderthal," Mike warned, "but the reality is we're animals with animal instincts. When I'm hungry, I know it. When I'm scared, I know it. And when I'm attracted to someone, I know it."

When it's time to end an interview, I know it.

"When I saw Amy on that train, I ached for her," he said. "Not just physically. Spiritually. You say I didn't know her, but corny as it sounds, I felt like I did know her. I sensed kindness, steadfastness, curiosity and intelligence. The same qualities I now admire in her on a daily basis."

He glanced instinctively toward a framed photo on his desk. I couldn't help doing the same. It was a snapshot of Amy at the Union Square farmer's market. She was looking over her shoulder with a deliriously happy expression as her hand reached for the camera. No, not for the camera. For him.

"If I hadn't trusted my instincts and acted on them, it would have haunted me," Mike said, still gazing at the photograph. "I could picture myself wandering the city, searching the Internet, hoping to find her again. I could still be doing that today instead of marrying the woman I love."

I no longer cared that most of what Mike said sounded hokey.

I wanted what he had. I wanted someone looking out of a picture frame with deep longing. Someone to talk with after turning out the lights. Someone to stand beside me beneath a wedding canopy.

"Meeting the right person is luck," said Mike. "The trick is acting on it. The moment you feel something, you need to act on it. Feel. Act. You need to practice doing that until it's muscle memory, like making a chip shot out of the rough."

I wasn't very good at golf either. "What if you act on your feelings with the wrong person?" I asked.

"There's no such thing."

"Trust me," I said. "There is."

"If it's the wrong person, you move on to the next."

"Doesn't it make more sense to try to pick the right person to begin with?" I asked. "If I'm going to expend the time and energy, it seems it should be with someone who wants me to."

"How are you going to know if someone wants you to?"

"That's what I'm asking *you*," I said. "At the very least, shouldn't I wait for a woman to send a signal that she's interested?"

"A woman doesn't have to show she's interested." He was emphatic. "All a flower has to do is be a flower. It's up to the bee to go to the flower. If she smiles at you, that's great. If she checks you out, even better. But she doesn't have to. You're the bee. You're the one who needs to show interest, even if you don't get any encouragement in return. You're still the bee, and a bee needs honey to live."

I thought a bee needed pollen, but I scrawled in my notebook like a remedial student cramming for a quiz.

"I usually charge a hundred fifty dollars for a session," Mike said, leaning back in his chair with a contented grin. "I'm just joking."

Then he handed me his business card.

Chapter Eleven

Be the Bee

Mike's bee metaphor was simplistic and chauvinistic—and utterly compelling. Bees cannot be flowers. Flowers cannot be bees. What could be more obvious than that? Yet I had spent years waiting for a flower to act like a bee.

I was determined to put this new insight to use immediately. I scanned Wooster Street through the light rain, but there was not a flower in sight. It didn't matter. For the first time in days, I felt empowered and optimistic.

That's when the flash flood hit.

There was a boom of thunder, and lightning slashed across the skyline. A deluge descended from the thick, dark clouds. I ran a few yards and took refuge on the covered stoop of a women's shoe store. New York downpours usually pass by in a few minutes. Twenty minutes later, I was still standing there as the wet wind whipped around me. Shivering, I contemplated an intricately strapped stiletto sandal that seemed more of an S&M device than a fashion accessory.

I looked up from the shoe display to see two statuesque blondes in black cashmere coats standing at the door and eyeing me eagerly. It was a sign from God. Or Mike Russo. Either way, it was time to make like a bee and get my buzz on. I gave my best Joey Tribbiani smile before I realized they were waiting for me to open the door for them.

"Are we supposed to tip him?" I heard one say to the other. After an awkward do-si-do, it became clear there wasn't enough room for all three of us on the stoop. I relinquished my space and sprinted down the block.

Spotting a coffee shop, I darted inside, only mildly drenched. I warmed my hands by an espresso machine and let the water drip off me before taking a place in line at the counter. I noticed it was three thirty, and I was running out of time for waiting out the storm. I was due at the office at four for a department meeting, which most likely was about some new cost-cutting plan. You can't make a turnip bleed, but you can certainly try.

I was silently berating the ambition-challenged latte boy, who seemed to be moving in slow motion. Then I remembered that this was precisely the kind of opportunity I was supposed to be taking advantage of: people waiting in a line. Sophisticated SoHo people who worked for art galleries and Web design companies. I checked out the five people in front of me. Not counting a German couple with a baby stroller, there was only one woman: a spry senior citizen in a yellow slicker.

Maybe I'd have better luck at the DMV. Then I heard an animated feminine voice behind me. In the back corner was a honey-streaked brunette with a swanlike neck and a ballet dancer's posture. She was sitting at a Formica table across from two hipsters in skinny jeans and matching dark eyeglass frames.

"I was in LA for six months, and my breasts are still the same size," she said with a throaty chuckle. "Though I think they exile you to Arizona after a year if you don't agree to augment by at least one cup."

"I thought you were in London," said Hipster Dude Number One.

"No, that was last year." She tore off a piece of a croissant from his plate.

There was a confidence in her physical movements and a skeptical intelligence in her gaze. I wondered if she was a creative director at a graphic design agency. Or a multinational architecture firm. I was intrigued, but hesitant about buzzing around in another bee's yard. Then Hipster Dude Number One licked latte foam off Dude Number Two's chin.

"Get a room," said the LA émigré. She laughed again. It was a welcoming laugh. Like she was inviting me over. All I had to do was walk fewer than three yards and tell a complete stranger that I was attracted to her, assuming that I really was. It was hard to be sure without knowing her religion, political views and SAT scores.

After convincing myself that standardized test scores were not a reliable measure of compatibility, I decided to go for it. What could she and her friends do to me?

Suddenly I was twelve years old, asking Julie Kaye if she wanted to "go around." I made my request over the phone, because it seemed more intimate than the school cafeteria. Though I had known Julie since we were six, the previous summer she had developed gentle curves and an insouciant pleasure in their deployment.

I was making a preemptive strike, hoping others hadn't

noticed her transformation from gawky orthodontic duckling to tween goddess. I received my answer on the school bus when Julie's blunt rejection was broadcast on Mark Roth's boom box from a tape recording she had secretly made of our conversation. The worst part was watching Mark's hand slip confidently into Julie's back pocket as they exited the bus together.

But I wasn't twelve anymore, and the hipster dude's hand was glued firmly to the thigh of his partner in all things retro. The worst-case scenario was sixty excruciating seconds, and I could always pretend to be a foreigner (*Je parle mauvais Anglais*).

I could feel my heartbeat accelerate as I contemplated what to say. What would get the attention of this potential female Frank Gehry? I watched as she took a tantalizing sip from her coffee cup and wrapped a long knit scarf around her open throat with a dramatic flourish.

"Sir?" A second employee appeared behind the counter and asked with feigned interest what I wanted. I ordered a large coffee and a brownie. I was going to need all the caffeine I could get to ask for her number. Though asking for a number seemed a little sleazy, regardless what Mike said.

I moved down to the register. As I took out my wallet to pay, I snuck another glance in her direction, but she was no longer sitting at the table. She was buttoning up a shearling coat and heading toward me, with the hipster twins close behind. I froze. And they were out the door.

"That will be seven ninety-eight," said the cashier.

I dropped a ten-dollar bill on the counter and ran after her.

The rain had yet to let up, so all three were huddled under the narrow awning. She was looking with dismay at the onslaught from above while pulling her hair into a loose bun.

"Hey!" I called out as I threw open the door. My pulse was

racing. "I was inside just now, and I couldn't take my eyes off of you. I think you're extraordinarily beautiful, and I would never forgive myself if I let you leave without asking you out to dinner."

Her mouth was hanging open at an odd angle, but it seemed closer to a smile than a grimace.

"Would it be possible to get your number?" I asked. Her friends watched her, waiting for a cue.

"I don't give out my number to guys on the street," she said, pulling her scarf tighter.

"How about your e-mail?"

"I don't give out my e-mail either," she said sympathetically before turning back to her friends.

Mike's voice reverberated in my head: "First thing out of your mouth should be where you work."

"You could e-mail *me* at The Paper," I blurted. "I work there. I write the wedding column."

"I love that column," Dude Number Two piped in. "I mean, I find it fascinating in an ironic way."

She turned toward me with renewed interest, so I forged ahead. "If you look up my columns online, you'll see my name, and if you click on my name, you can e-mail me." I held my breath, waiting for a response.

"So what's your name?" she miraculously asked.

"Gavin. Gavin Greene."

"I'm Téa." She held out her hand, and I held it lightly in my own. Dude Number Two eagerly introduced himself as well, but I didn't hear a word he said.

"What makes a good wedding story?" Téa inquired.

"Two people meeting during a rainstorm," I replied.

"The rain's letting up," said Dude Number One, sounding irritated. "We should get going."

"What are you doing tomorrow night?" I asked her.

"I have plans," she said.

"The night after?"

"I have a busy week coming up," she said, looking down at the wet pavement.

"Then how about tonight?" I surprised her. I surprised myself. Then again, some people don't like surprises.

"Tonight?" Her voice shot up two octaves. She turned to her friends. "What should I do?" she asked them.

"You should go out with me," I said before they could respond.

"I should?"

"Absolutely," I said.

She folded her arms across her chest and tugged at her scarf. "Twenty-four Carrots. Spelled like the vegetable. At gmail."

Score one for the bee.

"Do you want to write it down?" she asked as the hipster quotient ran up the street in their matching vintage sneakers, waving down a taxi.

"No need. I'll remember. I'll e-mail you." With my mission accomplished, I was at a loss for what to say next.

"Téa!" came a shout from down the block.

"Have a good ride," I said awkwardly, adding, "Stay dry."

She laughed as she took off toward the waiting cab.

"Twenty-four Carrots at gmail. Twenty-four Carrots at gmail." I repeated it over and over as I went back inside to claim my java.

The waiter placed two cups of sake on the minimalist birch table at Nobu (another cue from the Mike Russo playbook). Across from me was Téa Diaz, star of *All My Children*. Okay, not star. But regularly recurring character.

She had responded right away to the e-mail I sent her from work. "You really do write that column," she wrote. "I Googled you. You can Google me too."

Which, of course, I did. It's an odd thing to watch a steamy scene on YouTube of the woman you're about to go out with. My first thought was, *If I had known she was a soap opera sexpot, I wouldn't have had the nerve to approach her.* My second thought was, *Mike would be impressed.*

"I was once a reporter on *Days of Our Lives*," she said after we clinked cups, "but I didn't do much reporting. Mostly, I had sex with my editor, who was married to the daughter of a mafia boss. I was killed in a skydiving accident. Rule of thumb on a soap: When they tell you that your character is going skydiving, your 401(k) days are numbered."

Truth be told, I was a little disappointed she wasn't an architect, though I could almost hear Mike howl in disbelief. "My work's a little less dramatic," I said. "Less sex and death."

"In a newspaper?" She smiled seductively. "I doubt that."

"Less death, at least. It's the wedding pages."

Her neck was every bit as long and graceful as I recalled, emerging from an iridescent burgundy blouse with the hint of black lace at the lowermost vertex.

"So, do you travel round the world on the corporate credit card, looking for exotic weddings?" she asked.

"Not really. They're watching every penny these days." Why did I think this was information I needed to share? "I'm covering a wedding in Los Angeles next month, and my editor asked me today if I could stay with my brother." It was like my mouth was divorced from my brain.

"But you write one of the most popular columns."

"Yes, and the privilege of saying that is considered a significant part of my salary."

"Oh." Disappointment flickered across her tan face. I wanted to slap my own. Picking up a menu, she changed topics. "Nobu's one of my favorite places. It's great on a low-carb diet. I used to eat here once a week." *Wow. She must get paid well on soaps*, I thought. *Or dated well.* "What do you usually get?" she asked.

"It's my first time here," I mumbled.

"Oh," she said again, and this time the disappointment was mixed with apprehension. "I bet you get great meals at the weddings you go to."

The truth was, I didn't eat when on assignment. The Paper had an iron-clad rule about receiving anything that could be considered a gift. The concern was it could have an impact on objectivity, or, equally damaging, give other people the impression it had an impact. But I wasn't about to tell Téa that.

"What place had the best food?" she asked me.

"Blue Hill at Stone Barns," I punted, referring to the gourmet Mecca of the sustainable food movement, located on an organic farm an hour north of the city.

"I'm so jealous," she said. "Talk about a job with fringe benefits. I've been wanting to go there for years, but it's a hike getting to Tarrytown. I've heard they serve hand-picked individual tomatoes on a miniature wooden fence."

"They do. Ripe Sun Gold tomatoes with just a touch of sea salt." I had interviewed the publicist.

"You have to tell me what you ate. Course by course. And don't say you don't remember, because I won't believe you."

So much for punting. "I haven't actually eaten there," I had to confess. "But the food *looked* amazing." Mercifully, the waiter intervened.

"Do you know what you'd like tonight?" he asked enthusiastically.

The question was what could I afford. Nobu had been an

impulsive choice. I was already out thirty dollars for the sake, and I was hoping the evening would go well enough that I'd be ordering more. I scanned the menu for items in the lower stratosphere.

Téa was also deliberating: "I can never decide between the lobster salad and the black cod." The lobster salad was thirty-nine dollars and the cod was twenty-six dollars, so I was voting for the cod. "I'm feeling like something light," she said. There was an advantage to dating a woman who was a size two. "I'll go for the lobster salad, an order of ceviche, and three pieces of red snapper sushi." My eyes felt like rotating cash register digits, adding up the items: thirty-nine for the lobster plus seventeen for the ceviche plus twenty-one for the sushi.

"Light sounds good," I squeaked, without looking up, so that my face wouldn't betray the pinch I felt in my wallet. "I'll have the shiromi usuzukuri." I had no idea what it was, but it was only eighteen dollars and sounded more exotic than budgetary.

The waiter looked at me expectantly, asking, "Would you like something in addition to your sashimi?" Had I ordered sashimi?

"Saving room for dessert," I blathered. He looked skeptical.

Téa leaned toward me as he left, and I tried my best to keep my eyes on her face and not her lacy cleavage. "So, did you always dream of writing about weddings?"

Hardly. "I dreamed of playing backup guitar for the Rolling Stones."

"I'm not seeing it," she said with a smile and a sip of sake.

"I also dreamed of writing for *Rolling Stone* and decided that was more likely."

"So why don't you write about music?"

The question of the decade. "I wrote for *Spin* for a few years." I'd probably still have been writing for *Spin* if an old journalism professor hadn't introduced me to Renée. "The up-and-coming indie rockers I enjoy interviewing are too offbeat for The Paper, and more mainstream musicians aren't willing to open up with me. They just recite their press-release talking points, and there's no fun for me in being a glorified publicist."

"Uh-huh." She rearranged her chopsticks.

I was losing her. I tried to explain better. "What I thrive on is getting underneath a person's skin. I call it skin diving."

"Skin diving?"

I was reeling her back in. "When I sit down to write about a couple, I have up to twenty hours of tapes and sometimes a hundred pages of notes. I don't just read and listen. I submerge myself. Nothing exists but these two people, their thoughts and feelings."

"It sounds intense," she said. "It sounds sexy," is what she insinuated.

"I still get butterflies every time," I said, milking the thrill factor. "It's like going out on an early-morning dive. It's dark and cold. And staying on the boat seems a far more pleasant option. But I force myself to dive in."

"To what?"

"The couple's relationship. I explore the hidden crevices with a flashlight and a magnifying glass. Then I resurface with a sort-of prose sonar report, revealing the contours of their emotional bond." I didn't mention that I feared it was a substitute for forming my own.

"You must write about couples who have been together a long time."

"Not always," I said, looking deep into her vibrant aquamarine eyes. "A few weeks ago, I talked to a couple who met at camp when they were seven. He pushed her out of a canoe, and she had the preternatural wisdom to know that was a sign of affection. But the week before that was a couple who had known each other only six months."

"Have you talked to people who broke up and got back together?" Something about the question seemed a little rehearsed.

"Sure," I said.

"Do they end up okay?"

Did she think I was a reporter or a fortune-teller? "I can't really speak with any authority about what happens after the wedding reception."

She mulled that silently for a few moments. "Have you ever been married?"

Not my first-choice topic for first dates.

"No," I said, knowing what that sounded like coming from the mouth of a man my age.

"Have you lived with anyone?" was her next question.

I preferred when we were discussing restaurants I'd never eaten at. "Not in a formal kind of way," I answered, picturing Laurel in my bathrobe, drinking green tea from a Knicks coffee mug and working on the Sunday crossword puzzle. I expunged the image from my memory. "How about you?" I asked, more out of obligation than an active desire to know the details of her dating history.

"Pretty much the same," she said. "Never married. Though I had an on-again, off-again relationship with an investment banker for almost five years." She was trying to sound casual about it, but she wasn't entirely succeeding.

"Did you live together?" I asked.

She looked down at the table. "I'm supposed to move into his place tomorrow."

It was my turn to say "Oh."

"Or that's the plan. He's been pushing to move forward, and I've been very unsure. We've been back and forth so many times, and we haven't even been living in the same city for more than a few months. It's so easy to do something for the wrong reasons. Because you're scared. Because you're getting older. Because you don't want to make the effort to find someone new."

I nodded, wondering whether it was too late to cancel my sashimi.

"When you asked me out, I wasn't sure what to say, but I decided this is exactly what I needed. A chance to find out if there's someone else out there for me. Someone smart, sophisticated and successful."

That sounded more promising. I was ready to jump ship too soon. I was still getting this bee thing down.

"The truth is, I was dreading having the movers show up tomorrow," she said. "I feel so much better about it now. I really owe you."

The bill for dinner: $190. The emotional cost: immeasurable. As I walked home, I replayed the sequence of events in my head, wondering where I went wrong.

There was only one person to ask: Mike. After apologizing for calling so late, I launched into my tale of woe.

"A year ago," he said, "I hired one of the top marketing firms in the city to help me do a survey of what men and women look for in a mate." I wasn't even remotely interested in his survey. "What my research showed—which was quoted on *Oprah*—was that for men, the number-one concern was looks and the next was personality. For women, number one was financial success—"

"Meaning?" I asked, cutting him off.

"You need to date less-attractive women or start earning more money."

Chapter Twelve

Buzzkill

I dreamt I was getting married at Nobu.

I stood beneath a canopy of sashimi in front of a geriatric rabbi in an Elvis outfit, and a lobster salad sculpture of a giant koi. Beside me was my bride, but I couldn't see her face. She was hidden by a veil of newsprint. As I was about to say "I do," the waiter handed me a bill for the event and said my credit card had been denied. The bride screeched, and the rabbi beseeched the crowd, "If there is anyone present who can afford to marry this woman, let him speak now or forever hold his peace."

I bolted up in bed. I needed a raise.

I had never asked for one before. In fact, I didn't know if anyone at The Paper ever had. Newspapers aren't like banks. Your byline is your only bonus. I had always accepted that being underpaid and overworked was the natural order of things. Suddenly, I could see a future that included a bedroom. And stemware. It was like Mike had thrown open a damask curtain revealing an intoxicating new vista.

Feeling invigorated, I went for a short run and then charged uptown to work through lightly falling snow. When assigned to elevator B, I queued up with a sense of purpose and entitlement. I knew writers in the Entertainment section making double my salary. I wasn't going to ask for double, but I sure as hell was going to ask for my fair share.

Assuming I ever got upstairs. Elevator B was MIA.

Joe Mariano, a business columnist, was standing beside me. "If I wanted an extra half-hour commute, I'd move to Westchester," he said.

As if on cue, the errant but energy-efficient elevator arrived and whisked us upward. There was a newly installed digital screen where floor numbers could be displayed—*could be* but were not. When the doors opened, I poked out my head and scooted down the hall. I could hear Joe ask in his native Brooklyn patois: "Does anyone know what friggin' floor we're on?"

Moments later I was at my desk, but Renée was not at hers.

"Have you seen Renée?" I asked Tony.

"Target at twelve o'clock," he said without taking his eyes off his monitor.

Renée was in a glass conference room with Tucker Prescott, the head of the Lifestyles department. That was unusual. They had what I considered a unique working relationship: He barely tolerated her existence, and she pretended not to notice, which seemed to be working for them. Implicitly, interactions were kept to a minimum.

"I want to talk to her about a raise," I confided in Tony, testing his reaction.

"Good luck with that," he said, still glued to his computer screen. "They just announced layoffs."

"Who? When? Where?" I stuttered.

"I'm just reporting it as I'm reading it," Tony said.

My stomach churned as I quickly logged on. "Did they send out an e-mail?"

"Fat chance," Tony said. "I'm reading Gawker."

Gawker, the gossipy Web site devoted to all things snarky and sleazy in the media industry, was the best source of in-house news. When a music critic ripped the toupee off a copy editor and had to be restrained by a security guard, Gawker had the story with video before the rumor had circulated past the third floor.

I found it disappointing that people didn't have a greater sense of loyalty to The Paper. But at times like this, I was also grateful.

According to Gawker, unnamed sources at The Paper predicted the imminent elimination of 150 news staff jobs, which was roughly equivalent to recent announced cuts at the *L.A. Times* and the *Washington Post*. As if that was consolation.

With all the newspapers pulling back, it would be nearly impossible to find a job if I was laid off. I knew I shouldn't assume that I would be. In fact, there was no proof that anyone would be. Gawker often got things wrong. Fact-checking was not their forte. I needed to find out if other news sites were carrying the story. My phone rang, and I distractedly answered while scanning CNN's home page.

"This is Emily from the *Today Show*."

I freaked out. The *Today Show*'s standards were much higher than Gawker's. What did they know that I didn't?

"I have Roxanne Goldman on the line for you." False alarm. Roxanne was a segment producer whose Malibu wedding was the last weekend in February. I had a preliminary interview scheduled with her at two p.m.

"I need to take a rain check on our appointment," Roxanne said. I guess I *had* an interview scheduled. It was the third time she had canceled on me. Either she was a diva or she was getting cold feet about doing an article. She was marrying an Israeli gymnast she met while on assignment at the Athens Olympics. I had heard about her wedding from a publicist, and I was concerned the publicist wanted the piece more than she did.

"Do you want to do it later in the day?" I asked.

"I was thinking later in the week," she countered. It was Friday.

"Unless you want to do something this weekend, we're talking about next week," I said.

"Even better. Would you mind doing it in the evening?"

Of course I'd mind. "How about six on Monday?" I considered six p.m. a compromise.

"Let's do nine on Tuesday. Oops, that's Lauer on the other line. E-mail me if there's a problem."

It never ceased to surprise me how many women assumed their wedding was the most important event in *everyone's* life. Fortunately for Roxanne, it didn't behoove me to take an adversarial tone with a bride. A publicist was another story, and this one's client chose the wrong morning to piss me off.

I looked up the phone number for Brooke Brenner, the PR agent who'd been pitching me Roxanne's wedding for months. It was an LA area code. I wondered if it was too early to call, but by then I had worked up a head of steam and figured I'd just leave a curt voice mail. My attention was diverted by the sight of Renée angrily gesticulating in the conference room, and I was caught off guard when Brooke answered the phone groggily. I sheepishly identified myself, and she immediately perked up.

"We're so excited about the article," she gushed.

"Well, that's not exactly how it's coming across," I said,

deliberating if I should apologize for waking her or stick to playing the ticked-off reporter. I noticed Tucker seemed to be successfully placating Renée.

"What do you mean?" Brooke asked breathily. I pictured her batting her eyes at me. Not that I knew what her eyes even looked like, since we had spoken only on the phone. But she had a sexy voice with a disarming giggle. I was losing my focus.

"Roxanne's canceled on me three times, and she seems to think it's my job to work round the clock to accommodate her," I said, worried that I was coming off as peevish. "If we're having this much trouble scheduling the first interview, it makes me uneasy about getting the others in. Which is why I wanted to let you know that if she cancels again, I'm going to have to kill the piece."

"That is not going to happen," Brooke assured me. "I am so sorry you've been inconvenienced." Her soothing, apologetic tone made me feel like a jerk. "Roxanne's just been so busy with work and the wedding. But that is *so* not your problem. By the way, I loved your column last week. I cried."

"Really?" I asked. Flattery will get you everywhere.

"I had to get a Kleenex. Did he really show up at the airport and stop her from getting on the plane?"

"With a bouquet of wildflowers," I threw in.

"You didn't mention the wildflowers in the piece."

"It got cut," I said, still a little sore about the subject. Captain Al had extracted a pound of flesh for agreeing to leave my lede intact.

"Why don't I ever meet men like that?" Brooke asked. I made note of the fact she was single. Just being a thorough journalist.

"Roxanne will be available at whatever time works best for you. Just send me an e-mail, and I'll arrange it."

I glimpsed Renée and Tucker getting up from the conference

room table. Renée didn't look happy. So much for Gawker making things up. Whatever was going on was real. And seemed really bad.

"Can't wait to see your next column," Brooke said before hanging up. At this point, I was just hoping there would be a next column.

Renée emerged briskly from the conference room, her jaw clenched and her lips pursed. Though that was always how she looked after a conversation with Tucker.

He ambled out behind her. Standing over six foot four, Tucker Prescott had the kind of regal profile that belonged on Mount Rushmore. His weather-beaten, athletic frame resulted from years of mountain biking (and varsity lacrosse at Dartmouth). He was the bad sheep from a good Boston family, having traded in his docksiders for Birkenstocks after college, when he traveled through South America as one of the youngest foreign correspondents in The Paper's history. He had risen steadily over the past twenty years through a mix of political finesse and emotional indifference.

Renée once described talking to him as akin to bathing in motor oil: "It's not necessarily going to hurt you, but it's not going to help much either."

To his credit, under his guidance Lifestyles had become one of the most profitable departments, leading to the resentment of hard-news sections that were less popular with readers and the advertisers who covet them. In retaliation, Tucker was the whipping boy of weekly managerial meetings. He was openly treated with disdain and disinterest. Which was pretty much how he treated Renée.

If Lifestyles was the black sheep of the newspaper, Weddings was the black sheep of Lifestyles. Though everything we did was under Tucker's aegis, it was rare for him to read our pages.

Tony and I once had a bet over who could go the longest without being acknowledged by Tucker. The rules were we had to say "Good morning" or some other salutation every time we saw him. Tony won after twenty-one days, when Tucker asked me to pass him a hand towel in the bathroom.

True to form, Tucker didn't stop to chitchat after his meeting with Renée, and Renée was also silent as she plopped herself down at her desk and started reviewing page layouts. Tony and I convened at her cubicle in supplication, modern-day Oliver Twists beseeching her for a morsel of information.

"Take those lost-puppy expressions off your faces," she said, still focused on the layouts. "I got nothing for you."

"Did Tucker say there would be cuts in our department?" Tony asked. He was worried about supporting his children. I was worried about ever having any.

"No," Renée answered.

"Did he say there wouldn't be cuts?" was my follow-up, which received the same monosyllabic response.

Alison made her midmorning entrance. As she took off her wet parka, she said, "I heard Google is buying The Paper."

"Gawker predicted Murdoch," Tony lobbed.

Renée rocketed to her feet. "Gawker is a gossip rag," she said. "This is a newspaper. We stick to facts."

"No offense, Renée," said Tony, "but the fact is we saw you arguing with Tucker. We know something is up."

Renée scowled before declaring, "Tucker is disappointed in our 'Interweb' efforts." The terminology was Tucker's. We were never quite sure if he was being ironic or ignorant. "He suggested we start posting wedding breaking-news stories."

"Is there such a thing?" Alison asked. It was an impudent question, but a good one.

"He wants us generating more traffic to the Web site." Renée read from her notepad. "He wants more sticky eyeballs."

"I think my kids made those for Halloween," Tony said. He chuckled. Renée didn't.

"Tucker wants us to start a blog with five-hundred- to eight-hundred-word entries posted a minimum of twice daily."

"Starting when?" Tony asked, no longer laughing.

"As soon as we figure out what the hell we're going to fill a blog with. He wants a proposal next week."

"Will we get paid?" was my primary question. Renée gazed at me over the top of her glasses with a look one would give a brain-damaged child.

More work. No extra money. And diminished job security. So far the day was a career trifecta. My unborn children called out to me, begging not to be raised in a studio apartment.

The snow was coming down harder outside the building's thin glass walls as Renée planted herself back into her chair, signaling us that class was dismissed. "Is any of this negotiable?" I asked. I had started the day determined to ask for a raise, and I'd be damned if I didn't at least try.

"That depends," Renée replied.

"On what?"

"On whether you believe Gawker got their story right."

Chapter Thirteen

The Better Man

Manhattan is never quite as majestic as during a snow-storm. Skyscrapers melt into soft focus behind swirl-ing white powder that blankets the empty canyons of the traffic grid with car-high snowdrifts. The pristine accumu-lation makes the city seem cleaner and gentler.

Unless you're a bride.

In which case, each flake mocks and scorns. Amy was han-dling it better than many. No tears. No tirades. Just a complete emotional breakdown.

Her florist, Fabio, flagged me down as I emerged from the elevator on the sixty-fifth floor of Rockefeller Center, warning me there was more than one kind of turbulence at the Top of the Rock.

"The confetti's here, but the cake is not," Fabio informed me sotto voce, immediately slipping me his business card. "Her dress is locked in a warehouse in Queens, and her sister's been trapped in the Chicago airport for twenty-four hours. It's no wonder the poor girl is losing it."

I was already feeling pressured to deliver a killer piece in the hope of protecting my job. A stressed-out bride made for nervous bridesmaids, and nervous bridesmaids gave lousy quotes. It was going to be a long night. Who was I kidding? It was always a long night.

"She's just staring out the window," Fabio reported as he led me down a terrazzo-tiled hallway of glass-and-rosewood columns. "At one point she was counting snowflakes. The bridegroom is beside himself, and the best man, well, don't get me started on the best man." Fabio seemed to relish the opportunity to be a news source, but I suspected what he really wanted was to get his name in The Paper. "Did I give you my card yet?"

He pushed open a heavy paneled door, revealing Mike in a shawl-collared tuxedo, pacing a plushly carpeted room with a hangdog mien. Beside him was a largish tuxedoed man with thinning blond hair who had one hand on Mike's shoulder and a champagne glass in the other.

Mike seemed genuinely happy to see me and unexpectedly hugged me, which was both endearing and discomforting. It's hard to maintain objective distance while being embraced. As a journalist, I like to think there's an invisible shield surrounding me. I clearly watch too much Cartoon Network.

"This is Brody," Mike said, gesturing to the man beside him, "the best man."

"If I'm the best man, then why are you the one she's marrying?" Brody said with a loud laugh, then downed his champagne in a single gulp and deposited the empty glass on an ebony credenza before vigorously shaking my hand.

Mike smiled halfheartedly. "I'm worried about Amy," he

said to me. "I've never seen her like this. She just shut down. She won't even talk to me."

"Well, better get used to that part," Brody chortled.

"She wants to talk to *you*," Mike said, looking my direction.

"Me?" I looked behind me to see if someone was standing there. No one was.

"Do you mind?"

Amy was sitting in a curvy Art Deco suite straight out of a 1930s Hollywood film. I pictured a dozen aproned chorines attending to her and breaking into a Gershwin song as the snowflakes spiraled outside the panoramic windows.

"I'm not getting married," she announced, wrenching me out of musical-comedy land into melodrama.

"You're the easiest person to tell," she continued without looking at me. Bereft of her bridal gown, she was wearing a loose-fitting print dress over black leggings, with her arms folded tightly across her chest. "You're a reporter, so you can report it to everyone else."

I didn't know how to respond. Wrangling runaway brides was not part of my job description.

"Every bride gets nervous," I said, grasping for something impartial but helpful.

"I'm not nervous. I'm making a rational decision."

If I tried to change her mind, I'd be violating a journalism commandment: Thou shalt not interfere. It was imperative to only observe and never participate in an event being reported. On the other hand, if I didn't do something fast, there wouldn't be anything to observe. Not only would all the hours spent interviewing her and Mike be wasted, but I would be left empty-handed. Wedding or no wedding, I still had an article due and a job potentially on the line.

I had only one experience with a story falling through. It was three years back, when a bridegroom walked down the aisle and then kept on walking—out the side door of Our Lady of Perpetual Help. The priest ran after him and so did half the congregation, including the bride's Sicilian grandmother, who threw her back out throwing her cane at the bridegroom's Land Rover. While Nana was rushed to Victory Memorial, I made an emergency visit of my own to the marriage bureau at City Hall, where couples go for quickie weddings of minimal pomp and dubious circumstance. I interviewed a Ukrainian masseuse marrying her octogenarian landlord, and two eighteen-year-old high-school dropouts who were expecting their first child (shortly after their ceremony). Out of desperation, I chose to write about the teenagers, because they at least brought flowers. The Ukrainian brought her boyfriend.

I didn't think Amy should get married just to help me make my deadline, but a wedding definitely seemed mutually beneficial.

"You have a lot of guests arriving," I said.

"I have a lot of guests not arriving." She turned toward me, and there were dark smudges of mascara under her eyes. "My sister slept on a bench in O'Hare last night. My favorite aunt and uncle are stuck in Dallas. My cousins in Philly called a few hours ago to say the interstate was closed and they were turning back. I believe in signs, and this is beyond a sign. This is the universe sending me a direct message to stop what I'm doing."

"If people called off their weddings every time there was a storm, there would be a lot fewer married couples in the world," I said.

"This isn't just a storm. This is biblical."

To the best of my knowledge, there wasn't a lot of snow in the bible.

"I wanted to elope," she said. "I told Mike getting married here felt wrong. He should have listened to what I said."

"You specifically said that?"

"He should have listened to what I *didn't* say, and I didn't say I wanted this. I never wanted a big wedding. He couldn't possibly have thought that I did. Unless he doesn't know me, and how can I marry a man who doesn't know me?"

I assumed the question was rhetorical until she looked up at me with a wide-eyed expression beseeching some kind of response.

"Let's say, for the sake of argument, that you don't go through with the wedding," I said.

"I'm not."

"Then what?"

She didn't say anything. That was good. It meant she hadn't had a chance to think things through. Of course, neither had I.

"What do you do after everyone leaves tonight?" I asked, stalling for time. "What do you do tomorrow? What are you going to say to Mike?"

"I think it's really wrong of you to try and pressure me. I thought you were the one person I could talk to who wouldn't try to bully me into getting married."

I wasn't trying to bully her. It was an unfair accusation, and I resented it.

"I *don't* think you should get married." The words came out of my mouth before they had been cleared for takeoff. "If you don't love Mike and want to spend your life with him, then you shouldn't marry him."

"You don't think I should marry him?" she asked in a small voice.

"Not if you don't love him." I was flying on autopilot, unsure of my destination.

"I *do* love him," she said, not sounding very pleased about it.

"Do you feel that he loves you?"

"Of course I do. Or I wouldn't be here."

"Then I don't know how you can give up on that," I blurted. It was how I truly felt—and completely inappropriate to say. I had crossed the line from dispassionate observation to something primordial. "Mike can't take his eyes off of you. Even when he's working. He sits in his office and stares at your picture with a look of gratitude and awe. Do you know how many people are searching desperately to find someone who will look at them like that?" My voice was shaking. "You don't throw love away. I'm not saying getting married is an easy decision. I'm saying you're lucky that you have someone to make the hard decisions with."

I felt my lungs compress. I had to stop talking, afraid of what sound was going to come out of my throat. I was mortified to realize my eyes were watering. I could only hope that Amy was too immersed in her own feelings to notice my emotional distress.

"I still don't have a gown," she said after a couple minutes of looking out the window. "Or a maid of honor." She seemed to sink deeper into the upholstered wing chair. "If we had eloped, we wouldn't be having any of these problems."

"So elope," I said, my breathing coming easier.

"It's a little late for that."

Was it?

"There's a judge down the hall, already paid for," I said. "It's not like you're going to get a refund." She snapped her head my direction. I couldn't tell if she was insulted or intrigued.

Forty minutes later, I got my answer. Standing alongside the fifty guests who braved the inclement weather, I watched Amy walk down a petal-strewn aisle in her leggings and Ugg boots. Mike strode beside her, having traded his tuxedo for jeans and a plaid flannel shirt.

Judge Louise Flanagan led a short civil ceremony. No frills. No commentary. No different from if they were in her chambers. When she asked Mike if he promised to love and honor his bride, he spoke directly to Amy, as if she were the only other person in the room.

"Amy," he said, holding her hands in his, "you are the woman I want. Not someone in a fancy white dress. Not someone who pretends things are okay when they're not. You stole my heart from the moment I first saw you, and I don't ever want it back."

There were tears in her eyes as she responded. "I get scared, Mike. I get lost in my thoughts. Your love is the light that guides me out of the forest. You're the reason every day for me to find my way out of the forest."

I had heard so many flowery vows about metaphoric trees, soaring birds and sunny skies. But Amy was acknowledging the darkness. The effort it takes every single day to pull yourself out of yourself. Who wouldn't be grateful to have someone rooting for you and waiting for you? Someone willing to enter the darkness, Orpheus-like, and rescue you from yourself.

I wondered if I could have been that person for Laurel, and I found myself conceding that I hadn't been. Even in our most intimate moments, a part of me held back, afraid of being pulled under. Into what, I couldn't even put into words. It was a self-protective reflex. But without it, I could only imagine how much worse I would have felt when she left me. If it was possible to feel worse.

I watched Amy and Mike place rings on each other's fingers. He laughed when he couldn't get hers on, and she tenderly helped him. I understood why they were together in a way I hadn't before. It wasn't that they were a perfect couple, but that they balanced each other. His optimism was the antidote to her nervousness. Her caution tempered his bravado.

The judge pronounced them husband and wife, and a boom box blasted as Mike scooped Amy into his arms. Like a certain green ogre and his bride, they kissed to the accompaniment of "I'm a Believer."

The Russo family didn't believe that less was more. The reception was a ten-course Italian-style banquet, and it was family tradition for everyone to give a toast.

Amy's father started the ball rolling, asking if he still had to pay for the bridal gown. Mike's parents recited a lengthy list of relatives who hadn't been able to make it to the event (some of whom I suspected were long dead). Then the microphone was indiscriminately passed to assorted cousins, neighbors and a Rainbow Room bartender. We were well into the third hour of speeches when Brody took the microphone hostage.

"Love means never having to shave your back," he declared. Wearing his tuxedo jacket over a T-shirt and torn jeans, Brody seemed to be auditioning for a stand-up comedy show. On cable-access in Latvia. For twenty-five minutes, he rambled on. The longer he talked, the more he drank. The more he drank, the slower he talked.

I shifted my weight from one leg to the other, trying to

mitigate the ache in my lower back from the five hours I had been on my feet. When waiters started serving the roast duckling entrees, Brody got the hint (or got hungry). It was time to make my exit. However, I was stopped by the sound of a clinking wineglass. Amy was standing at her table.

"Everyone knows how much I hate talking in public," she said, "so I'm going to make this very short." She thanked Mike, their parents and their fifty hardy guests.

"And I want to thank Gavin Greene, who's hiding behind a mirrored column in the back of the room." I wasn't hiding so much as cringing. "I put him in an impossible situation, and against his better judgment, he offered me some very good advice. Sometimes it truly is harder to give than it is to receive, and I want him to know that I'll always be grateful."

She had potentially just destroyed my career. If anyone at The Paper learned how far I had strayed from my observer's role, the story would be killed along with my reputation.

I had made a foolish choice. Yet a warm feeling emanated from my chest. I felt flattered and appreciated. More than that. I felt proud. I had somehow managed to say the right thing when I hadn't even been sure there was one. Maybe writing about so many weddings had taught me something about relationships. Maybe Mike should be the one asking me questions. The future seemed a lot less foreboding than it had only hours earlier.

As I was on my way out of the room, Brody grabbed me by the arm, a glass of whiskey sloshing precariously in his other hand. "Hey," he said, "you didn't interview me yet. Don't you want the best man's take on the big event?"

I had purposely been avoiding him, but since Brody had grown up with Mike in Boston, there was a chance he had a good anecdote to share. I reluctantly opened up my pad, flipping to my last page of notes. "So, why do you think Amy is the right person for Mike?"

"Who said I thought she was right for him?" he tittered, taking a gulp of his whiskey. "I'm just joshing with you. I think she's great. I think they're great together. I hope they have an amazing time tonight. Because it doesn't last."

"Excuse me?" I wasn't sure I heard right.

"You know what you should do? You should do a column about what happens after the wedding. You should do a column about what happens six months later. Six years later." I noticed a pale band of skin around the ring finger of his left hand. "Now, that would be something useful to read."

The drunk and bitter best man was not a Hollywood myth but a flesh-and-blood reality. I had learned to approach with the same wary respect a mail carrier must show an unleashed pit bull.

"Thanks for the suggestions," I said. "I'll pass them along." I was finished with the interview, but I was concerned that closing my pad would be taken as an act of aggression.

"Are you married?" Brody asked me. I didn't answer. He violently grabbed my left arm again and thrust it into the air.

"No ring!" he bellowed. "What the hell are you doing writing about weddings? Are you some kind of wedding Peeping Tom?"

My arm was wrenched above my head and my back was against a wall. I tried to pull away, but he was clutching my arm tightly and not letting go.

I was eleven years old again, being blocked in a back hallway of middle school by an older bully who wouldn't let me get to my class. No, I was a reporter for The Paper. He couldn't do this to me.

"What do you know about what Mike's getting himself

into?" he persisted, daring me to retaliate, but there was no way I was going to let him goad me into a fistfight. "What do you know about devoting your life to someone and getting your heart ripped out in return? You want to write about something, then get yourself on the front lines and learn about it firsthand. Have someone take your home and your life savings and see what you think of some asshole writing romantic fairy tales." His mouth was only inches from my nose. Each word was expelled with a sour odor that made me gag. I wanted to punch him. I wanted to scream. I wanted to disappear.

"This is bullshit," he said, abruptly dropping my arm. "What the fuck do you know about marriage?"

Chapter Fourteen

In the Wee Small Hours
of the Morning

I was a fraud. It was obvious to Brody. It was obvious to the cashier at the Westside Market, where I stopped a little before midnight to pick up a rotisserie chicken for dinner. I saw myself reflected in the store window. My thin black tie and pressed white shirt were visible beneath my wool coat as I emptied my grocery basket of the chicken, milk, eggs, Frosted Flakes and a jar of tomato sauce. A New York Lifestyles reporter living it up on a Saturday night.

The cashier, a kind-faced Hispanic teenager, seemed to look at me with pity as she rang up my meager items. She probably had a hot date lined up after her shift. She gave me an encouraging smile when she handed me my change, as if to say, "You're not such a bad-looking guy. A little scrawny for my taste, but I'm sure there's a woman somewhere who would be willing to go out with you."

As I trudged home, I needed moral support. I started dialing

Hope's number before allowing myself to consider if it was too late to call.

She answered her phone breathlessly. "I'm on a date."

I assumed she wouldn't respond well if I asked how that was possible.

"Match-dot-com," she said as if reading my mind. "You should join!"

I had forgotten that Hope had been preaching the gospel of Internet dating since her third coffee date in two weeks. I had refrained from reminding her that the last time she was on Match, she had two dozen coffee dates but no second dates.

"So you've graduated past coffee," I said, sounding only half as churlish as I felt.

"I was instant messaging with a guy, and he invited me for a midnight drink at Lansky Lounge."

"That's not a date. That's a booty call. He's a player."

"He's a pediatrician. And am I better off staying home alone?" A flurry-flecked couple passed me on the sidewalk, holding each other close. "He said, 'A snowstorm is a terrible thing to waste.' Isn't that sweet?"

"Very," I said sourly. "So, why are you answering your phone?"

"I can't find him. I've been looking for fifteen minutes. It's very dark."

"The outlook?"

"The room!"

I felt guilty about teasing her, and I was going to feel even worse if the guy turned out to be a no-show. A blast of wind caught me as I climbed the steps leading to the front of my apartment building.

"Maybe he's waiting for me outside," she said with a quiver in her voice.

"Maybe," I said, though it seemed doubtful. She deserved

better. Much better. If I blew off transcribing my notes from the wedding, I could jump in a taxi and be at Lansky Lounge in ten minutes.

"Or maybe," Hope's voice rose an octave, "he's sitting at a fireside table with two wineglasses and an open bottle of cabernet. Oh, my God, he's standing up. He looks even cuter than his picture. And taller!" She bubbled over with delight. "Gotta go."

I sat down in front of my computer without taking off my suit. Without putting away my groceries. I opened my Web browser and typed in www.JDate.com.

I had mostly avoided online dating because I found it too much like shopping and I'm not a good shopper. I tend to get overwhelmed in stores and leave empty-handed or rashly buy something just to validate the time invested.

Come to think of it, that was how I dated.

I stripped the chicken of white meat while intently scrolling through pictures of single Jewesses. I chose JDate because given my relationship track record, I thought it might be a good idea to start with something in common, and since there wasn't a dating site for people with literary aspirations who were soon to be unemployed, JDate would have to suffice.

I quickly learned that unemployed would be a deal breaker. Even employed, I wasn't necessarily going to make the cut. At least not for Manhattan women with svelte figures and Ivy League degrees (though I was, admittedly, setting my sights a little high). A six-figure income was a popular prerequisite for initiating e-mail contact. "Tall" and "successful" popped up regularly along with "comfortable in a tuxedo or blue jeans." (Were they looking for James Bond or a date?) But the number-one desired attribute was "a guy's guy." *As opposed to what?* I wondered. *A girl's guy?* And if there was such a person as a girl's guy, wouldn't that be a good thing?

George Clooney's name was mentioned so often as the ideal mate that I questioned people's grasp of reality. Not that I was any better, compulsively clicking on any woman's photo that vaguely resembled the Semitic beauty of Natalie Portman.

There was something sordid about it. Like I should be wearing a raincoat as I hunched over my keyboard, trolling through profiles by the bluish light of my screen.

Then at one a.m. I saw her. Her. The one. ComeFlyWithMe was her screen name. She had the almond eyes and olive skin of Emmanuelle Chriqui from *Entourage*, with the same dark, flowing locks (and the cleavage). She was a graphic designer addicted to Frosted Flakes, and she worked off the carbs by running along the Hudson and dancing late into the night. Her favorite place to be was an international airport, "because there are so many possibilities." She said she was looking for a smart, funny guy with "passion to burn and a song in his heart."

I was SO that guy.

All I needed was a chance to prove it. I set to work composing a witty, unaffected, confident yet humble, erudite and effervescent e-mail. It didn't go well. It was hard to be clever without sounding fey. Even harder to be both seductive and sincere. After an hour of effort, I was tempted to just say I was "a guy's guy" and leave it at that.

It was past two by the time I finished the e-mail to ComeFly-WithMe. Then I had to come up with an amusing subject line. It was another half hour until I settled on "I've Got a Crush On You." Sinatra reference in place, I finally hit SEND. A pop-up balloon appeared on my screen, informing me that ComeFly-WithMe was online. A flashing icon propositioned me, asking, DO YOU WANT TO CHAT LIVE?

It had taken me almost two hours to write one e-mail. I couldn't take the pressure of instant messaging.

But what if she also got a message saying I was online? Would she wonder why I wasn't writing? Her smile beckoned from a shot of her in a sleeveless yellow sundress. Though it wasn't her smile I was staring at.

"Nice photo on the beach," I wrote.

There was no response. For more than a minute. Then: "What are you doing looking at my pictures in the middle of the night?"

I felt like a five-year-old caught looking up a girl's dress. (It happened only once, and I was picking up a stray marble.) I had blown it. Then I received a second IM:

":-)"

It was on. "What are *you* doing messaging strangers at strange hours?" I wrote.

"Someone has to take pity on all the lonely men at their computer monitors," she quickly replied, upping the dare level.

"I thought that's what your pictures were there for." I marveled at the amount of damage I could do with a mouse and a keyboard.

There was radio silence. I started typing. "I do much better on delayed telecast."

"Are you hungry?" flashed on my screen. Followed by, "Get your mind out of the gutter. I know a great all-night kebab place."

My phone rang, and I jumped, thinking it was her before remembering that it couldn't be.

"Gavin!" It was my grandmother. She had a habit of calling late when she couldn't sleep, forgetting that, unlike Gary, I was in the same time zone. "I'm so glad you're there."

"So what's your feeling about skewered meat?" ComeFly-WithMe queried, as if I needed more enticement.

"I like meat," I typed, cradling the phone against my shoulder.

"How much?" was the response.

"Bernie had some kind of seizure." My grandmother's voice was shrill. "I think it starts with a 'P.' I can't remember the name." She sounded frantic.

"It's okay, Grandma."

"No, it's not okay. I'm telling you he had a seizure."

"I mean it's okay you don't know the name." I glanced at my screen. "How much?" appeared a second time.

"Ostrovsky. I think that's the name," my grandmother said.

"Of the seizure?" I asked.

"Of the doctor. A young doctor. He talks very fast. He said Bernie needs emergency surgery."

Images of skewered flesh and surgical instruments flashed through my mind in disturbing combination. Multitasking wasn't working.

"I'm sorry, I have to go," I typed, wincing with every keystroke. "I'd really like to *meat* some other time." The pun seemed funny in my head, which is where I devoutly wished it had stayed, since ComeFlyWithMe didn't write back.

"Gavin, I don't know what to do." My grandmother was near tears.

"I'm going to call the doctor," I said, already Googling the hospital. A craving for kebabs lingered in the pit of my stomach.

"The nurse gave me a paper to sign, but I don't have my glasses."

"It's okay." I repeated gently, "I'm going to call the doctor."

"Tell him I don't have my glasses."

I remembered being five and bawling in her arms. It was after a traumatic tricycle incident with an unrepentant palm tree. She told me it was okay to cry, that crying got all the pain out, and she rocked me back and forth while I buried my face in her sweater.

"It's okay, Grandma." I said. "Everything's going to be okay."

Chapter Fifteen

Turbulence

My flight to Fort Lauderdale was rain delayed. While the plane lurched between tempestuous altitudes, I gripped the armrests and imagined my parents waiting for me at the airport gate. They hadn't been able to do that since I was a kid, but as the plane pitched and dipped, I was nine years old again, running down a jetway into their arms. My father threw me in the air, his coat smelling like cigarettes even though he didn't smoke.

"Did you have a good time with your grandma?" he asked.

"Uh-huh," I said. "She said I can come to Florida by myself again anytime Gary has soccer playoffs during Thanksgiving."

"Any collisions with fast-moving palm trees?"

"That was years ago!" I protested.

My mother's lipstick was candy-apple red, and she rubbed some of it off my cheek after kissing me.

"Did you miss us?" she asked.

I shook my head.

"Not at all?"

I shook my head vehemently. Then I threw my arms around her neck.

Upon a bumpy but gratifying landing, I tried to remember the last time I told my parents that I loved them. I hurried through the Delta terminal, uncharacteristically eager to do so. Thirty minutes later, my warm feelings were wilting in the Floridian heat. My carry-on duffel bag hung from one shoulder and my laptop case from the other, as I paced the pick-up zone, searching for the metallic lavender cruise ship my parents considered a car. I had already called my mother's cell phone twice, but it had gone straight to voice mail. After another twenty minutes, I was beginning to worry and called again.

"Gavin," my mother answered cheerfully, "it's so nice to hear your voice."

"Where are you?" I asked, suspecting I wasn't going to like the answer.

"I'm putting you on speakerphone in the car. Can you hear us?"

"I can hear you. Where are you?"

"Gavin, tell us if you hear us," she repeated.

"WHERE ARE YOU?"

"You hit the mute button," I heard my father say.

"That's impossible," she said. "I don't even know where the mute button is."

I hung up and called back.

The phone rang several times before my mother picked up. There was much amplified jiggling, as if the handset were being scraped against every surface in their vehicle.

"Why are you calling?" my mother finally asked. "Did you miss your plane?"

"My plane landed an hour ago," I said with the adolescent whine nurtured over years of waiting for them curbside. "Are you anywhere in the vicinity of the airport?"

"You're not supposed to be here until two," my father said.

"I told you he was coming at noon," my mother scolded.

"You never said that," he replied.

"Dad," I said with as much affection as I could still muster with sweat dripping down my neck, "I specifically called you this morning to remind you." Bad choice of words. At seventy, he was sensitive about his memory.

"I don't need you to remind me of anything," he snapped.

I wasn't going to convince my father he was mistaken, and I knew I shouldn't want to. I vowed silently to be a better person, but what I said out loud was, "If you don't need me to remind you, then why aren't you here?"

"I need you to give me the right time!"

"I said noon!"

"YOU NEVER SAID THAT!"

It wasn't supposed to be like this. I was going to be loving and demonstrative. They were going to be . . . functional.

"Did you congratulate Gary?" my mother asked. I had no idea what I was supposed to be congratulating him for. "Gary and Leslie are celebrating their seven-month anniversary."

"Who celebrates a seven-month anniversary?" I asked.

"People in relationships," my mother said pointedly.

"Gary's in a relationship with another girl every year," my father groused. "The whole advantage of being single is not having to put up with being in a relationship."

"Just what have you had to put up with?" my mother wanted to know.

He proceeded to recite a list, which I assumed was

chronological, since he started with the seating arrangement at their wedding reception.

While they prosecuted crimes and misdemeanors of the previous century, I sat on the curb. It was the closest I had come to resting in two days. I had spent most of the flight working on my column about Amy and Mike, which had gotten short shrift on Sunday as I coordinated both my trip and Bernie's medical care, while also checking hourly for JDate messages from Come-FlyWithMe. I had sent an e-mail explaining what had happened, but I hadn't heard back from her.

I did, however, hear from SaneJane, who didn't seem all that sane. Her name was Janet, but she liked the rhyme. The first e-mail she sent was a simple hello, saying she liked my profile. The second e-mail was checking to make sure I got the first e-mail, because she had some kind of computer glitch. The third e-mail was apologizing for the second e-mail. She attached a photo with a live python wrapped around her, suggesting a fondness for danger or bestiality. In either case, I decided it was best not to respond.

But I was in continual contact with my grandmother, who wavered between feisty optimism and atypical despondency. I tried my best to comfort her and promised I would be there as soon as possible. What was stopping me was my parents.

We had been on the phone for twenty minutes, and the only thing quickly approaching was my article deadline. If I was going to be on the phone with anyone, it should have been with Roxanne Goldman, the *Today* producer I was supposed to finally interview the next morning. I should have called her to reschedule before calling my parents. Or I should have called her publicist. But what I really should have done was rented a car.

"How far are you from Fort Lauderdale?" I interrupted.

"Fort Lauderdale? We're on our way to Palm Beach," my mother said.

"Why on earth are you going to Palm Beach?"

"Because that's where you said you were coming in," my father said. "You told us two o'clock at the Palm Beach airport!"

"He said noon!" my mother interjected.

"In Fort Lauderdale!" I howled.

They responded simultaneously: "You never said that."

My grandmother seemed smaller than I remembered and almost girlish in her sweatshirt and leggings, with her silver hair pulled back in a ponytail. She was sitting at the side of Bernie's hospital bed, where he laid inert with his mouth open, eyes closed and various vinelike tendrils mooring him to equipment along the perimeter of the room. A soft beeping pulsed as my grandmother attempted to feed him from a small glass jar.

"Come on, Bernie," she said, bringing a spoon to his lips. "Open wider."

"Grandma, they're feeding him intravenously," I said.

"That's not food. I made him a beautiful tuna casserole with green beans and walnuts and celery. Just the way he likes it."

"He's going to choke."

"I put it in the blender and made it nice and smooth. Do you want some?"

"No."

"It's delicious."

"It's pureed."

She leaned toward him as if anticipating him sitting up and voicing an opinion. He remained stationary, taking shallow breaths with a raspy rumble of phlegm in his throat—probably from the casserole.

"I need you to help me wash him," she said. I had told her I'd do whatever she needed, but I'd been thinking more along the lines of grocery shopping.

"Wouldn't it be better to let the nurses do that?" I asked.

"I waited until you were here because I hurt my back the last time," she said, dipping a washcloth in a plastic cup of water.

"That would seem a good reason to let the nurses do it."

"Did you come to help or aggravate me?"

She untied the top of his gown and pulled it forward, exposing pale skin hanging lifelessly from his formerly barrel-chested frame.

"Lift his left arm," she said. I would have preferred to feed him blended tuna.

I tried to remember if I had ever touched him before, other than to shake his hand. I was nineteen when they married after a two-year courtship. I had often accompanied them on dates, and he had never complained, showing up in his bold-colored jackets, eager to take the slender arm of my grandmother, who strutted out of her bedroom in short skirts and high heels that showed off her runner's legs. As a suitor, he never arrived empty-handed, brandishing flowers, jewelry and once a refrigerator. And always with chocolate-covered peanuts for me. He had a thing for chocolate-covered peanuts. He would toss me a bag, still proud of his pitching arm.

"Raise his arm," my grandmother said impatiently. I couldn't explain my hesitation to her, but I felt I was violating his privacy as I took hold of his left elbow.

She wrung out the cloth before gliding it slowly along the length of his arm in short strokes. There was something unsettling about the maternal way she caressed him, as if he was now her child rather than her spouse. Ill at ease, I looked out the window.

The Delray Medical Center was a sprawling low-rise complex of generic eighties architecture. Despite the sunshine, it seemed a dreary place. If it wasn't for the occasional (very stationary) palm tree, it could have just as easily been in Jersey. Given the makeup of the local population, that might have been a comforting thing.

"I haven't seen your parents today," my grandmother said, which was her roundabout way of asking where they were.

"I thought they drove you here this morning." My grandmother didn't drive, having been too poor when she was young for a car (or lessons) and never learning once she was older.

"I took a taxi after my run," she said.

"Why didn't you wait for them to pick you up?"

She raised an eyebrow. "Why didn't you?"

I had flown more than a thousand miles, rented a car and still made it to the hospital before them. "They're on their way," I said, not sure if I was trying to convince her or myself.

"They're always on their way," she said. "It's about time they got somewhere." She pursed her lips as she massaged Bernie's fingers, tracing the hills and valleys between them. "You write about all these weddings. So when am I going to dance at yours?" It wasn't the first time she had asked, but the question always left me tongue-tied.

"When I find the right person," I stammered.

"I didn't go out with Bernie because he was the right person. I went out with him because he asked me." Her tone was kind, but the words stung. Questioning my judgment was usually my parents' domain, and I couldn't understand why a woman ministering to her fourth ailing husband would be proselytizing about marriage.

While I adjusted Bernie's appendages as instructed, my thoughts drifted to my unfinished article. I wondered if Amy and Mike knew what they had potentially signed on for when they promised their devotion "until death do us part." Would they have made a different decision if they were standing where I was now?

"I need you to hold him up so I can do his back," my grandmother said. I recoiled at the unavoidable awkwardness. I envisioned myself lying in Bernie's place, helpless, half naked and suffering the indignity of being infantilized by a wife and grandson. But would I even have a wife and grandson?

My grandmother pressed a lever on the bed, partially elevating his torso, and I positioned myself behind him. I gently pushed him forward, but he slumped to the side.

"He's going to fall," she yelped.

"He's not going to fall," I said, running around to the other side of the bed to keep him from falling.

"You can pull him up by his wrists," she suggested, but when I tried, his head fell back at a painful angle.

"Grandma, I really think you should wait for the nurses to—"

"If you don't want to help me, I'll do it myself."

"Indomitable" was a word I often used to describe my grandmother. "Stubborn" was another. Against my better judgment, I climbed onto the bed and straddled Bernie's legs. Then I hooked my arms under his, careful not to yank loose any tubing, and pulled him toward me, cradling his head in my hands.

That's when I remembered the first time we had physical contact. I was visiting my grandmother during spring break, and he invited us to dinner at Arturo's, a fancy Italian restaurant in Boca. He was the new beau. I was hungry. When he picked us up, I scooted into the back of his silver Mercedes, leaving the front seat for my grandmother. He turned around and swatted the top of my head. "You always hold a door for a lady," he said before bounding out of the car and over to the passenger's side, where my grandmother was blushing.

"His skin color's better," she said, delicately swabbing the back of his neck. "It's pinker."

It looked greenish to me.

"That's good," I said. His cheek brushed against mine. It felt like sandpaper. But slack. As if there was no muscle beneath it. More like Jell-O. Jell-O covered in sandpaper.

This was not the same immaculate man who had his hands manicured with clear polish once a month. In Judaism there's a period of shivah, where you sit in mourning with the bereaved. I felt like I was mourning Bernie while he was still alive, while he was hanging limp in my arms.

I recalled the way my grandmother used to giggle at his racy jokes, and how her leg would kick up when he pecked her in my presence. I found myself mourning her as well. Mourning the younger her and how they used to be together.

"Who's going to take care of you?" she murmured in his ear.

"He can't hear you, Grandma," I said tenderly, watching her fingers glide along the curve of his shoulder.

She shook her head. "I wasn't talking to him."

Chapter Sixteen

Ripe for the Picking

"She was standing in moonlight in a red sundress." Ari Oz was describing for me the first time he saw Roxanne Goldman. It was at the *Sports Illustrated* Olympic party, the night before the closing ceremony in Athens.

"You must—how you say?—picture frame it," he said, his Israeli accent adding to the evocative setting that was already spurring pangs of envy. "Orange half-moon. Dance club on the beach. And a tall woman with lips the color of pomegranates."

I'm going to die alone.

It was my persistent thought since returning to New York. Like a neon sign inside my brain, lighting up at irregular intervals. I didn't have control over when it illuminated, but couples gushing about how they met was a fairly reliable trigger.

"She had a martini in her hand," Ari continued, "and her hair—how you say?—floated in the wind."

"It was a gin and tonic, and my hair has never floated," said

Roxanne, who made it clear her frizzy locks were a source of lifelong frustration.

We were on a conference call. Not my preference, but I couldn't blame Roxanne. I had canceled our previous interview, and now she was in Los Angeles and Ari was in Tel Aviv. His cell phone kept going in and out, as did my concentration while he rhapsodized about his first impression of her thick, dark, corkscrew curls.

"I thought she was Israeli," he said.

"I thought he was twelve," she bantered.

Though boyish and gymnast height (he claimed to be five-seven), Ari was twenty-four when they met and she was twenty-eight. They would be twenty-seven and thirty-one at their wedding in two weeks. Ari made a point of saying he was the oldest of his friends to get married. I wanted to punch him.

"In Israel, I'm considered an old maid," Roxanne affirmed.

I'm going to die alone.

I pictured myself lying in a cavernous hospital room, emaciated and solitary, while an endless line of graying couples ambled slowly by the open doorway. They were all couples I had written about, and they whispered to each other as they passed, "Look, dear. That could be us if we hadn't found each other." Then they would shuffle on, hand in hand in IV stand.

I was never going to know someone so well that I could predict when they needed chocolate. I was never going to be woken by a child bouncing on my bed and squirming under the covers. I was never going to keep my job unless I stayed focused.

"I told him he had nice pecs for a twelve-year-old," Roxanne was saying.

"I told her, 'So do you,'" Ari said, snorting as he laughed.

"He still thinks that's a good line. He's so lucky he's no longer single."

Fortunately, Roxanne and Ari's story wasn't very complicated. Glamorous party. Balmy evening. Two people with perky pectorals. Other than a couple layers of flimsy summer clothing, there didn't seem much standing between them and the Olympic dream of international unity.

"I didn't think I ever see her again," Ari said.

I had missed something crucial. "What happened after the party?" I asked.

"I told you I left," Roxanne said impatiently. "It was a work night for me."

"You left?" I scrolled through my notes, trying to see where I had lost them.

"Without give me phone number," Ari said. "She was playing—how you say?—hardball to get."

However, she had told him she'd be watching the closing ceremony in the NBC box, so instead of joining the other athletes on the field, he parlayed his way through security with flowers and an Israeli team pin as a gift for her. "But she not give me the box number," he said. "I run door-to-door, and I ask, 'Is this NBC?'"

"How was I supposed to know he'd be crazy enough to do that?" she said. "I didn't think he'd remember me five minutes after I left the party. There were a hundred thirty thousand condoms handed out to athletes in Athens. So let's just say he wasn't lacking for pleasant opportunities."

"I didn't want someone pleasant," he said. "I wanted you."

I'm going to die alone.

"Misery makes great copy," Tucker proclaimed, pounding on his desk for emphasis. "Our readers don't want touchy-feely crap.

They want stories about people who've been raped, murdered or censured by a congressional ethics committee."

It was the most he had spoken in my presence in months. Renée had just pitched our latest blog proposal about "Dream Weddings." It was our third attempt in as many weeks, but this one had potential. Our plan was to post multimedia interviews with upscale wedding vendors, incorporating photos and videos from their recent events. Basically, wedding porn. Tucker was less than dazzled.

Renée persevered. "It's an opportunity for us to provide readers with information about the latest trends in designer bridal dresses, celebrity florists and—"

"My eyes are glazing over," Tucker said. "I mean, in this day and age, who really cares about weddings?"

Oh, the millions of people who read our pages each week, for a start.

"With the number of divorces, everyone knows weddings are a sham." It should be noted that Tucker was on his third marriage. "I don't want to read about some Wall Street bozo marrying a swimsuit model. Or what dress she wore. I want to hear about what happens when she runs off with her personal trainer."

"That sounds a little tabloid," Renée tut-tutted.

"Well, weddings aren't anyone's idea of hard news," he said with what could be described as concealed contempt only if he had tried to hide it. "You can't go to a wedding without thinking of a bad Hollywood movie. Speaking of which, there's some flick coming out about a bridesmaid gone bonkers." He grabbed a press release from a pile on his desk and tossed it toward Renée. "Even Hollywood knows that breakups make for better stories than people mooning over each other. I can't tell you how many times friends ask me, 'Why don't you run a column about divorces?' So now I ask you: Why don't we?"

He pointed his finger directly at me. I had assumed I was there mostly to offer Renée moral support.

"Well, Tucker," I stalled. "We rely on couples being willing to share intimate details about their lives, and I don't know if people getting divorced would be willing to do that."

"Real reporters make people talk about things they don't want to." *Real reporters!* This was from a man whose last byline was about martini trends in Miami. In Tucker's mind, he was still a sharp-shooting, trash-talking foreign correspondent slumming it in Lifestyles until his inevitable rise up the managerial ladder.

Tucker decreed that we should take another stab at the blog proposal, combining our concept with his. The lack of a common denominator didn't faze him. I was dismissed, but he asked Renée to stay behind. I tried not to dwell on any ominous implications and returned to my desk. Before I could even look at my e-mail, an instant message from Tony distracted me.

"Check out Gawker."

I wasn't in the mood for reading about other people's misfortune, as I felt more than sated by my own. Gawker's victim of the week was one of our fellow Lifestyles reporters. He was being raked across the coals of public ignominy for a mass e-mail he had sent out requesting an invitation to a sex party. The fact that it was for a story he was writing got lost in the tittering and Twittering.

My phone rang. It was Tony. Sheesh.

"What do you think?" he asked.

"I think you need a new hobby."

"Did you read it?"

I clicked on the Gawker link he had sent.

The Paper Announces Buyouts.

"Shit."

"Keep reading."

There was a letter from our publisher, which looked suspiciously like an e-mail I had deleted earlier in the day after only a cursory glance. But after several paragraphs of hyperbole about our "hard-working staff" and "award-winning journalism" came this gem:

By this time next year, there will be significantly fewer people working in our newsroom than there are today. How many fewer, I don't know yet.

Fear crept up my esophagus.

Through attrition and buyouts, we're looking to collect the low-hanging fruit. If necessary, there will be layoffs.

There it was in black and white. No longer a rumor. Now the only question was, Who were the lowly plums and which of us were lofty coconuts?

"It's a scare tactic," thundered Renée, looming over my shoulder. She was standing in what Tony called her battle-ready pose, shoulders back and jaw defiant. "They won't do layoffs. Even in 'eighty-seven, after the stock market crash, there were no layoffs in the newsroom."

"They already started," Alison piped in. "Have you heard about Darius de Santis?" She was referring to an admired fashion writer. "He hasn't been seen in two weeks."

"I heard he pitched a pilot to ABC," said Tony. There was a hush. Few things inspired greater awe than a reporter getting a Hollywood production deal. It was like going up to the Heaviside layer in the musical *Cats*, but with better residuals.

"Enough," Renée declared. "Buyouts are not layoffs. Rumors are not facts."

"So you think we're safe?" I asked.

The word "safe" seemed to undo her. "There's no such thing," she sighed, deflating before our eyes. Her shoulders sloped. Her cheeks sagged. She was no longer a sergeant leading her troops. Just a woman approaching her eighth decade with a bad hip and a "rumored" heart condition who had dedicated her life to her career. No, to a newspaper, and everything it stood for.

"I would never bet against The Paper," she said, lumbering back to her desk. "But I'd sure as hell fasten your seat belt."

Chapter Seventeen

Flying Solo

For the second time in a month, I was flying. Looking out the plane's window at the grid of snow-flecked ground below, I felt untethered. I wondered where I was going. Not literally. I was on my way to LA for Roxanne and Ari's wedding, but to what end? I was a bean count away from unemployment. Even if I survived the gauntlet, there was a limit to how many weddings someone single could attend before imploding. The couples seemed to be getting younger and younger, reinforcing my fear that I was past my prime bachelor days and on my way to becoming a male spinster. A spinet. A freestanding male on an interconnected planet.

I was on a path I didn't recall choosing. Gary was always the one who swore he'd never get married. Not me. Though it was embarrassing to admit, I was the kid who daydreamed about fantasy honeymoons (from watching too many episodes of *The Love Boat*). I even once made a clandestine list of potential baby names that went well with Greene. When I imagined myself as an adult, I envisioned marriage being central to my existence. And it was. Except it was other people's marriages and not my own.

I feared I had made a wrong turn somewhere and diverged from my destiny. Perhaps one of the speck-sized houses I was passing over contained someone living the life I had intended. Someone with a ring on his fourth finger and a life companion who offered the affection and ballast that I yearned for—and that I briefly had with Laurel.

I still couldn't go near the lake in Central Park without my stomach rebelling, and I couldn't even look at green tea. Ironically, she had been the one to pursue me. She even made the first call. Gary said that was what doomed us. Of course, he also said she was a heartless shrew. But what he meant was that she could be painfully blunt, which was why I trusted her. Right up until the three a.m. newsflash that she had found someone else.

Here it was, more than three years later, and I still hadn't. Not really. Not unless I counted Melinda. And how could I? I barely knew her. Yet I still caught myself thinking about her, and I needed to stop. I needed to set my sights lower. My new goal was improving my love life and finding someone to marry me before my chest hair turned gray.

Online dating had been a bust. ComeFlyWithMe had flown the coop, and most of the other profiles seemed to blur together. As did my belabored e-mail exchanges about what I liked to do with my free time. Hope said I needed a more positive attitude.

"It's a good thing A.J. was more optimistic about online dating," she had said. A.J. was the pediatrician with a penchant for late-night cabernet—more specifically, he turned out to be a Stanford-educated pediatric surgeon and volunteer fireman who had spent two years in the Congo with Doctors Without Borders. He had her at "Doctors Without Borders."

"He cares about people," she told me with the tone of voice one would usually reserve for Mother Teresa and Bono. I'd rarely seen Hope fall for someone so quickly. She was already seeing A.J. twice a week, and she talked about him *ad nauseam* (emphasis on the "nauseam").

I was happy that she had found someone, but her success made me all the more aware of my failure. I knew that "failure" was not a politically correct or psychologically helpful word to use, but that's what it felt like. I had failed in the most basic of life's tasks. Oh, I know: In our evolved, multicultural world all lifestyles are equally valid, but for the billion or so people who don't watch *Oprah*, being alone violates societal and biological norms. From a macroeconomic perspective, living by myself in a Manhattan apartment was a waste of limited housing and energy resources. Taking an even broader view, according to Darwin (and Richard Dawkins), I was on this planet solely for the purpose of procreating, and to the best of my knowledge, I hadn't done so. It was no longer just a matter of losing out on two-for-one airline deals; I was letting down the species.

I usually tried not to think of living alone as being an anomaly. Or, more accurately, I tried not to think about it period. After so many years, solitude had become as familiar to me as the plaid wool blanket I wrapped around myself on winter nights. When I was in my twenties, I would pretend there was someone waiting for me in my apartment. On my way home, my pulse would quicken. As I turned the doorknob, I would have a momentary vision of her hair, her neck, her voice. I don't remember when I stopped fantasizing about her presence, but it seemed a healthy choice at the time. It was disconcerting that Laurel was the only girlfriend who ever had a key to my place. Yet I habitually slept on only one-half of my full-size mattress, leaving room for a better or at least a different future.

There was something about arriving at LAX that invigorated me. It could have been the three hours gained. Or the VIP treatment I was getting from Brooke Brenner, Roxanne's publicist. She texted me within moments of landing that she was waiting for me outside the baggage claim to chauffeur me to the wedding. Gary was picking me up afterward to ferry me to his place in Burbank for the night. I was hoping that saving The Paper money on a hotel and car rental would score me some brownie points.

Since I had never met Brooke before, she had e-mailed me a photo—of her car. A red convertible MINI Cooper. Sitting inside it, slurping a Starbucks iced latte, was a tan woman with silky blond hair and oversized Chanel sunglasses. Her smile was broad. Her teeth were white. I caught myself thinking of the iconic Farrah Fawcett poster. Not that Brooke was wearing a bathing suit, but her clingy, white sleeveless top was barely more concealing.

"Jump in," she said with an inviting twirl of her hand. I tossed my shoulder bag into the backseat and was still buckling up when she zipped out from under the overhang into the glorious sunshine.

"What's with the jacket?" she asked. I was dressed for the wedding in a light gray suit and tie. She was obviously not. The wind whipped through her hair as she wove between lanes. "Loosen up. You're in California."

I caught a glimpse of the ocean while standing on the narrow balcony of Brooke's apartment in Santa Monica. She lived a few blocks from the beach, and I could see a small patch of azure waves between the neighboring buildings.

"You're sure you don't mind waiting while I change?" she asked for the third time, even though I had assured her I was fine. "When I was a kid, I hated it when my dad would make unannounced pit stops. Hated it. I hope I'm not turning into him."

Clad in cut-off jeans and sparkly flip-flops, she didn't look like anyone's father. I said something to that effect.

"You're a keeper," she said with an ingratiating giggle. I was tempted to think she was flirting with me, but that's what publicists do. They flirt. They charm. They do anything within their powers to persuade you to write nice things about their clients, and I knew better than to take it seriously.

"I'll be back in a flash," she said. "Make yourself at home."

I closed my eyes and surrendered to the sun's warmth. It felt good on my face. I wanted to take off my clothes and go running along the beach. Or swimming in the figure-eight-shaped pool below. It somehow felt wrong to be in California and not be lounging poolside. I was glad I had taken Brooke's advice and removed my jacket.

I heard her voice from the back of the apartment somewhere. "I forgot to ask you if you'd like to freshen up."

"Is that your polite way of saying I have convertible-car hair?" I asked, eyes still closed and staying in my Zen zone.

"I think of it as organic volumizing." Her voice sounded closer. "People pay hairstylists a lot of money for that."

I opened my eyes and she was standing beside me—in a white towel. And not a particularly large white towel.

"I think it's working for you," she said. "See for yourself." She held up a hand mirror she was carrying, but it was hard for me to take my eyes off her tan lines.

"Not too much damage," she said, teasing my hair. She was

more than a half foot shorter than me, so to do that, she had to stand very close. Her towel brushed against me, and she smelled like fresh taffy.

I held the mirror. Or rather I held my hand around hers. I wanted to caress her shoulders. I wanted to kiss her lips, her chin. I wanted to nuzzle in the crook of her neck.

"I decided to take a shower," she said. I hoped she was going to say, "Do you want to join me?" I had an irresistible urge to remove her towel. All it would take was one finger.

I had an hour before I had to be at the wedding. I had condoms in my wallet.

I had to stop.

She was the publicist for my article. It was hard to conceive a worse ethical breach than sex with a source. This was not the time to be taking chances with my job. Not to mention I was one false move from a serious charge of sexual harassment. True, she was undressed, but this was LA. Being half naked was a way of life.

Brooke wasn't the slightest bit self-conscious. She didn't seem to notice I was attracted to her. Or she didn't care. Or she was pretending she didn't care. I wanted to know which.

She absentmindedly picked up a stack of mail before putting it back down and heading back to her bedroom.

"I gotta get cleaned up," she said.

I didn't want her to go. I needed to say something smart and sexy.

"Are you a dirty girl?" That wasn't it.

She laughed but didn't turn around, saying, "Oh, God. That's something my brother would say."

Driving north on the Pacific Coast Highway, we were buttressed by the Palisades as we snaked along the shoreline. Brooke had put the MINI Cooper's top up before heading to the wedding.

Big hair didn't go with her slinky, backless dress. I had tried not to gape while helping her with her wrap.

Now she was silhouetted against the vast expanse of gleaming sea and Western sky. I kept glancing in her direction, taking in the view. If she minded, she didn't let on. I allowed myself to imagine what it would be like to be really going to the wedding together as a couple. Walking in arm in arm. Me holding her wrap while she set stray blond strands in place. Her rubbing lipstick off my lips with the tips of her fingers. There was something to be said for California dreaming.

A valet took the car when we arrived at the entrance to the Malibu estate Roxanne's parents had rented for the event. A palm-lined pathway led past a pool and a petting zoo, where bleating sheep wore pink ribbons round their necks. It was a cross between wedding kitsch and animal cruelty.

The six-thousand-square-foot modern white beach house emerged from the lush vegetation. I followed Brooke inside, enjoying the sway of her hips. Waiters provided champagne flutes while guiding guests to the bi-level wraparound terrace, where a string quartet was playing Vivaldi.

Brooke grabbed two glasses of bubbly. Tempting as it was to linger in a fantasy version of my life, the reality didn't allow for imbibing.

"I'm on the job," I demurred.

"Don't be such a martyr." It wasn't Brooke speaking. Roxanne was towering over me with the train of her Vera Wang lace slip dress hoisted over her shoulder. "I promise not to post pictures online if you do anything outrageous."

"You look beautiful," Brooke said, kissing her cheek, which unexpectedly made me flush.

"This *shmatte*? I picked it up secondhand. That's not for print." She winked at me.

Usually brides are hidden away before the ceremony, not broadcasting their thrift-store bona fides. Roxanne wasn't at all what I expected from the daughter of a Beverly Hills surgeon, and she had an imposing physical presence. She was close to six feet, not counting her hair, which sprouted upward into a cornucopia of tightly coiled ringlets, easily giving her a half foot of added height.

"It's nice to finally meet in person," I said awkwardly.

"I should have warned you that I'm an Amazon," she said. "And I'm not even wearing heels, because I'm marrying a munchkin. If there's anything you need, just let me know. I'll get you a copy of our vows after the ceremony, and I can wrangle people for interviews during the reception, if you tell me who you want to talk to."

I usually avoided harassing brides on their wedding day, and I was rather looking forward to reconnoitering with Brooke. "I think you've got a few other things on your plate," I said.

"Are you kidding? I'm a producer. This is what I do. My only task is to walk down the aisle and say 'I do' without falling on my face. Do you really think that's going to be a problem for me? I'm asking him, not you," she said, turning to Brooke with mock indignation. "Brooke has known me to be vertically challenged on occasion."

"Only with a bottle of Manischewitz in your hand," Brooke said.

Roxanne howled with laughter. "Did she tell you we went to Hebrew school together?" It was news to me that Brooke was Jewish.

Dating a source suddenly seemed less reprehensible.

"But we usually cut class and smoked cigarettes in the girls' bathroom," Brooke said.

"Don't believe anything she tells you," said Roxanne. "I was a model child. And if Rabbi Snyder asks, I have no idea what happened to the missing case of Manischewitz at the seder in 'ninety-two." With that, she was off to micromanage the photographer.

Brooke and I strolled toward the terrace. Beneath us were rows of white chairs set out on a manicured carpet of lawn that extended to the edge of a dramatic bluff, with wooden steps zigzagging down from the precipice to a private cove.

"Sounds like you had some wild and crazy school days," I said, almost groaning at how uncomfortably forced that sounded.

Brooke didn't respond. I wasn't sure if she was embarrassed, bored with the subject or bored with me. I decided that it didn't matter. I wasn't going to put my job at risk for someone just because we were the same religion and she looked good in a towel.

"Do you want to get seats?" she asked.

"I usually just stand in the back," I said.

"That works for me." I wondered if she was trying to assist my reporting efforts or ensure that we spent more time together. I reminded myself it didn't matter.

As the sun sank below the horizon, Rabbi Snyder began the ceremony, taking his place beneath a wedding canopy of bamboo and palm fronds. Five tawny bridesmaids carrying tapered white candles paraded by in form-hugging pink sheath dresses, which I couldn't help notice showcased impressive cleavage on each woman. Then I realized it wasn't just the dresses that were identical; the bridesmaids had matching breasts.

"Yes, they all went to the same doctor," Brooke whispered. "That's off the record," she added, grinning mischievously.

She was adorable. I was in trouble.

Every time I looked at Brooke, I regretted not kissing her in her apartment. So I avoided looking at her, which just made me want her more. I felt like a starving man in the presence of a glazed pastry. My first instinct was to gorge myself, but even thinking that way was disrespectful to Brooke—and The Paper. After the ceremony, I vowed to focus on doing my job and keeping my distance.

I mingled with the guests as they migrated to a candlelit tent containing a lavish buffet of smoked sable, rack of lamb and a myriad of other delicacies. There were a dozen linen-covered tables interspersed with floor lamp–style propane heaters. Chinese lanterns hung overhead, glowing like crimson-colored sentinels.

Buffets were challenging environments for me, because doing interviews required competing with the food for people's attention. At a Jewish event, there was no contest. Standing between guests and stuffed portobello mushrooms was a good way to get myself trampled.

"Is this the silliest wedding ever?" asked Roxanne, resting her head against her husband's. Though her words were irreverent, her body language was not.

"Not by a long shot," I said reassuringly. Looking around the space, my gaze gravitated immediately toward Brooke. I purposefully turned away.

"Is this what you—how you say?—expectated?" Ari asked. Naturally, the only two people I didn't need to interview were the only ones willing to converse.

"I anticipated seeing more gymnasts," I said. I also expected to see Matt Lauer, but I didn't want to sound like a star fucker.

"My teammates do training," said Ari, who had short-cropped hair and deep-set eyes. Though only a couple of inches shorter than me, he seemed almost twice as broad.

"Ari's only in the States until Tuesday," Roxanne said. "We're putting off the honeymoon until after Beijing."

It would have seemed more logical to put off the wedding as well. I wondered if she was pregnant. "So why get married now?" I asked.

"We didn't want to wait," she said.

"You waited three years," I pointed out.

"I waited," Ari said. "She debated."

Roxanne blushed. "I had a plan for my life," she said, "and my plan didn't include a guy who lived on the other side of the planet and was a half foot shorter than me."

"Not half foot."

"In heels," she said, stroking his cheek. I averted my eyes and caught sight of Brooke again. "Being together didn't make any sense. It still doesn't."

"Why are you not eating?" Ari asked me.

Bridal couples rarely understood that what was a party for them was a work night for me. It was also difficult to explain The Paper's strict rules about accepting anything that could be construed as a gift.

"It's not a gift. It's food," Roxanne said, "and no one's going to know. There's an extra seat at Brooke's table. You'll be her date."

It was out of the question and wildly inappropriate. So why did it sound so appealing? "I think Brooke might have an opinion about that," I said, trying to make light of the subject but feeling a tightness in my chest.

"Advice from married man: Never ask woman's opinion."

"You won't be married long giving out advice like that," said Roxanne.

"You see? You get without asking. You must stay and be our guest."

"I assure you that Brooke will be delighted," Roxanne added.

"Thanks for the kind offer," I said, wondering if she had

inside information on precisely how delighted Brooke would be. "But I can't accept." I felt a sharp pain underneath my ribs as I insisted I didn't want what I specifically did.

"You need to let go," Ari said emphatically. "It is—how you say?—secret agent of life."

"When he retires from gymnastics, he's going to get a job making—how you say?—Chinese fortune cookies," Roxanne joked while running her fingers through his hair.

"I am serious," he said. "Life is like being on the high bar. There is time to hold on tight, and there is time to let go." As Ari spoke, he embraced Roxanne firmly in his thick arms. "You ask why we get married now. The answer is simple: She let go."

Roxanne kissed him gently on the lips, holding his face in her hands. "That's exactly what I did," she said, her voice cracking. "I let go."

"The valets won't let me near the place." It was Gary calling from the front gate. "Sorry I'm late. Are you ready to leave?"

The honest answer was no, but I wasn't ready to stay either.

I'd been deliberating while interviewing guests. Deep down I knew that Ari was right. There were times when you needed to let go and take a chance, but I hadn't decided whether this was one of those times.

Of course, it wasn't supposed to be something I decided. It was supposed to be spontaneous. I liked being spontaneous. I just preferred to do it with some preparation.

In fairness to myself, this wasn't a no-brainer about having fun and maybe hooking up with someone. It meant violating rules that could have severe repercussions. But were there really any rules when it came to sex and love? Thousands of years of history from Adam and Eve to Bill and Monica said no. Then again, they all suffered for their indulgences.

I watched Brooke sashay toward the dessert table, and for a moment I couldn't remember what it was I was deliberating. The only important question was whether *she* wanted me to stay, and there was only one way to find out. I was advancing toward her, on the verge of asking, when Gary had phoned. I took that as divine intervention. Though it might have just been bad luck.

Gary was standing on the side of the street next to his Prius. He looked good in a green hoodie and jeans. He had the same ex-soccer player build, but his face was somewhat fuller than when I last saw him. He was wearing silver eyeglasses, which was new for him, and as he embraced me in a bear hug, I saw he also had some silver in his dark brown hair and small laugh lines around his eyes. It was jarring. What happened to my baby brother running down the stairs of our house in his footed pajamas?

"Leslie was going to come with me, and then she wasn't. Then she wanted to know if there was any food you would want, and I said what you would want was to get picked up on time. Then she got hurt, and I got pissed. Or vice versa. Either way, I had to apologize, which took more time, and here I am with my lame excuse."

I wanted to stay. It suddenly hit me. I really wanted to stay with Brooke. I deserved to have what Gary had. What everyone seemed to have. Someone in their life to torment them. To love them. To keep them company. I didn't know if Brooke could be that person for me, but if I left I'd never know.

I told Gary about her, and it occurred to me he might think I was choosing a woman I barely knew over him. There were fault lines in our relationship since childhood, and as the younger sibling he often accused me of taking him for granted. It had been the standard outburst whenever I missed his soccer tournaments. Blowing him off on a Saturday night after he drove across town to pick me up could trigger an eruption of buried resentment.

He looked wounded. I was being a terrible brother. "It's not important," I said. "I go to these weddings and get caught up in the romantic atmosphere. Occupational hazard. Sorry." I was in town for less than twenty-four hours. What kind of a jerk tells his brother he doesn't want to spend any time with him?

"Is she hot?" he asked, cutting to the core of the matter, as far as he was concerned.

"She's very cute."

"Cute as in, 'She has nice dimples' or 'She looked smokin' in the towel'?"

"Smokin'."

"You have to stay."

I was grateful to hear him say that, but I still felt guilty. Noticing my hesitation, he said, "If you don't stay, I will."

He was joking, but not entirely. He seemed preoccupied. I wanted to find out what was going on with him, but it wasn't a conversation to have on a street. "I'm not sure Leslie would appreciate that," I said.

"Well, the Leslie thing is getting old. You know?"

"It's been only seven months."

"Almost eight," he said. "There's a lot of women in the world who look good in towels. Even more who look good out of them."

I was afraid I was being a bad influence, which was an odd role reversal. "She obviously cares about you," I said.

"I care about her, but that doesn't necessarily mean she's someone I want to spend the rest of my life with." How could two such different people come out of the same womb?

"Get back to your party," he said, smacking me on the back. "Remember: 'Better to be a king for a night than a schmuck for a lifetime.' That's a DeNiro quote. Look it up." He slid into the driver's seat and lowered the window. "Call me if you need a place to stay tonight, but I'm warning you, I'll never let you live it down."

As he sped off into the night, I could hear Kanye West championing the good life over the DJ's loudspeakers. I half ran back to the tent, eager to see Brooke. Her table was in the back, and I hurried over. But she wasn't there. I didn't see her standing nearby. Or at the bar. A crowd had gathered on the dance floor around Ari and Roxanne, who were rocking out to Kanye's rapping, but Brooke wasn't among them.

Outside, guests were wandering around the property. It was hard to make out faces from a distance in the darkness. The lanterns that were hung along the periphery contributed more shadows than illumination.

I checked the terrace and inside the house. A woman was entering the white marble bathroom on the main floor, but it wasn't Brooke. I started to panic. It occurred to me I had never asked Brooke how late she was staying. Was it possible she had left?

I raced to the front gate. A couple was waiting for their car. More people were approaching. No sign of Brooke. I tried calling her, but it went straight to her voice mail. I didn't even know if she had brought her phone with her. She could be back in the tent. She could already be gone. She could have left while I was talking to Gary, or while I was searching for her. I paced back and forth, unsure what to do next. I risked missing her if I went anywhere else, but standing out front for the rest of the night was ridiculous. Sweating and dizzy and incapable of making a rational decision, I dashed back to the tent.

Rihanna's latest single was playing, and Ari was doing back-flips to hoots and catcalls. It was like watching someone perform an Olympic floor exercise in a tuxedo. I still didn't see Brooke anywhere, but I made eye contact with Roxanne, who was standing on the sidelines.

"A woman should never marry a man more limber than she is," she said, raising a champagne glass in my direction.

"Have you seen Brooke?"

"I think she went down to the beach," she said as Ari grabbed her round her thighs and lifted her into the air. "Ari!"

It was easier to see the edge of the bluff by daylight. Finding the steps at night was no easy task, and getting down them even less so. It was a good thing I hadn't been drinking, because there were a hell of a lot of them. I huffed and puffed my way downward on pure adrenaline, holding on to low shrubbery for balance. I couldn't see Brooke or even where the steps ended. I pitched forward when I hit sand, grateful to have made it to the bottom and not at all looking forward to the return trip. Letting my eyes adjust to the dim light, I spotted Brooke sitting near the undulating surf, and I stumbled toward her, catching my breath.

She looked up, startled, as I collapsed by her side. "I thought you left," she said.

I shook my head.

"So, you're happy you decided to cover the wedding?"

I nodded.

"I told you they had a good story. I have a client getting married in May with an even better one, if you're willing to put up with my pitching you another piece."

I nodded again.

"Are you off duty now?" She lifted an open wine bottle that

had been half-buried in the sand beside her. "I pinched a party favor from the bar. It's not Manischewitz." She laughed as she handed me the purloined pinot, and I took a swig. I watched the waves lap at the shore and exhaled deeply.

"Can I ask you something?" I said. It was her turn to nod.

And I kissed her.

The universe didn't burst into heart-shaped confetti. I had taken her by surprise, and she pulled away. I was crestfallen. Then she threw her arms around my neck and drew me to her. We kissed again, and this time there were cymbals and electric guitars. My hands found the smoothness of her spine while high above us Rihanna pleaded, "Please don't stop the music."

We didn't make it to her bedroom. We barely made it back to her apartment without having to pull over on the highway, and as soon as the door closed behind us, we were tangled in each other's limbs.

"You're so beautiful," I murmured, slipping a thin strip of fabric off her shoulder and replacing it with hungry kisses.

Soon we were rolling naked on her living room carpet. We rocked in slow motion. Nothing existed but her eyes, her breath. Her lips, her neck. Her touch.

"Do you have condoms?" she asked, her arms and legs wrapped tightly around me.

Fortunately, my wallet was within reach. Rising to my knees, I held her to me like a second skin while grabbing for my pants. I whispered in her ear, "Let's go to the bedroom." She shook her head coquettishly while stroking my back. I nibbled on her ear-lobe and attempted to stand.

She shook her head more emphatically. "No," she said,

pushing me backward to the carpet. "I don't let guys in my bed until we've been dating at least a month."

Then she got on top of me.

Sunlight was flooding the apartment when I opened my eyes. Sheer curtains billowed in the morning breeze. My back was stiff from sleeping on the floor, but otherwise I felt good. *Very* good.

I got the towel off, I thought to myself with bemused pride. But that wasn't what was making me feel so light-headed. Something had happened over the course of the night that I hadn't anticipated. Something beyond the physical. Though that was how it began, as we clung to each other, wordlessly revealing secret longings. Then we lolled in each other's arms and talked late into the night. About pizza cravings and fish tacos and Los Cabos and last relationships and what we wanted in our next ones.

It was the first time I'd talked about Laurel without my chest constricting. I was even able to joke about her criticism of my recycling habits. Maybe I was moving past the pain. Or maybe I was moving forward. Luxuriating in the memory of Brooke's embrace, I felt deep affection. I turned over to snuggle, but she was gone.

She wasn't on the sofa or in the kitchen making coffee. Assuming she was in her bedroom, I put on my boxers and ventured toward the inner sanctum. I stood in the doorway opposite a pristine queen-sized bed with a voluminous white duvet. I knocked, but there was no response. I listened for the telltale sound of rustling clothes or running water. Nothing.

Then I saw her sitting on the bedroom balcony at a table with an open laptop, her cell phone to her ear. She was in a white terrycloth robe with her hair haphazardly clipped high on her head. She looked effortlessly enticing. I opened the glass door and kissed the nape of her neck, imagining what it might feel like to do so every day.

"Good morning, sleepy head," she said, smiling up at me. She covered the phone with the palm of her hand. "Are you feeling charitable?"

It was an odd question. "Very," I said, fondling a loose lock of her hair.

She pressed a button on her phone and set it on the table. "Alexander, I'm putting you on speakerphone. Gavin, meet Alexander. Alexander, meet Gavin." She playfully hooked a finger under my waistband, and I wondered just how charitable I had volunteered to be.

"Gavin," a tinny voice exclaimed. "Brooke has said amazing things about you."

She tapped my arm. I looked down, and she was typing something on her laptop. "Don't hate me," she wrote. "Alexander is the client I told you about, and he was begging to talk to you."

Did she tell him I had slept over? I was torn between machismo pride and professional concern. Pride won out as Brooke massaged my inner thigh.

"I would love to tell you about my upcoming May wedding," he said. Of course he would.

"He met his fiancée on a plane in Spain," Brooke interjected.

"It wasn't raining on the plane," he quipped. I resisted the impulse to groan.

"He got off in Madrid, but he couldn't get her out of his mind." Brooke's sky blue eyes lit up while narrating the story. "He drove five hundred miles to surprise her at her hotel in Barcelona, and proposed two days later."

"Very romantic," I admitted. Also a little crazy, but I was

beginning to think the two were synonymous. I was already contemplating a return trip to LA as soon as possible, and wondered whether I should tell her.

"You two should set up a time to talk," Brooke said, shifting a little too easily into full PR mode. A calendar appeared on her computer screen. "How's next Thursday?"

My neck stiffened. It flashed through my mind that Brooke had slept with me only to get another story in The Paper, but I felt guilty for even thinking it. Working at The Paper was making me cynical.

It was going to cost me only an hour to meet with Alexander, and not even that if I got a story out of it. I agreed to lunch before we hung up. Brooke jumped into my arms and exuberantly kissed me good morning.

"So what do you want to do now?" I asked, gripping her waist in a way I hoped suggested what I'd most like to do, but I would have been happy doing anything as long as she was by my side. "How about a walk on the beach?"

"I would love to," she said, caressing my pecs (which I instinctively flexed). "But I have to meet a client in an hour."

"How about after?" My plane didn't leave until late afternoon.

"Unfortunately, I have a haircut."

"That sounds like something that could be postponed," I said, sliding my hands down around her hips.

"Not really," she said. Not what I was hoping for. "It would take a month to get another appointment," she explained.

"Then I'll go with you," I said, proud of my quick thinking.

"I can't imagine a more boring way for you to spend a day in LA."

"Maybe you're underestimating the allure of curling irons," I said, stealing another kiss.

She didn't respond right away. To the kiss or the plan. "It's really crowded at the salon," she finally said. "Half the time I can't even find a seat."

I blinked several times, like a foreign exchange student trying to comprehend what she was saying.

"I was thinking about coming back to LA next month," I blurted.

"Great." That was all she said. Just "great." No suggestion of who in particular it might be great for.

"I had a really nice time last night." I was attempting triage.

"I'm really glad," she said, "and I'm really glad you're going to meet Alexander." Somewhere on the planet was a guy who wouldn't take that response as a blow to his manhood. I desperately wanted to be that guy.

"I've got to take a shower," she said. "Do you want the number for the airport shuttle?"

I dressed quickly, and she gave me a brisk hug, like I was the runner-up on a reality dating show. I waited until the door closed behind me before slamming my fist into my thigh as hard as I could. *How could I be so stupid?*

I reminded myself I had sex. I had great sex. I put on my aviator sunglasses, determined to look tough. Or as tough as I could look standing on the side of the road in a wrinkled suit, waiting for a shuttle bus.

"I'm flying United," I said to the baby-faced driver. He nodded as he ripped my ticket, inadvertently flaunting the gold band on his left hand.

Chapter Eighteen

Dork Is a Four-Letter Word

There was no way I was going to write a story about Alexander's wedding.

"Then why are you meeting with him?" Hope asked. I had called her for solace, not syllogism. But after three tracheal intubations in one morning, she was not at her most sympathetic.

"I don't want Brooke to think I'm angry," I said as I raced to make the light at Broadway and Houston, hurtling myself across eight lanes of traffic.

"You *are* angry."

"An angry person wouldn't go to the meeting."

"Neither would a sane person."

All week, I'd done everything I could to hide any sign of being hurt. I bent over backward to ensure there was nothing in my column about Roxanne and Ari that hinted at hard feelings.

As far as Brooke knew, I hooked up at weddings every week. Perk of my job. All those bridesmaids. All those publicists. She had no way of knowing how much I had tormented myself before kissing her, let alone how much I had thought about it afterward. And she never would.

"I promised to meet the guy," I said, galloping past Dean & DeLuca, "and that's what I'm going to do."

"Well, since you're so hell-bent on meeting new people, I want you to meet A.J." I just ran right into that one. "You could join us for dinner next week."

I could also attend a seminar on septic-tank maintenance, but it's not something I would volunteer to do. It wasn't that I was biased against A.J. I just didn't think I had the stamina for being with a couple in the throes of new love. They had been dating only six weeks. My preference was to wait—until they broke up.

"Sure," I said, hoping the high pitch of my voice suggested enthusiasm. "But can we discuss this when I'm not ten minutes late for an interview?"

I had agreed to meet Alexander at Balthazar, a SoHo bistro that many consider *un morceau* of Paris in New York. An overrated *morceau*, with the Gaul-ing combination of French attitude and New York prices. It was very popular among people who didn't blink at paying fifteen dollars for a bagel and cream cheese. I wasn't sure how appropriate it was for Alexander to indulge in such luxuries, since he was on the city payroll as a deputy mayor. I was planning on sticking to just a cup of *café* before making my exit and rushing back to the office for a departmental staff meeting.

The powwow was set up to counteract rumors about the buyouts. Of course, it was having the opposite effect, but it gave me an excuse to keep things short with Alexander. A quick in and out, and I would be done with Brooke. It wasn't that I regretted what happened in LA, but it made me doubt the reliability of my instincts—and my charm.

The hostess at Balthazar displayed only a trace of disdain as she escorted me past the zinc bar through the noisy and unduly crowded, dark-paneled dining room. Approaching Alexander's table, I was surprised to see he had brought his fiancée with him, and even more surprised by her age. An elegant woman with gray-streaked hair pulled back from her face, she appeared to be in her late fifties, while Alexander was a strapping Bradley Cooper look-alike more than twenty years her junior.

They sat side by side on a red banquette, his hand in hers, and I had to admit, their story had just become a lot more interesting. There were quick introductions, and she said her name was Genevieve. "Do I detect an accent?" I pulled out a notepad. I hadn't intended to, but the journalist in me couldn't help asking a few questions.

"Boarding school in Switzerland," she said. "You're good." She seemed sincerely impressed.

"So, I'm guessing you've traveled a lot."

"My father said I was born with a Baedeker in my bassinet." I liked that she wasn't embarrassed to show her age. "Alexander is the same way. We're very similar."

"Two peas in a pod," Alexander said, kissing her hand.

My stomach convulsed at the excessive display of affection, but if I judged all bridal couples on the gag factor, I would rarely write an article.

"Alexander speaks four languages," she informed me.

"My mother taught me well," he said.

"She must be very proud," I said reflexively.

"I am," said Genevieve.

Holy maternity! She was his mother? I'd seen my fair share of inappropriate parents, but this was borderline clinical.

They Eskimo kissed. *Ew!*

"We're so excited that you're going to be writing something about our celebration," she said.

OUR celebration? Boundaries, people. Get some boundaries.

"Unfortunately, it turns out, I don't think I'll be able to fit you in," I said to Alexander, segueing into my prepared spiel. "May is a busy month for weddings. We get submissions from three hundred couples a week."

"But none of them are as interesting," Genevieve said.

No. I write only about boring people. I smiled through gritted teeth.

"You can't imagine how much my mother's been looking forward to this," he said. "I hate to disappoint her."

How did a man so unhealthily attached to his mother find someone to share his life while I couldn't? I wondered what his fiancée was like and if the fourth plate setting on the table was for her, but I didn't plan on staying long enough to find out.

"I'm sorry, but it's my editor's decision." Fortunately, Renée gave us carte blanche to pin blame on her whenever we encountered resistance.

"Well, he'd be crazy not to include Alexander," Genevieve opined.

"*He* is a she," I said, trying not to sound contemptuous.

"Good for her. I so admire working girls."

My phone rang. It was Captain Al, who was editing my column. "I'm sorry," I said, "I have to take this."

I turned away, but I couldn't hear amid the cacophony of conversations. I would have left right then, but if it got back to

Brooke that I'd been rude, it would have defeated my entire purpose for being there. I headed down a back hallway toward the lavatories with my cell phone held to one ear and a finger stuck in the other.

"I liked your story," Captain Al grumbled. It was a rare compliment. I wished I could have savored the moment somewhere other than a men's room.

"You need to rethink the lede," he said.

He giveth and he taketh away. I assumed his complaint was that I had used a quote for my first line, which was highly discouraged. The question was whether it was a good enough quote to be worth fighting for:

"Dorks like us don't have Hollywood love stories," said Roxanne Goldman.

The irony was that it *was* a Hollywood-style love story, and I found it charming that a successful television producer raised in Beverly Hills considered herself a dork.

"I think it makes the reader like her," I said. "It's quirky. It's unexpected."

"It's obscene."

That was harsh.

"The word," he said. " 'Dork.' It's slang for the male sexual organ."

That was news to me. Though I wasn't about to admit it.

"Look it up in the dictionary, and come up with a new lede. You have thirty minutes."

"Thirty minutes?"

"You're lucky I'm giving you that. We're shutting down in an hour so everyone can go to the department meeting. I need the column clean by then."

I hustled back to the table to grab my pad and go. A dark-haired woman was sitting across from Alexander and

Genevieve. I felt like warning her to run, but I had problems of my own.

"I want you to meet my fiancée," Alexander said as I reached for my coat.

One look at her and the air was knocked out of me. I staggered backward when she flashed a dimpled smile.

"Gavin, this is Melinda."

Chapter Nineteen

Facts and Figures

I had found her. I had lost her.

A thick, jagged line sliced downward across the auditorium's projection screen. "This graph displays The Paper's advertising revenue for the last decade," said Tucker, standing at the front of the jam-packed room.

The budget problems at The Paper were far worse than I had realized. Even if layoffs were averted in the near future, online ad rates were only a tiny fraction of print ads, which meant in the long term, there would be only enough money for a fraction of the staff.

What was I going to do? About Melinda. I couldn't get her out of my head. I superimposed her face on every photograph displayed, and reformatted each pie chart as a compilation of her attributes: 25 percent charm, 17.8 percent altruism, 14.3 percent ingenuity (I could intuit her ingenuity), 19.6 percent beauty (I considered her 100 percent beautiful, but I was trying not to view her solely from a sexual perspective).

My mathematical glorification was interrupted by a promotional video with high-tech graphics and peppy music. Talking heads praised The Paper's longevity and integrity, as if those qualities could shield the company from financial reality. Then again, we could all use a break from reality.

A couple was shown walking on a beach, and I imagined it was me alongside Melinda, her curves filling out a tropical green bikini and sarong. Then I reminded myself about Alexander. How could she be with someone so spineless? That was judgmental. Someone so soulless.

The video ended and a slide appeared with the words THE SOLUTION IS YOU.

"You are the ones who will make us relevant in the twenty-first century," Tucker said. "We want you thinking outside the box. We don't just want you thinking; we want you blogging. We want you chirping." He looked down at his note cards. "I mean, tweeting."

The slide quickly changed to OTHER SOLUTIONS. There were only two bullet points: DONATIONS and MEMBERSHIP. Neither screamed out "game changer."

Under DONATIONS there was a list of luminaries, including Bill Gates, Warren Buffet and Oprah Winfrey. "There are many generous benefactors who we think could be interested in supporting our newspaper and the ideals we uphold."

"We're expecting people to donate their money to a for-profit company?" an editor asked.

"After careful consideration, we've determined that donations are an unlikely solution," Tucker said, reading from another note card.

Yet there it was, officially part of a PowerPoint presentation. It wasn't that I'd been expecting revelatory disclosures. Oh, who was I kidding? Yes, I had.

I wanted to know: How were we going to overcome the odds? How were we going to reinvent ourselves as trailblazers? How was I going to see Melinda again?

The most obvious reason to contact her was if I was writing an article about her wedding, but I'd already said I wasn't. It would seem odd for me to randomly change my mind, in addition to being disingenuous. However, I wasn't coming up with a better alternative.

"Another option is membership," Tucker droned. "We see great potential in the idea of having customers purchase memberships to the newspaper."

"They're known as subscriptions," someone in the back called out to scattered laughter.

"This is different," Tucker said with a thin-lipped smile. "We want to create a sense of community. One with bonuses for belonging. Something along the lines of PBS, where you pay a membership fee and receive umbrellas or baseball caps. People love baseball caps."

I was working at a company with some of the smartest, savviest people on the planet, and they were delusional.

So who was I to be otherwise?

I decided to do the story. I couldn't claim it was admirable or even rational, but I needed to see Melinda again. I needed to know if she was thinking about me. It had nearly killed me running out of Balthazar after barely saying hello. I had sputtered something about not expecting her to be there. The understatement of my life. But there was little else I could say in front of Alexander. She had played it cooler, not giving any hint that we knew each other or that she even recognized me. Unless she didn't.

"Are there any more questions?"

What if she didn't recognize me?

"Are there going to be layoffs?" someone demanded.

Was it possible Melinda didn't remember me?

"Never ask a question if you don't want to hear the answer."

Chapter Twenty

Up, Up and Away

Traffic uptown wasn't moving. Eighth Avenue was a parking lot, thanks to the St. Patrick's Day Parade three avenues over. Temporary insanity was my only excuse for being in a taxi.

I was meeting Melinda at a Starbucks near Lincoln Center, and I was counting the minutes. Still, I should have been grateful to be out of the office, where it was wall-to-wall anxiety as fear of layoffs took the form of conspiracy theories and desecrated vending machines.

With only a week until the buyout deadline, there wasn't a conversation that took place that didn't end with "So, are you thinking of taking the 'you know'?" Decisions needed to be made or bets placed. Our workplace had been transformed into a casino, with management posing the question, Do you feel lucky?

Yet, at that moment, I could think of little else but my

pending rendezvous. I had wanted to arrive early so I wouldn't be nervous. Or so I'd be less nervous. I hadn't slept much the previous night, as I contemplated disaster. And by "disaster," I really meant any scenario that didn't include her swooning into my arms.

I was fully aware that I was setting myself up for disappointment. When my phone rang, I jumped. Or I would have if I hadn't been seated. It was more of a head-to-toe muscle spasm.

"Can we reschedule?" Melinda asked.

"No," I said, before remembering that inflexibility wasn't an appealing trait. "I mean, when did you have in mind?"

"Maybe tomorrow. Or the day after?"

These were not the words of a woman eager to see the man she's been secretly pining for. Or were they? Maybe she was afraid to be alone with me for fear of revealing her feelings. I needed to hold my ground, which was hard to do when I was barely holding down my lunch. I focused on keeping my voice in a low register.

"I'm already in transit," I said.

"I'm sorry. I don't want to flake out on you." She sounded distressed. "This shouldn't be your problem."

"I have some experience with bridal problems," I said. "Is it something I can help with?" This was good. I was being empathetic and flexible while still sounding like a baritone.

"No. Well, maybe. This is embarrassing." She seemed about to confide in me—a huge step forward in our nonexistent relationship. "You have to promise you won't tell Alexander." Even better. "I locked myself out of my apartment, and it's the second time this month. Which is bizarre, because I haven't done that in years."

"Lots of people lock themselves out," I assured her.

"They don't have a very sweet but anal-retentive fiancé who

taped a sign to the front door saying, 'Do you know where your keys are?' Which is why I didn't call him, but now I'm stuck waiting for the locksmith on my front stoop. It's been over an hour."

"I can do an interview on a stoop," I said. If I didn't know myself better, I'd think I was a pretty smooth guy.

"I can't ask you to do that," she said.

"You didn't."

Melinda was sitting on the stone steps six inches from me. Her hair was longer than when we first met, but otherwise she looked exactly how I remembered. Her perfume hinted at gingery spices. I wanted to kiss her. Instead I clenched my notepad.

She talked about Alexander and Spain. She talked about the master's degree she had put on hold while planning the wedding and the writing class she was teaching at a homeless shelter. But she had yet to acknowledge our previous meeting. I purposely dressed in the same jacket and jeans I had worn on New Year's Day, hoping it would trigger a reaction. I could have just asked her if she remembered me, but if I had to ask, the answer seemed a foregone conclusion.

I looked for signs of familiarity and seemed to be finding them. She was smiling. She was bantering. She was also shivering.

"Are you cold?" I asked. After several days of springlike temperatures, the weather had abruptly boomeranged to a bitter winter chill.

"Guess I didn't dress well for an outdoor play date." She had a diaphanous scarf around her neck and a flattering but thin suede blazer. "But I can't leave until the locksmith comes."

I took off my plaid wool scarf and handed it to her. "Now you're going to be the one who's cold," she said.

"I'm impervious to cold," I said. She laughed with such warmth, I half expected the sun to emerge on command. Her arms were still clasped around her chest, and her teeth were chattering. Again, I had to resist the urge to embrace her.

"Which apartment is yours?" I asked, standing up.

She pointed to a third-floor windowsill next to the fire escape. "The one with the pot of overgrown basil."

"With the open window?"

"I think it helps the basil."

I climbed onto an industrial-sized garbage can next to her stoop.

"What are you doing?" she gasped.

I jumped up and reached for the fire-escape ladder. It looked easier when Matt Damon did this kind of thing. I briefly imagined how embarrassing it would be if I fell. I grabbed hold of the bottom rung and pulled myself up (all those chin-ups at the gym finally paid off), and I was soon scrambling up to the second-floor platform.

"Gavin, I'm fine. Come down!"

I was going up, not down. I was on a mission. I made it to the third-floor platform, and her window was less than two feet away.

"You're going to get yourself killed," Melinda shouted. A discouragingly possible outcome.

I had never envisioned myself risking life and limb for someone, let alone another man's fiancée. But something about Melinda made me want to be better than I was. Braver. And a little stupider.

I leaned over the railing and reached for the window.

"Gavin!"

My hands were inside her apartment. My feet were still on the fire escape. It was neither a flattering nor comfortable pose.

"Are you stuck?"

I wasn't stuck. I was just awkwardly suspended, gripping her window ledge for dear life. I looked more Michael Cera than Matt Damon. The latter would have crouched on top of the railing and flung himself through the window, but that kind of move works better with a stunt double and a safety net.

I heard something rip as I shimmied slowly forward. I pictured my butt hanging out of the window with the seam of my jeans split open. I wanted to reach back and check, but I also wanted to live.

I pulled myself through the window, careful not to topple the basil. What I didn't notice was the cat's water dish beside it. The plastic saucer tumbled to the floor, as did I.

I lay there for a moment, letting my heart rate decelerate and hoping the spreading wetness I felt on my leg was from the spilled water. I did a quick inventory of body parts and was relieved that other than a banged knee, my only wound was not to flesh but fashion. What was left of the front right pocket of my jacket was dangling at an acute angle. (The seat of my pants was, mercifully, intact.) I suspected the average twelve-year-old could have done the same maneuver with sartorial integrity. So much for my Bourne-like bravado.

I retrieved the dish from under my thigh. I had already soaked up most of its contents, but I wiped the floor with my knee to be sure. I looked around the room. Not in an invasive kind of way. Just taking it in. There were fresh tulips in a Turkish vase on an antique desk, and large, framed photographs covering the peach-colored walls. The pictures were mostly outdoor shots of exotic locations, but there were also detailed close-ups of unusual objects such as a broken umbrella upended on a cobblestone street and a handwoven basket filled with balls of colored yarn.

Her dining table was piled high with bridal magazines and

boxes of wedding invitations, as were two worn leather club chairs. It was weird being alone in her apartment. It was like I had broken in. I realized I sort of had.

A buzzer blared.

Melinda must have been wondering what was taking me so long. I placed the dish back on the ledge before rushing over to the front door of the apartment and hitting the intercom button.

"Are you okay?" she asked.

"Piece of cake," I said, pressing the button that unlocked the entrance to the building. I felt awkward about welcoming her into her own home, yet standing in the open doorway, I felt something surprisingly natural about waiting for her return.

She was laughing as she got off the elevator. "Who knew that Clark Kent covered weddings?"

I basked in the compliment as she dashed by me into the apartment. I was in the process of following her when we collided. She had a coat in one hand and her keys jingling from the other.

"We've got to buy you a new jacket," she said, pointing at my pocket.

I was pretty sure that Clark Kent never shopped with Lois Lane, but the thought of Melinda picking out clothing for me had a certain intimate appeal.

"I owe you," she said. "I'm getting off cheap compared to what the locksmith was going to charge me. Plus it will be fun."

The way she squealed the word "fun" convinced me I was perilously close to gal-pal territory, and I didn't just scale a building so we could get facials together. "Thanks, but I'm fine," I said. "Really."

"Okay." She seemed miffed.

"So, shall we continue the interview?" I asked a little over-enthusiastically.

"Absolutely," she said, closing the door in my face and swiftly double locking it. "But not here." She tossed me my scarf before darting toward the elevator, and I had no choice but to follow.

"This is a highly unusual location for an interview," I said while taking off my shoes.

"Do you only climb fire escapes?" Melinda asked, a daring twinkle in her eye.

We were in a warehouse-sized gymnasium beside a three-story ladder leading to a circus trapeze. When she told me in the taxi she needed an energy boost, I assumed she was talking about an espresso.

"I thought you were afraid of heights," I said, then bit my tongue. That was information I obtained on New Year's, but it was too late to take it back. This was the moment of truth.

There was no flash of recognition. No incredulous smile. It was all too clear she didn't know we had met before. A tiny voice in my head said, *Tell her. Tell her now. Tell her everything.* But what was there to say if she didn't remember meeting me? And why should she? I had blown it out of proportion. We had spent less than a half hour together. She traveled around the world, and I was just some random guy who helped her down a staircase. Now she was probably trying to figure out how I knew about her phobia. "Alexander mentioned something about it," I mumbled.

"Oh," she said, completely unaware of my inner turmoil. "Well, I'm not afraid when I'm wearing a harness and attached to rigging. I wish I could go through my entire life that way. We have safety belts in cars, but what's supposed to protect us the rest of the time?"

I couldn't really think about that, because I was still registering the concept of Melinda in a harness and trying not to picture her in bondage lingerie.

"I took a trapeze lesson in Switzerland a few years ago, and I've been hooked ever since," she said. "I was thrilled when I found this place in New York. I come here when I'm stressed."

"Are you stressed now?" Was I stressing her?

"You try planning a wedding in less than four months. It was only two days after New Year's when I met Alexander."

She couldn't have known how excruciating it was for me to hear that. "Why were you in Spain?" I asked, my warbling voice betraying me.

"I was going to my college roommate's wedding in a small town near Barcelona, and the last thing on my mind was meeting a guy."

Right. Last thing on the mind of a woman attending a wedding alone. "I'm not sure my readers are going to believe that," I said, jealous of Alexander's perfect timing.

"Well, it's the truth," she flared.

"A single woman on a transatlantic flight wasn't interested in checking out who was sitting nearby?"

"I was still sleep deprived from the holiday and checking out empty seats. Not physiques. At first, I was annoyed when Alexander started talking to me, but he won me over." I couldn't imagine how. Or maybe I just couldn't bear to.

"It never crossed my mind that it was anything more than a pleasant conversation," she insisted. "When we parted at the airport, I thought that was it. 'Nice meeting you. Have a nice life.' I've never been more surprised than when I opened the door of my hotel room and saw him standing in the hallway with two dozen red roses."

I wanted it to be me. Me on the plane. Me with the roses.

A whistle blew, and she bent over and touched her toes. "They recommend stretching before using the trapeze."

"Do they also recommend taking out life insurance?" I said while reaching for my ankles.

She laughed, and I could have spent all afternoon folded half upside down, watching her do so. However, I needed to appear fully engaged in the task of interviewing her, which was also my opportunity to probe the depth of her feelings for Alexander. "If you just met in January, what's the rush to get married?"

"There isn't one," she said. "If I stopped and thought about it, I'd say we're being ridiculous. We barely know each other." So I had reason for hope. "But I guess this is what happens when your first date is at a wedding."

"You were able to bring him to your friend's wedding at the last minute?" Some guys have all the luck. Others forget to even ask for a phone number.

"It was one of those events where the whole town is invited," she explained. "The bridegroom's family had lived there for centuries, and everyone escorted him uphill through the winding streets to the town square, where the bride was waiting by a five-hundred-year-old stone fountain. Alexander proposed along the way, and I thought he was joking. The next day he got me a ring. Are you taping this?"

"Huh?"

"I noticed you're not writing anything down."

Oops. I tapped my head. "It's all in here."

"You can really remember everything I say?"

She had no idea.

"I'm impressed," she said, clasping her hands together behind her back and stretching her arms.

"I still don't understand why you had such a short engagement," I said, suspecting there was something she wasn't telling me.

She rolled her shoulders evasively, but she was just loosening up. "Alexander felt if we were going to get married, why not just do it rather than spending a year of our life planning it? And I agreed, since I'm a big believer in not putting things off to the future. I don't like to tempt fate."

So it was Alexander's idea. Or maybe it was Genevieve's. "Alexander and his mother seem very . . ." I searched for the right word. "Close."

"Isn't it wonderful?" Melinda enthused. Not the reaction I was looking for. "I wish I was as lucky." Something flickered across her face, and she turned away. Maybe she wasn't as hunky-dory with Alexander and Genevieve's relationship as she claimed. Another whistle blew. "Let's go flying," she said.

After a quick lesson on essentials (e.g., remember to hold on to the trapeze bar), we were strapped into our harnesses, which were more like weight-lifting belts clipped to multiple rappelling ropes. We were soon ascending the aluminum ladder like adventure-seeking marionettes.

Compared to my earlier escapade, this was going to be a walk in the park, but when I looked down, I got vertigo. It reminded me of climbing a high-diving board—without the board. I felt an undeniable thrill at the prospect of "flying," but I was also getting increasingly queasy, pretty much identical to my response to high-diving boards, which is why I hadn't been on one in decades. From the age of eight, I was willing to forgo pleasure if it came with pain. Something for me to think about.

Melinda must have sensed my apprehension. "You don't have to do this if you don't want to," she said, glancing down over her shoulder. "I was terrified my first time."

The only thing I was terrified of was looking wimpy in her eyes.

"I've missed out on too many things because of being afraid,"

I heard myself say out loud. "I'm beginning to think 'fear' is just another word for 'desire.'"

Why had I said that? It wasn't even a ready-for-primetime thought, let alone something to share. Melinda looked at me like she had just caught me peeing with the bathroom door open. Then she continued to climb.

What was I doing here? Did I really believe I was going to bond with her by quizzing her about her fiancée? It was absurd. And masochistic. I had made no impression whatsoever on New Year's. I needed to get off of this apparatus. Take a cold shower. And focus on finding a way to save my job, because a buyout wasn't an option. I'd been offered little more than unused vacation time, which wasn't half as insulting as the growing rumor about management axing the entire wedding section. Renée was hoping our popularity with readers would protect us. But that hadn't saved the engagement section, which was eliminated in 2000 after the dot-com crash.

The whistle blew, and I stopped, as I'd been instructed. Seconds later I saw Melinda soaring across the tent. Like a lithe angel. Graceful and strong. She lifted her legs up over the trapeze bar, released her hands and swung upside down. Back and forth and back and forth, her hair a halo of feathery curls. Then she slid from the bar, effortlessly doing a double-somersault dive into the trampolinelike net.

Another whistle, and it was my turn. I would have preferred to be teleported back to my desk as I stood at the top of the ladder, where there was just a narrow platform and open air. An aerialist instructor stood beside me in a space the size of a bathtub, with the net spread thirty far feet below.

The instructor handed me the bar. It was heavier than I expected. I lurched forward, but he held firmly on to my harness. "I've got you," he said. So much for being Superman.

"Jump!" he said. I looked down. Bad idea. I couldn't move. It was like I was back on Melinda's fire escape but jumping *away* from the building.

"Look up," he said. Like that was going to help. But on the far wall was a huge window with a view of water and sky and burgeoning sunlight. "Jump!"

And I did.

I was flying. Not as gracefully as Melinda, but I was swinging on a bar. I pumped my legs, gathering speed and height. And damned if I didn't feel like the happiest five-year-old alive.

I dropped into the net, bouncing a few times before flipping myself off of the edge. It was weird being back on the ground. I was wobbly and disoriented. I toppled onto a mat where Melinda was waiting for me. She gave me a small smile, so all was not lost.

"I've been thinking about it," she said, "and I'm not sure I believe fear always comes from desire."

I was counting on her forgetting about my detour into pseudopsychology. "I don't know where that came from. I think I had altitude sickness."

"I owe you a better answer to your question about Alexander." The last thing I wanted to talk about was Alexander. "When I was ten, my mother was diagnosed with breast cancer," she said, hugging her knees to her body. "I was twelve when she died."

I didn't know what to say. "I'm sorry" seemed trite. "What was that like for you?" I asked, immediately thinking "I'm sorry" would have been exponentially better.

"It was hideous," she said. "Thanks for asking. I mean that. People usually don't. They want to be polite, but there was nothing polite about the experience."

"I can imagine," I responded for lack of anything useful to say.

"No, you can't." She looked down at the mat. "She baked kick-ass snickerdoodles and sewed funky, homemade Halloween costumes. What I hate is, I have memories of her bald and screaming for morphine that occupy space in my brain. I didn't think anything could be worse. Until my dad was diagnosed with colon cancer four years later. The day he told me, I insisted it wasn't possible. We already had our turn. It was double jeopardy, and I had learned in my eleventh-grade government class that was unconstitutional."

I wanted to have been there for her. It wasn't logical, but it was what I felt. I wanted to take care of her. I wanted to make things better for her. "I'm so sorry."

"See, that's what people usually say," she said with a rueful smile. "I should be the one apologizing. This is not what you signed on for. I think all the wedding stuff is—" Her voice caught in her throat. "It's just bringing things up to the surface."

"How could it not?" I asked.

She looked up and scrutinized my face. There were tears in her eyes. So much for making things better. I always felt helpless when a woman cried, but this was worse. I couldn't begin to fathom what Melinda had been through, but if it was possible for me to fall even more for her, I had just done so.

"Can I ask *you* something?" she said after wiping her eyes with her sleeve. There was a seriousness of purpose in her voice.

"Sure," I said with a slight waver in my own. There was something happening between us. Something significant. This was the moment I had been waiting for since New Year's.

"Would you be interested in coming to our engagement party?"

Chapter Twenty-one

Male Pattern Boldness

My first thought when Melinda invited me to her engagement party was that I'd sooner staple my eyelids to a telephone pole. Then I thought again, and the next day I was in Tucker's office, pitching him a new blog premise.

"What if the blog was about following individual brides on their path to marriage?" I was talking fast to keep his attention. It was part eagerness. Part survival instinct. The worst-kept secret in the building was that there was already a list circulating of layoff candidates. The best way for me to stay off that list was by convincing Tucker I was indispensable. "We could call it 'Destination: Wedding.' Get it? It wouldn't be about the location of the wedding, but the journey getting there. It gives us an opportunity to really delve into all the issues a wedding forces upon people. Not just the obvious stuff like choosing a dress and a caterer. But deciding if they want to change their name. Dealing with in-laws. Bachelor parties. *Engagement parties.* And all the feuds and fits along the way. It could almost be like an online reality show." I was appealing to Tucker's desire for glory on the "Interweb."

"What happened to the idea of covering breakups?" he asked, unmoved.

I was way ahead of him. "That's one of the things that can happen along the way. Not every couple is going to make it down the aisle." I paused for effect. "You get to have your wedding cake and eat it too, so to speak."

He groaned.

"It's a broad enough topic to generate the amount of material we'll need to maintain a daily blog," I said, bringing it back to meat-and-potato issues. "And it will allow us to serve readers looking for romantic stories as well as those looking for more cynical ones."

" 'Destination: Wedding.' " He mulled it over. "I don't hate it. Do you have a bride in mind?"

I pictured Melinda in a silky white gown. "I do."

"Are you out of your mind?" asked Hope. I assumed the question was rhetorical.

"It's like I'll be an embedded reporter," I enthused.

"Your desire to be 'embedded' with her is the problem," Hope sniped while fussing with a bubbling saucepan on her sleek induction stove.

"Tucker likes the idea." I didn't know why I had to defend myself. I never told Hope how to go about sewing someone's finger back on.

"Tucker doesn't know you have the hots for your interview subject." Hope was irritable because A.J. was late for dinner. Though she had told me it was just going to be a casual get-together, the fresh-baked pear and goat cheese tarts on puffed pastry suggested otherwise.

"This isn't the first time I've had to write about a woman I find attractive," I said, dipping a celery stick in homemade salsa.

"There's a big difference between thinking someone's cute and wanting to abduct a bride."

I had to confess I had dreamed about grabbing Melinda as she walked down the aisle and carrying her, fireman style, to a waiting taxi, but I could distinguish between dreams and reality. I was taller in my dreams.

"You have no business writing about Melinda. It's unprofessional and unhealthy." Hope had a point, but I had no intention of admitting it. "I'm going to call your brother. Maybe he can talk some sense into you."

"Gary would be the first person to encourage me," I said.

"To pursue a married woman?"

"She's not married."

"She's engaged!"

"To a creep!"

"Has it occurred to you that you might be biased?"

Actually, it hadn't. I prided myself on my objectivity. "If I thought Alexander was worthy of Melinda, I would step aside and wish them both well."

"Bullshit."

Hope rarely swore. I was bearing the brunt of A.J.'s transgression. He was supposed to have been at Hope's place by eight. It was nearing nine. The goat cheese tarts were congealing, as was her mood.

"If I'm wrong about him, they'll be married the first week of May," I said. I didn't mention I had requested a background check on Alexander. It was standard procedure—for suspected felons and war criminals.

The phone rang, and Hope went into her bedroom to answer it. I stirred the pomegranate sauce for the chicken that was still roasting (or, more likely, dehydrating) in the oven. I deliberated whether Hope was right, knowing full well that she was. I weighed the pluses and minuses of my situation, trying to come up with some pluses.

"A.J.'s on call at his clinic," Hope said when she returned, minus her heels and sparkly earrings. "Did I mention he used to work for Doctors Without Borders?"

Thirty-seven times and counting. I dipped a tasting spoon into the pot.

"He's a caring and compassionate person," she said without much conviction, "so why couldn't he have mentioned he was on call tonight prior to five minutes ago? I don't understand him. No, I don't understand men, period. Why do you do the things you do?"

I have never felt representative of my entire sex, but rarely less so than when slurping a spoonful of simmering fruit sauce. "Hey, I was here early," I said.

"There is no logic to male behavior. Just when I think I've got the primary motivations down to sex, money and fantasy football, the whole paradigm gets rearranged. What possible reason do you have to write about Melinda's wedding?"

I thought we had moved on to lambasting A.J.

"Do you really believe no one's going to notice that you're head over heels for this woman?" Hope was growing more agitated. "You keep saying how everything's so precarious at work, then you go and purposely put your job at risk."

"I'm not putting my job at risk," I said, suddenly worried that I was.

"Then what is it that you think you're doing?"

It was less a question than an accusation, and I resented it.

I was doing the only thing I could to be with Melinda. If I didn't write the article, I wouldn't have a reason to see her, and I couldn't bear that.

There it was.

Not such a complicated paradigm at all. I was doing what felt right. Even if it happened to be completely wrong.

"Maybe A.J. didn't tell you he was on call because he wanted to be here if he could," I said with newfound appreciation for complicated choices.

Hope collapsed onto her creamy leather sofa and picked at a desiccated tart. "You really think so?"

It was only a theory, but I was sticking to it. "From everything you've told me, he seems to really care about you."

"It's just so hard. Finding someone. Trusting someone. I know you like Melinda, but do you really want to be the guy who tries to break up an engagement?"

"No." Not when she put it like that. "But I also don't want to be the guy who wonders 'What if?' If Melinda decides she's making a mistake, I'm not going to feel bad about it. Let the best man win."

"What if he's the best man?" Hope softly inquired, adding, "for her."

I didn't have an answer for that. "It makes me happy to be around her," I said, stating the simple truth. "Really happy."

Hope sighed and took a small bite of the tart. "For how long?"

Chapter Twenty-two

There Will Be Blood

Gawker was having a field day with my blog, and I hadn't even started it yet. The headline of their article christened it DESTINATION: DIVORCE.

Is there any sadder indication that romance is dead than The Paper expanding its wedding coverage to tales of love gone wrong? Harlequin writer—we mean, columnist—Gavin Greene, bereft of enough nauseating courtships to fill his quota, has decided to devote a new blog to the brokenhearted. Bravo, Gavin. Will you also be reporting on the breakup sex?

I didn't know if I was more upset about someone leaking false information or the Harlequin crack.

My phone didn't stop ringing all day. From the *New York Post* to *Entertainment Tonight*, everyone wanted to know if it was true

I was starting a divorce column. Then the publicists descended. It seemed that every high-profile divorce lawyer had a publicist and an ax to grind. I was offered salacious stories about wife swapping in Westchester and botched penile implants.

I spent the day declining and disclaiming, when I should have been finishing my article about two former reality-show contestants who had met while competing on *The Amazing Race*. At eight thirty, I was still at my desk instead of at the Upper East Side townhouse where Melinda's engagement party had already started.

Well, physically I was at my desk. Mentally I was picturing Melinda in a strapless black dress and plotting ways to get her alone at her party. An impossible feat if I didn't get out of my office.

I was ready to beg Renée for an extension on my deadline, but she had slipped out without my noticing. Often she worked late into the night. In fact, we had some of our best conversations well past midnight. Bleary-eyed, she'd reminisce about the old days when pneumatic tubes carried stories (and the occasional reptile) to the press room, where printers (the unionized kind) set articles word by word in "hot type" metal plates.

But Renée was gone. As was everyone in the department, which was unusual. But it had been an unusual week. An unusually tense one, as the deadline for voluntary buyouts came and went. Those who chose to take them were both ridiculed and envied by the rest of us, who chose to stay and play an adult version of musical chairs, in which chairs would soon be eliminated one by one, along with computers, security passes and paychecks.

People were tiptoeing around, waiting for the music to stop. They were afraid of drawing attention to themselves, so they made their escapes each night as quickly and quietly as possible. I was the only person working late in the entire wing, and the automated overhead lights kept going off. Every fifteen minutes, I had to get up and do jumping jacks to convince the motion and heat sensors that I was, in fact, a human life form in need of illumination.

Metaphorically, of course, I remained in the dark. I didn't know when the layoffs would start. Or if they would start. Maybe Renée was right when she said it was all just a scare tactic. If so, it worked. I would never have taken solo responsibility for a blog if I hadn't been worried about losing my job.

I grimaced while doing my umpteenth word count. I had only seven hundred words of what needed to be a thousand-word story. I needed to get the piece done and get uptown. The lights went out again, and this time the sensors deemed my in-place calisthenics insufficient proof of my existence. So I ran up and down the hall between the cubicles, waving my arms in the air. I was confused to see Renée's computer was still on and a coat was on the back of her chair. I stopped when I noticed her purse was also hanging there.

"What are you doing?" I heard Renée before I could see her approaching in the darkness.

I was about to tell her that I wasn't snooping when the fluorescents flickered on, and I was jolted by what they revealed.

It wasn't the blood itself that was so shocking, as the amount of it. Renée was holding several saturated pieces of Kleenex to her nose, but viscous red fluid was still oozing down to her chin.

"What happened?" I asked, sprinting to my desk to get her more Kleenex.

"I'm bleeding," she grunted. She was also crying. "I get nosebleeds. It's nothing."

I had never seen Renée cry. It was more disturbing than the blood. As I handed her a box of tissues, I remembered reading somewhere that nosebleeds were a symptom of leukemia. *Could Renée have been diagnosed with cancer?*

"They fired me," she rasped, and collapsed into her chair. "The bastards fired me."

I didn't know what to say. I didn't even know what to think. For weeks we had been warned, but I still wasn't prepared. Even if I had felt prepared, I would never have expected Renée to be let go.

"Heidi Takahashi called me into her office." Renée's body heaved as she spoke. Her words came out in staccato bursts between sniffles and convulsions. "First thing she did was introduce herself as a managing editor. Like I don't know who she is. Like I haven't been here since she was in diapers."

My mind was racing. If Renée was expendable, I was a goner.

"When I started working here, there was no such thing as a female editor, let alone a female managing editor." Her eyes reddened as her tobacco-cured voice rumbled with gritty indignity. "Women weren't even allowed in the newsroom. We were exiled to Ladies Fashion or the secretary pool. It took me ten years to get my first A-section byline, and now this snub-nosed pipsqueak in open-toe pumps has the gall to tell me 'The Paper is no longer in need of your services.' She couldn't even tell me what those services were, because she hadn't had time to review my file." Renée wiped at her eyes with the wad of Kleenex, distributing a bloody smear across her face.

"I'm so sorry," I said, wanting to say something more useful. I had the urge to embrace her, but I knew better. It was one thing for her to show her vulnerability and quite another for me to acknowledge witnessing it.

She pulled more tissues out of the box and plugged her nose. Tears trickled down her cheek. "This isn't how I wanted to go out."

I couldn't imagine The Paper without her. Not only had she worked there for almost half its history, but she also personified its core values. Her exacting standards for accuracy safeguarded what she considered a sacred pact between the newspaper and the public. If The Paper had a soul, it was because of Renée and a handful of others. Take them away, and it was just an office building with unconventional elevators.

"Don't give your life to this place," she said, pointing a bony finger at me. "It will suck you dry and feast on your sinew." She seemed less a scrappy newswoman than an Old Testament prophet as she rose unsteadily to her feet.

"Renée, do you want me to take you to a hospital?" I asked, alarmed by both her warning and her wobbling.

She shook her head slowly with a melancholy gaze. "The problem with loving a newspaper is it can't love you back."

With Renée's words reverberating in my brain, I paid the taxi driver and dashed toward the columned portico of a beaux arts townhouse. I had one goal: to find Melinda. I had no idea what I was going to say to her, but doing my best Stuart Smalley imitation, I silently affirmed that I was good enough, I was smart enough and my best chance of winning her over was while I still had a job. An elderly security guard was standing in front of the massive carved door, nonchalantly smoking a cigar.

"Where's the fire?" he asked as I ran up the front steps.

"I'm a little late," I said, trying to get by him.

"The party started at eight," he said. "At eight fifteen you were a little late. At nine thirty, you're early for Thanksgiving." A real character. Just my luck. And he wasn't budging.

"I'm here as a reporter for The Paper," I said, pulling out my notepad.

"I thought they did everything on computers these days," he said, taking another puff on his cigar. "You sure you're a real reporter?"

"That's what it says on my paycheck." I was impatient to get inside.

"Well, then, you can't be working for The Paper. They don't have any money left to pay people." He grinned, enjoying himself at my expense while purposefully blocking the doorway. He looked to be in his seventies with an impressive thatch of white hair and the stance of a former prizefighter eager to prove he could still go mano a mano. "So is every fancy-shmancy party considered news these days?"

"Only the shmanciest," was my flippant response as I considered crawling between his legs. He erupted in a fit of phlegmy coughs. I wasn't sure if he was choking or laughing.

"You better get inside," he said. "There could be a breaking story on the tortellini."

He pushed open the door, revealing a grand expanse of limestone walls and marble floor, with society types sipping from crystal goblets and a jazz trio playing in a corner. I navigated through the sea of mingling guests, looking for Melinda, but my height was working against me as I tried to peek over padded shoulders and French twists. At the far end of the room, an ornate winding stairway swept upward, and I headed toward it for a bird's-eye view.

"Gavin, we missed you at dinner." It was Genevieve, descending like the plague. I pivoted my head from side to side, scanning the room for the one face I was seeking. "The mayor already left, but he said you can call him for a quote."

"I'll do that," I said while maneuvering around her, but she hooked her arm through mine and guided me back down the stairs as she whispered forcefully in my ear.

"Now, you didn't hear this from me, but the mayor has promised to endorse Alexander for city council next year."

"Alexander's running for councilman?" It was the first I had heard of it.

"He didn't want to throw too much at Melinda all at once, but she's going to be a wonderful asset for him." I bristled, though Genevieve didn't seem to notice. "Not only for the council race," she continued. "You may not know this, but my great-grandfather was governor and two uncles were state senators. It's sort of a family business."

She was steering me toward a solitary socialite standing at the bar. I cranked my neck so far around, I feared I was going to pull a muscle. Out of the corner of my eye I saw a flurry of activity among a group of people near the base of the stairs. The waters parted, so to speak. Melinda emerged and ascended in a red wrap dress that caressed each curve even more than the black strapless one I had imagined.

"Gavin." Genevieve tugged impatiently on my arm. "I want to introduce you to Libby Rockefeller."

At The Paper, the rule was there was no difference between a Rockefeller and a Rastafarian, but that didn't mean it was ever advantageous to be rude to one of the former. Yet even saying hello would obligate me to endure chitchat while Melinda disappeared, so I deployed the strategy I learned from a foreign correspondent I had briefly dated.

"I'm sorry," I said, "but I'm just getting over a tapeworm infestation and need to find a restroom." While Genevieve shuddered, I fled.

There were several people standing on the second-floor landing, but Melinda wasn't one of them. I poked my head into the nearest room. It was the kind of oak-paneled library I had only seen in movies, with antique leather club chairs, Tiffany lamps and thousands of hardcover books.

"Thinking of buying the place?" Alexander thumped me on the back, startling me.

"Your parents have a beautiful home," I jabbered.

"Thanks, but my parents' brownstone is a fisherman's shack compared to this place. No, this is Melinda's home."

I had been to Melinda's home and still had the bruises to prove it. "I thought she lived on the Upper West Side," I said.

"You know how some kids put up tents in their backyard to feel like they're roughing it? Melinda's apartment sort of serves the same purpose. This is where she grew up. Her bedroom's down the hall, and she hasn't changed it since she was in high school."

I was a little dizzy. I flopped into one of the chairs, wondering how much I didn't know about her.

"Pretty amazing, isn't it?" Alexander sat opposite me. "When I realized who she was, I almost shit in my pants. There I was on this plane to Madrid, sitting next to the Altman department store heiress. Beautiful *and* loaded." I knew I was focusing on the wrong point, but my first thought was that Altman was a Jewish name.

"You asked me how I decided to blow off my conference and drive to Barcelona." Alexander leaned in toward me. "The only question for me was whether I should drive or take a plane. I wasn't going to let her have a chance to meet any other man. Ever. I mean, only an idiot would let a woman like Melinda get away. Right?"

"There he is!" A thickish thirtysomething guy with an anorexic twentysomething spouse burst into the room. "Alexander, we have to take off."

Alexander jumped to his feet, and the two men pounded each other's backs. "You're not staying for dessert?"

"Do I look like I need dessert?"

I wandered out of the room and down the hall, my mind reeling. Melinda was an heiress, and I was a fool. Not because she was an heiress. Because I let her get away. I should have grabbed hold of her on that rooftop and vowed eternal devotion. No, I should have just kissed her. How could one mistake keep boomeranging back to haunt me? Oh, that's right—because I chose to put myself in a situation where I'd be forced to deal with it over and over. I could hear Hope's voice in my head, berating me.

I passed a half-open doorway and caught a glimpse of a pink coverlet on a canopied bed. I leaned against the door, and it swung open. I told myself I didn't belong there. I vowed to start making better choices—as soon as I took a quick look around. There were volleyball trophies, a poster for a school play and two framed pictures on a white bureau: a young girl on a man's shoulders, and the same girl sharing a milk shake with a woman who looked a lot like a darker-haired version of Melinda. I heard a floorboard creak and hastily turned round with a guilty expression on my face.

Melinda was standing in the doorway, her Bacall-esque silhouette backlit by a hallway chandelier. "I'm on to you," she said.

There were so many problematic ways she could have meant that. I was at a loss for how to respond. She flipped on a light switch and eased into the room. I could swear I heard her shimmering dress gliding along her skin.

"I saw Gawker today," she said, reminding me of one of the day's many events I was attempting to forget. "You've gone to the dark side, and I don't mean Fox News." Her dimples made a brief appearance. "Here I thought you were the last romantic."

Was she flirting?

"I am," I assured her, launching a charm offensive with what I hoped was an irresistibly disarming smile. "Well, not the last, I hope."

She laughed. "Then what's with the divorce blog?"

"It's not a divorce blog."

"Whatever it is, it sounds ghoulish. Like ambulance chasing. Where are you going to find people willing to talk on the record about their marriages breaking up?"

"Some people belong together and some people don't," I said meaningfully. "For those who belong together, getting married is an amazing experience, but for others, going their separate ways can also be a happy event."

"That's not what most brides want to hear." Her face flushed, and she turned away from me.

What the hell was I doing talking to her about divorce at her engagement party? I changed the subject. "So, this house is where you grew up?" I asked.

"Hardly," she said, still facing away. "I grew up in a six-hundred-square-foot, one-bedroom apartment on the Lower East Side. My father was what one could call a very stubborn man." Her fingers lightly grazed the top of the picture frame. "My grandfather took me in after he died."

Good one, Gavin. Take the conversation from divorce to death. "I think this bedroom might be six hundred square feet."

She laughed again. "I think you're right. It's a bit much. When I was young, I used to think my grandparents lived in a foreign kingdom. Even though it was only a few miles away. We would visit for holidays, and I felt like a fairy-tale princess with velvet dresses and silk pajamas." She curled her fingers around a bedpost and swung girlishly from it for a moment. "You're very easy to talk to."

"I hope that's a good thing," I said, meeting her gaze with brazen longing.

"It's like talking to my therapist." Maybe I was barking up the wrong bedpost. "Why aren't you married?" she abruptly asked me.

"Is that something you ask your therapist?"

"My therapist is married."

I would have loved to have had an epiphany about my life at that moment. Something I could have shared with her, but epiphanies are hard to come by.

"I wish I knew why I wasn't married," I said. "It seems like something I should know." There were the obvious reasons. Poor choices. Heartbreaks. I thought of Laurel and how it felt watching her pack her tea infuser and her dental floss in a recyclable Whole Foods grocery bag. It felt like I had failed. That was the part I couldn't get over. That and the fear of not knowing how to prevent it from happening again.

Melinda crossed her arms and scrutinized my face, like an artist deliberating how she wanted to paint me. "I think you know the answer, but you're keeping it a secret from yourself."

I only wished. "That sounds highly unlikely."

"You're just going to have to trust me," she said with a playful tilt of her head.

She seemed to be flirting again, so I flirted right back. "Oh, now I'm supposed to trust you, but a week ago you wouldn't tell me where you really live."

"I never tell anyone where I live," she said.

That wasn't true. "You told Alexander."

"Are you kidding? I didn't even tell him my last name until after he proposed. I'm a little paranoid." Her caution was endearing, but completely contradictory to what he had told me. "The first time Alexander came here to meet my grandfather, he nearly had a coronary. He was very upset with me for not coming clean with him."

Either she was lying to me for some reason, or Alexander was lying to her.

"Speaking of coming clean, there's something else I should admit to you." Her voice dropped an octave. She *was* lying about something, and I dreaded finding out what. "I should have told you this before, and I guess I'm a little nervous how you're going to react." That made two of us.

"The truth is that when we were introduced at Balthazar, it wasn't the first time we met." My mouth opened but words didn't come out. "You probably don't remember with all the people you meet, but we were at a party together on New Year's Day. Well, not together, but we were both there, and we spoke. Not much. Just small talk about travel and Thomas Mann. I don't know why I didn't say something sooner. I think I was just embarrassed that I remembered and you didn't."

I was such an idiot.

Waves of desire pelted my nervous system. Nothing had changed, yet everything had changed. Or at least changed enough for me to take a gamble and tell her how I felt about her. It was like everything I wanted was right in front of me, and all I had to do was seize the moment. "Melinda, I—"

"Melinda, your husband is looking for you." It was the security guard, once again standing in a doorway and blocking my progress.

"He's not my husband yet," Melinda corrected him.

"Well, he acts like he is." The old guy must have been some kind of butler rather than a guard. A crusty family retainer who liked to put his nose in everyone's business.

"Gavin," Melinda said, "have you met my incorrigible grandfather?"

Oh, God.

"We met," he harrumphed before quickly changing the topic. "Alexander wants to make a toast before dessert." He followed this announcement with another spate of coughing. Melinda put a protective arm around his shoulders.

"Did you take your medication?" she asked.

"It's just allergies," he said, waving her off. "Now, if you put off dessert any longer, they're going to be serving the gelato with straws."

She hurried out of the bedroom. In a daze, I followed down the stairs and through a limestone archway into an immense candlelit dining room where everyone was gathering. I was uncomfortably aware her grandfather was just a few feet behind me while I tried to process everything that had happened. I must have had an odd expression on my face, because the fellow standing next to me kept staring at me. He looked vaguely familiar, with acne scars and unruly dark hair.

"Aren't you the bloke from New Year's?" he inquired. The Australian accent was the giveaway. The evening was becoming an excruciating trip down memory lane.

I halfheartedly extended my hand to Jamie, my once imagined rival for Melinda's affection. If only things had been that simple.

"What are you doing here?" he asked, seeming perplexed by my continued existence on the planet. I explained my job at The Paper, but he remained mystified. "Blimey! What are the odds?" I couldn't answer that one for him. "You know she totally had a thing for you."

"Excuse me?" I said, unwilling to believe I heard right.

"Melinda," he said like I was daft. "Did you guys ever hook up?" All I could do was shake my head. "Too bad. Have to admit, I was a wee bit jealous. I never got anywhere with her, and not due to a lack of trying. But if a chick doesn't fall for you when she's pissed on plonk on a beach in Goa, it's never going to happen." He looked at me for confirmation. I was still too stunned to speak. "You must have the magic mojo, because I could barely get her out the door of that party on New Year's, and then I had to stop her from going back inside."

I had to stop myself from throttling him. "She wanted to go back to the party?"

"I had to drag her into a taxi. Don't know what she was thinking. Was a lame party if you ask me, but she thought you were quite the Jackaroo. She couldn't stop yabbering about you until, well, until she met Alexander."

There was a bell-like ringing in my ears. I saw Alexander clinking his champagne flute with a small spoon. "I just have a few words I want to say," he said with a Cheshire cat grin, dramatically unfurling his prepared speech.

The room was spinning. On more than one axis. Like a gyroscope. Like I was inside a giant gyroscope. I was sweating. My breathing was shallow. I was afraid I was hyperventilating.

"I'm the luckiest man on the planet," Alexander exalted.

The luck-a-luck. The luck-a-luck. The words reverberated in my head. Round and round. *She totally had a thing for you. Just small talk about travel and Thomas Mann. Only an idiot would let a woman like Melinda get away.* Faces mixed and matched and blurred together with the candles and the champagne. And Melinda's smile. Melinda's lips spreading apart. Alexander's lips drawing toward them. *The luck-a-luck. The luck-a-luck.*

"When you meet the woman of your dreams, you don't waste a moment," Alexander said as their profiles merged and the crowd cheered.

I turned around. I couldn't watch anymore. But it was even worse seeing the beaming reactions of the other guests. There were tears in her grandfather's eyes, and he was holding his hands to his heart.

No, he was clutching his chest. *Shit*.

I ran toward him while calling 911 on my cell phone. His legs seemed to collapse, and I scrambled to catch him before he hit the ground. As I held him in my arms, he whispered hoarsely, "Promise me you'll take care of Melinda."

Then he passed out.

The sliding doors opened and closed, and another bloodstained gurney was wheeled into the emergency room. Still no sign of Melinda.

I had been pacing for twenty-five minutes. I didn't know if I should stay or go. I wasn't sure she remembered I was there. I was even less sure that I should have been. It all happened very quickly. One minute I was checking her grandfather's pulse, the next I was jumping into the ambulance with her while Alexander was offering to stay behind and take care of their guests. But when we had arrived at the hospital, she was escorted by the paramedics into the ER, and I was left to fend for myself in the waiting room. A place that made the Port Authority bus terminal look inviting. The harsh lighting, uncomfortable seating and proximity to mortal ailments made me jittery. The two cups of coffee also weren't helping.

I couldn't stop thinking of what her grandfather had said to me. He was obviously confused. Probably delirious. Yet I couldn't resist thinking it was some kind of sign.

The glass doors opened again, and I saw Melinda's mascara-stained face.

"He's in the ICU," she said as she tottered toward me. "No one's telling me much of anything."

I wanted to comfort her, but I wasn't sure what was appropriate. I reached out my hand and she took it. I awkwardly patted her elbow with my other hand, and she slipped her arms around me, burying her face in my shoulder. I let myself enfold her. I could feel her heart beating. I could smell the faint scent of mandarin oranges in her hair. I was a terrible person.

"I'm sorry," she sniffled.

"For what?"

"For being such a wreck," she said. "I appreciate your being here. I know it's not what you get paid for. Or maybe it is. Comforting nervous brides."

With her body pressed against mine, I wasn't thinking of her as a bride. "I thought I was comforting a nervous granddaughter."

"I'm both," she said. As much as I wanted to be supportive and compassionate, that was the opening I'd been waiting for.

"Are you having doubts about marrying Alexander?" I asked. If it wasn't destiny for us to be together, I was going straight to hell.

"How could I not?" she said, her head still resting on my shoulder. "I know how ridiculous it is to marry someone I barely know. He made this big romantic gesture, and I either had to say yes or risk being the girl who was afraid to take the leap."

That didn't sound like true love, but I didn't want to get my hopes up.

"I've been looking for the right person for so long, you know?" She looked up at me. "How do you ever know it's the right person? And how long do you wait? I'm already thirty-two. My mother was dead at thirty-five." She retrieved a tissue from her purse and blew her nose. We were no longer touching, and I already missed the warmth of her breath.

"Of course, there are things that bother me about Alexander," she said quietly. "I wish he was here now. I wish he had taken my hand and stayed with me and said to hell with everyone else, but he's very responsible. It's one of the things I love about him. So how can I be upset?"

She had every reason to be upset, but I was grateful Alexander wasn't there.

"You must hear this kind of thing all the time," she said, gnawing on the nail of her index finger. She looked nervous and vulnerable. I didn't want to say anything that would make her feel worse. "Lots of brides get cold feet, right? I'm not saying I've got cold feet, but if I did, what would you say to me?"

There wasn't a question of what I should say. I had the words in my head. Words I had used with Amy about trusting her feelings. And trusting love. It was the right thing to do. The noble thing to do.

I just couldn't do it.

"Don't marry him," I said. Melinda's eyes widened. "He's not worthy of you. Do you really believe he didn't know about your money? Or that he stayed at the party for anyone's benefit but his own? He's not here with you right now because he didn't want to be. Because you're not his priority. And you deserve to be with someone who *always* makes you his priority."

It all came pouring out without time to organize my thoughts. I was harsher than I intended to be. It was hard to hide my animosity for Alexander, but there was something I had left out. Something important, if I could just think of what it was.

"I'm such a fool," she said.

"No. That's not what I meant to say at all." I had done this all wrong. There was something crucial I hadn't told her.

"You must really hate me."

Hate her? I'd just realized how much I loved her. That's what I'd forgotten to say! I completely left out how I felt about her.

"I saw that article on Gawker," she said, "and it didn't even occur to me what you were doing."

What did Gawker have to do with anything? "Melinda, there's something I need to tell you."

"You said enough. I get it. What better way to get a wedding-breakup story than to break it up yourself?"

"WHAT?"

"My grandfather could be dying, and all you care about is your pathetic blog."

"No!"

"I have to hand it to you," she said, her jaw tightening. "You're very good at what you do. That whole sensitive-writer thing. Getting people to open up. You got me. You got me good."

"That's not what I was doing." I had to find a way to convince her.

"Were you going to write about the poor little rich girl with abandonment issues? Or were you going to lead with how I didn't trust my fiancé with my last name? Well, that's not news. I never trust anyone. But I trusted you."

Paramedics wheeled in a stabbing victim on a crimson-stained gurney.

"Melinda—" I reached for her, but she swatted my hand away.

"Stay away from me and stay away from my fiancé!" Anger flashed in her eyes. And betrayal. I had hurt the person I most wanted to protect.

"I never want to see you again," was the last thing she said.

The doors slid open, and she ran into the ER. She kept running down a long hallway. I watched her get smaller and smaller, until she was just a dark smudge in my shriveled world.

Chapter Twenty-three

No News Is Good News

"Nothing good ever happens in a hospital," my grandmother said, sounding even wearier than I felt. I had
called her on my way to work, as was my habit,
because if I hadn't, she would have sensed something was wrong.
And I didn't want her worrying about me.

"They've got Bernie hooked up to all these machines, and
they're draining the life out of him," she said as I lumbered
uptown under dense April clouds.

"The machines are helping," I said, forcing my voice into a
cheerful register.

"I don't see them helping," she replied testily.

Our conversations were, more typically, short and upbeat.
She'd pretend Bernie was improving, and I'd pretend I didn't
know better. This wasn't a good day for changing our routine.
This wasn't a good day for anything. My goal was to get through
it without breaking down completely. I had dragged myself out

of bed, wanting to call in sick but knowing that would be a terrible mistake. The last thing I needed was for Melinda or Alexander to call The Paper before I had a chance to explain my actions. Not that I knew how I was going to do that.

"I'm sorry, Gavin," my grandmother said. "I'm just a little tired. Tell me about your new bog."

"It's called a blog," I said, though her name was more accurate. I had the urge to divulge what had happened the night before. I wanted her to tell me that all I had to do was eat a slice of her apple strudel and everything was going to be all right. But she hadn't baked strudel in twenty years, and nothing was going to be all right. I had lost Melinda, and I was likely to lose my job. "The blog is going well," I lied.

"Are you dressing warm?" she asked. We were back on familiar ground.

"It's sixty-eight degrees here."

"That's cold," she said. Spoken like a true Floridian. "I'm sending you a sweater."

It wasn't my birthday, and my grandmother had never cared for knitting. "That's okay, Grandma. I have sweaters."

"I bought Bernie a cashmere V-neck the day before the accident," she said, her voice becoming more pinched with each word. "He's not going to be needing it."

I had known since February that Bernie wasn't going to recover, yet hearing my grandmother give up hope was still unsettling, like being on one of those amusement park rides where the floor gives out from under you.

I stood across the street from The Paper for ten minutes, letting its immensity loom over me. I dreaded going inside. It would have been humiliating enough having to admit my poor judgment to Renée, but the thought of telling Tucker was unbearable. I wondered if the Army recruiting station in Times Square was open.

Soldiering on, I pressed the elevator call button, for once grateful I could count on several minutes of delay, but there were none. The elevator arrived instantaneously, taunting me with its eager, open-door salutation. If I didn't know better, I would have sworn I heard the gears snickering.

Paranoia wasn't going to help me. I had plenty of real problems without viewing inanimate objects as antagonists. Yet as I walked along the fifth-floor corridor, the walls seemed to be sloping inward.

Approaching my cubicle, I could see the message light on my telephone flashing. In and of itself, this was not unusual, but it was nonetheless fraught with perilous possibilities. The moment I sat down, the phone abruptly rang. *It's alive*, I thought. *The whole building's alive. And it knows everything.*

Tamping down my rising hysteria, I recognized the number on the display panel. It was Roxanne's. There were two reasons brides contacted me after articles were printed: to express gratitude or to complain, and thank-yous almost always came by e-mail. I let Roxanne go to voice mail. Then I closed my eyes, took a deep breath and exhaled.

When I opened my eyes, Tucker was hovering over me.

"Could you come by my office for a few minutes?" He asked it so nonchalantly, a third-party observer might assume it was a casual request.

"Sure," I said, attempting to be equally casual. Like my body was functioning normally and my adrenal glands weren't broadcasting a system-wide alert: *All hands on deck!*

I followed Tucker the ten yards to his office, fighting the impulse to run the other direction and never look back.

His secretary glanced up as we passed. I detected pity in her eyes. Or maybe it was fear. Tucker settled himself behind his desk and gestured. "Have a seat."

Were there three more ominous words in the English language?

"I received an interesting call this morning," he said, using the word "interesting" as a synonym for "career-ending." "From a Genevieve Bigelow. I take it you know her."

My life was over. "Yes," I mumbled, reminding myself even criminals have the right to remain silent.

"She claims you urged her son's fiancée not to marry him," Tucker said. "Do you make a habit of demanding brides call off their weddings?"

"I wasn't demanding anything," I said feebly. "I was answering a question."

"Isn't it your job to be the one *asking* questions?" He was just playing with me. I was a dead reporter walking. Well, sitting. "Did you threaten her?" he asked.

"No."

"Did you offer her anything in return for canceling her wedding?"

"No."

"Then why would Ms. Bigelow say you did?"

I found myself contemplating the many benefits of beheadings. A swift execution was a merciful one.

"The bride saw Gawker's article about our blog," I attempted to explain, "which might have confused her about my intentions."

Tucker's eyes narrowed. "Well, she couldn't have been that confused, because they still want us running a story. They just don't want *you* writing it." He flicked his thumbnail against his index finger, a nervous habit that usually surfaced when he was about to blow.

"They want me to assign another reporter," he said, leading up to the part about reassigning me permanently. I had an impulse to throw myself at his feet and beg him to let me keep my job. Working at The Paper wasn't just what I did; it was who I was. I was the guy who wrote for the number one newspaper in the country. No, more than that. I was the guy who wrote about weddings, and I was good at it. It was the one thing in my life I took pride in.

And I had blown it.

"The problem is I don't like being told how to run my department." Tucker slammed his fist on his desk. "The nerve of these people. I don't know how you have the patience to deal with them."

Huh?

"I'd tell them all not to get married." His lips briefly formed a smile. "But not until I filed my story."

I'd been reprieved.

Tucker was taking my word against Genevieve's. I wasn't going to be a pitiful unemployed writer living on unfiltered vodka and tuna fish. I was shocked. I was grateful.

"You're staying on the piece," he said.

I was screwed. Staying on the piece wasn't an option. I couldn't do that to Melinda. Or to myself. "Tucker, don't you think it would be difficult for me to continue to work with them?"

"I'm sorry," he said. "Did you sign up for the easy journalism career?"

There was a nasty edge in his voice. Still, I had to remember how thankful I was for the prospect of continued employment and branded alcohol.

"It's not just about it being easy or not." I fumbled for words. "The truth is I think I've lost my objectivity. Just on this one story. I'm sorry. I should have said something sooner." I was admitting to violating one of The Paper's bedrock principles. But I was being honest about it, and I hoped that counted for something.

Tucker leaned back in his chair, mulling the implications. "Well, that changes everything, doesn't it?" I nodded. "Objectivity is the most important thing," he said, pausing for emphasis. "*If* you were writing about a real news event. But you write about weddings. There's nothing whatsoever for you to be objective about. You jot down when couples met, where they married, and you're out of there."

"That's all you think I do?"

"A trained monkey could write your stories, if a monkey knew the names of bridal gown designers." I didn't know if he really believed what he was saying, but he seemed to be taking great pleasure in disparaging me.

That's the price one pays to work at a place like The Paper. You put up with whatever is dished out, because there's nowhere to go but down. Renée did it for almost fifty years. And I saw what that got her.

"Now, I have a job to do," he sneered. "No, with Renée gone, I have two jobs to do." He spoke as if it weren't implicit that he was actively involved in her dismissal. "She left me with a two-thousand-word story to edit on a movie about a freaking bridesmaid. God help me. So I suggest you get busy doing *your* job. While you still have one." With that he turned his attention to his computer monitor.

"There's just one thing, Tucker."

"Yes?" he said, without looking up.

"I quit."

Chapter Twenty-four

The New Me

"No one ever leaves The Paper," said Renée. "Ever."

I had invited her to breakfast at an Upper West Side diner to see how she was doing, and she seemed to be doing pretty well as she chastised me between forkfuls of egg-white omelet.

"They dragged me out of there kicking and screaming," she said. "What on earth were you thinking?"

I was thinking she'd be more supportive. Tony and Alison had taken me out for drinks. Even Captain Al had reached out. I'd been hesitant to open his e-mail, anticipating one last complaint about my punctuation. But what he wrote made no mention of my predilection for commas: "Gavin, I was saddened to learn of your departure, and I consider it The Paper's loss. It's been a privilege to work with you."

High praise from a man who despised sentimentality. So

why was Renée busting my newfound balls? Especially since my action was largely motivated by the shabby way she was treated. I would have liked a little recognition of that. But what I really wanted was access to her Rolodex. I needed a new job ASAP.

"You made a *huge* mistake," she said.

Quitting The Paper or buying her a meal? Her lack of empathy was beginning to piss me off. "Why, Renée? Why was it such a *huge* mistake?"

"Because I arranged for you to get a promotion."

My first thought was, *How?* (My second was, *How much?*)

"It was one of the last things I did," she said, giving me a look that suggested she deeply regretted the effort. It was a cruel joke to be indebted for something I didn't even get to enjoy.

My phone rang. As I hurriedly switched the ringer to vibrate, I saw Roxanne's number displayed. She had already left me two cryptic messages insisting I call her back as soon as possible, but her complaints were no longer my concern.

"Tucker didn't say anything to you?" Renée asked, chomping on her last piece of toast. I shook my head despondently. "Figures. You just saved him ten thousand bucks."

I wished she hadn't told me that. It felt almost criminal to have walked away from a five-figure raise in this economy. Unlike Renée, I had no pension to fall back on. I started thinking again about the thousands of laid-off journalists across the country, all competing for the same few positions, and I lost my appetite.

"You can still go back, Gavin," she said. "You're good at what you do, and Tucker knows it. He's a prick, but he's not an idiot."

"He's not going to let me just waltz in and have my desk back."

"No, he'll make you beg for half your salary. But you'll be employed."

"Until the next round of layoffs."

Renée flinched. I hadn't meant to be insensitive. But a fact is a fact. What happened to Renée showed that despite the idealistic rhetoric, The Paper was no different from any other corporation. I thought that's what she had tried to warn me about. I had expected her to applaud what I did. Applaud and share her Rolodex.

"You're the one who told me to get out while I could," I said.

"I never said that." She dabbed her lips with her napkin.

"Not in those exact words—"

"If you're going to quote someone, quote them accurately."

"They took advantage of you." She turned her head away. "I'm sorry, Renée, but that's what you said. And you were adamant I not let them do the same to me."

"It's the best job on the planet," she said, pushing herself up from the table. She stood facing me, and this time there was no wobbling. "I'd go back in a heartbeat."

"There's more than one Rolodex in this city," I said to Hope as she inhaled a Venti-sized Starbucks espresso in preparation for working the night shift. "I respect Renée, but she doesn't necessarily know what's best for me. I have to trust my instincts and not second-guess myself."

This was the new me. Acting on my feelings. Letting go. And not dwelling on the past. My life was a big arrow pointing forward.

"Have you called Melinda?" Hope asked, dragging me back into the primordial muck.

"I was talking about my job."

"You don't have a job." Not a helpful response. We were walking to St. Vincent's Medical Center. Correction: She was going to St. Vincent's. I was only going as far as the front door, since I couldn't handle being inside another hospital.

"You need to call Melinda," she said, continuing to guzzle her iced Café Americano.

"You were the one who said not to contact her in the first place."

"That was before I knew you loved her."

"How can I love her? I barely know her." The whole situation was preposterous. "I think love is something you imagine," I hypothesized. "When two people imagine it at the same time, it's real. But if only one, it's not."

Hope was unimpressed by my philosophizing. "Either you have feelings for her or you don't."

"It makes no difference what I feel. She doesn't want to see me. And she definitely doesn't want me to call."

"Don't underestimate the power an apology can have on a woman." We weren't necessarily still talking about Melinda. A.J. had been MIA since the missed dinner. There had been no calls and no apologies, but Hope was, well, hopeful. "One fight doesn't have to be the end of everything. But you can't expect someone to read your mind. You need to tell her how you feel about her."

Hope had no idea how many times I'd picked up the phone to do precisely that. "You didn't see the way she looked at me," I said, shuddering at the memory. "It would be selfish to call her. She's getting married in less than two weeks. I need to let her go."

But Hope was the one going away. We had reached the

entrance of the emergency room. My phone vibrated in my pocket. It was Roxanne again. She wasn't taking a hint.

"I'm focusing on moving forward," I said to Hope as we hugged good-bye.

"I wish I believed you." This was why Hope was still single; she didn't know when to lie.

My phone continued to buzz. Roxanne was like the Ghost of Stories Past, rattling her chains. The old me would have fretted about what mistake I had made in her article, but the new improved me decided that article was ancient history. I wasn't on The Paper's payroll, and Roxanne wasn't my responsibility.

However, it occurred to me that she was Tucker's responsibility. I couldn't think of a better going-away gift than letting him have the pleasure of placating an angry bride. Especially one who worked for the *Today Show*. I answered the call.

"You've been avoiding me," Roxanne said as salutation. "And don't think I don't know why."

If she knew I quit, why was she bothering me? The sooner I gave her Tucker's phone number, the sooner I could put her and The Paper behind me.

"Whatever *Good Morning America* is offering you for an interview, I'll beat it," Roxanne said. I wasn't about to broadcast my unemployment on either show, and I was surprised she thought it was newsworthy. She must have had a lot of airtime to fill. "I can get you better placement, bigger limousine—you name it."

"I'm not appearing on *Good Morning America*," I assured her.

"Are you doing *Regis and Kelly*? No insult, but they're total size queens. The bigger the name, the more screen time. I guarantee you they'll spend the entire segment with James Marsden, and just put you on as an afterthought."

I had no idea what she was talking about. "What does James Marsden have to do with anything?"

"Have you even seen the movie?"

"What movie?"

"Are you playing with me? Or do you really not know there's a movie out about you?"

She had to be mistaken. Didn't she? I grabbed my paper and flipped to the film ads. *American Zombie, Horton Hears a Who, 10,000 B.C.* I was pretty sure any movie about me would not include loincloths.

Then I remembered Tucker had mentioned something about an upcoming movie, but he didn't say it had anything to do with me. He said it was about a bridesmaid.

"*Always a Bridesmaid* is the number-one movie in America this week," Roxanne said. "Where have you been?"

I spared her the details as I spotted the full-page ad. Six color photos of Katherine Heigl wearing six different bridesmaid dresses.

"I hate to break the news to you, Roxanne, but I've never been a bridesmaid, and I don't look anything like Katherine Heigl."

"Don't be a dope," she said. "Heigl's character is the bridesmaid. She falls for a guy who writes the wedding column at a newspaper that looks a whole lot like The Paper. It's you. Right down to your skinny tie."

Roxanne had no reason to make this up. Someone must have really made a movie about me. Who? Why? It was exciting. And disorienting. Not the kind of thing you expect to hear while standing on Seventh Avenue with ambulances going by and panhandlers asking for spare change. I felt like shouting out, "I'm going to be hanging with Matt Lauer on the *Today Show*."

I couldn't ask for better proof that my life was heading in a bold new direction and away from the past.

"I'm guessing you must know the screenwriter," Roxanne said. "Her name's Lori something. No, I'm wrong. It's Laurel. Laurel Miller."

God hated me.

Chapter Twenty-five

Always a Bridesmaid

I sat in the near darkness, gazing upward. There were only a half dozen other people in the matinee showing. I could hear them munching popcorn and wondered if they noticed that James Marsden and I were wearing identical blazers.

He was me. Or me with whiter teeth. (I made a note to myself to buy whitening strips.) He was like my personal wardrobe avatar. James/I looked dorky in a fedora, but our jeans-and-jacket look totally rocked. Of course, there were obvious differences between us. I would never wear jeans to a wedding. Laurel knew that.

What was she thinking? Not about the jeans. About the whole thing. I had steeled myself for something unflattering, but the movie was a valentine. I was sensitive and romantic. Or James was. But Laurel didn't consider me either. Not by the end. I'd never forget the icy look on her face the night she told me she was leaving.

I'd been thinking about proposing. I'd been specifically thinking about it while in jewelry stores examining diamond rings. I'd never contemplated spending so much money on a single item, and I became overwhelmed by doubts. What if she didn't like it? What if she said no? What if she wasn't the right woman for me?

My vacillations proved providential when she told me she had met a patent lawyer who played drums for a Springsteen cover band. Turned out I'd been "Dancing in the Dark."

So why did she write about me? She walked out and never called. No e-mail. No nothing. Then three years later, I'm her idea of a romantic hero. It didn't make any sense.

Unless she still had feelings for me.

I would never have considered it possible, but there was Katherine Heigl, clinging tearfully to James Marsden as she apologized for running away and telling him how much she loved him. Maybe the movie was Laurel's way of reaching out to me.

If she could pen a twenty-million-dollar peace offering, I could make a phone call.

Laurel looked good. Her face was fuller, and there were a few small creases in her brow. But her thick auburn hair still fell in lustrous waves past her shoulders.

She wasn't the kind of woman one would think of as beautiful at first glance. Her features were a little too soft, her cheeks a little too round. But there was a sparkle in her eyes, an inner fire belied by her placid exterior.

I couldn't tell whether she was nervous. I never could.

She had responded promptly to my voice mail and seemed happy to have received it. I suggested lunch at Cornelia Street

Café, a cozy bistro in the West Village. It wasn't until I walked in the door that I questioned my sanity.

I couldn't look at Laurel without remembering a thousand moments I had spent three years trying to forget. Sharing a chocolate fondue at a country inn in Stowe, Vermont. Sulking on separate benches on a Fire Island ferry. It was like opening a booby-trapped footlocker. I apprehensively kissed her on the cheek.

"You're still wearing Drakkar," she said. Yes, I'd been wearing the same cologne since college, but I happened to like it. I didn't think I needed to do a makeover for lunch with a woman who'd dumped me. "You smell great."

My bad.

"I'm glad you contacted me," she said, getting right to the point as she always did. It was one of the things I'd admired about her. In addition to her intelligence. Her creativity. Her perceptiveness. "I wasn't happy with how we had left things."

"Neither was I," I said, and we both smiled. Partially from discomfort, but mostly because of sincere fondness. I truly liked Laurel. That hadn't changed since the day I met her at a friend's book party. It felt natural to be sitting across from her, and I was grateful to her. Grateful for the movie and the opportunity to set things right.

"It's not that I hadn't thought of contacting you before," I said, and I couldn't remember why I hadn't, though it had seemed implicit until moments ago.

I looked at her looking at me. The open expression on her face, like she was listening closely to what I was saying. Laurel had always been a good listener. And a good talker too. No one could milk a joke the way she could. Or get as riled up about the latest political scandal. I had missed her more than I'd realized. It occurred to me that maybe everything I'd experienced with Melinda was for a reason, and the reason was to end up here, back with Laurel.

Melinda was a mirage. Someone I imagined more than someone I truly knew. Maybe the reason I was still single was because I preferred the fantasy of a relationship to the real thing. I wrote about marriage, but my stories ended on the wedding night, before any complications set in. I wasn't just a hopeless romantic; I was a professional one.

But Laurel was real. I knew she snored in her sleep. I knew she liked to eat Cherry Garcia ice cream out of the container. I knew how it felt to kiss her when her lips were still cold from the ice cream.

I proposed a toast with my water glass. "To new beginnings," I said. She laughed nervously and clinked her glass against mine.

That's when I saw her wedding ring.

"You're married?"

"Almost two years," she said.

Then what the hell was she doing there? What was *I* doing there?

"Do you remember Jeffrey?" she asked.

"The drummer from the D Street Band?"

She glared at me. "His band's name is Born in New Jersey."

As if that was better. "That's not a credential I'd necessarily want to advertise," I said, which I concede was a little hostile.

"We live in Hoboken," she fumed. *Oops.* "With our six-month-old son." *Ouch.* "Are you going to ask to see pictures?" *I would prefer to shoot myself.*

"Of course I want to see pictures," I said, trying not to choke on my water.

She pulled open her purse and took out her iPhone. Several minutes of awkwardness followed as she clicked through a succession of generic baby photos. Though I had to admit, he was a pretty cute little tyke with thick bed-head hair.

It hit me that he could be mine. Not literally. The math didn't allow any question about that. But I could be the father of a boy with big brown eyes and fat cheeks in a blue jumper. Well, in my family, maybe not the fat cheeks. I looked longingly at the last shot of him gurgling. If I had a uterus, it would have been aching.

"I don't understand why you accepted my invitation for a date," I said.

"A date?" She looked appalled. "I didn't come for a date. I came for an apology."

She had to be joking.

"I've been waiting for three years," she said.

"*You* left *me*," I said. "Not the other way around."

"You can't leave someone who wasn't really there."

I could feel my face getting red. "If I wasn't there, where was I? Because someone got left behind when you walked off into the Jersey sunset, and I seem to remember it being me."

"Because you think everything's about you."

"And what about your movie? Was that about me or some other guy you dated who writes a wedding column?"

"It's not like I wrote *The Devil Wears Drakkar*."

I felt like I'd been stabbed. "But you obviously thought about it."

"Of course I thought about it. I was angry and hurt."

No! She didn't get to turn our entire relationship inside out and rewrite history. "You're the one who walked out without any warning."

"Your unlucky-in-love act is getting old," she had the audacity to say. "Poor Gavin. Everyone leaves Gavin."

"Not everyone. You. Specifically you."

"You don't give yourself enough credit," she said. "You always complain how you've been so unsuccessful at getting married, when the opposite is true. You've been completely successful at avoiding it."

"That's bullshit." Now she was some two-cent psychoanalyst. I wanted to take back every compliment I ever gave her about being perceptive. "It just so happens that when you took off with your Springsteen wannabe, I was looking at rings."

"Looking!" she erupted. "Not buying!"

She opened her purse and pulled out a Kleenex. "You weren't even able to be honest with yourself, let alone with me. When Jeffrey and I first got together, he was consoling me."

"I bet," I said, more to the tablecloth than to her. When I looked up, I saw her eyes were bloodshot.

"You're so stupid."

There are many things that I can be accused of, but being stupid isn't one of them.

"If I had believed there was any chance of you proposing, I would have stayed. How can you not know that?" She buried her face in her hands. "I can't believe I'm crying."

Neither could I. She wasn't the one who was single, childless and heartbroken. If anyone should have been crying, it should have been me. But all it took was a few tears for her to trump all of that.

"I didn't think you would get to me," she said, and a small part of me took pride in the fact that I still could. But mostly I wished I'd never called her. "I came here feeling sorry for myself because of how I let you treat me. But the truth is, I feel worse for you, because you're going to end up living your life alone."

I couldn't tell if she was pitying me or gloating. "Don't you think I know that!" Three years of pent-up hurt and frustration came gushing out. "What do you think is my biggest fear?"

"Gavin." She caught my outstretched hand in hers. "Your biggest fear isn't being alone. It's ending up like your parents."

Bernie's funeral was on a particularly steamy Florida day. As the temperature neared ninety, I didn't feel like I was wearing my black suit so much as stewing in it.

About sixty people were gathered under a green canopy that seemed more suited for a swim party. My grandmother sat stoically in a folding chair beside the raised casket, and I stood behind her, between my parents. Gary and Leslie stayed farther back, on account of Leslie having an allergic reaction to my father's new cologne. (It was suspected my father was also allergic, since he had been sneezing all morning.)

"Isn't it nice that Leslie came?" my mother whispered as the rabbi began chanting a Hebrew prayer.

"What's so nice about it?" my father asked in his attempt at a whisper, which was pretty much his normal voice, except louder.

"It's nice Gary has someone to go places with," my mother persisted.

Yes, I thought, *having a date to bring to a cemetery is a top reason for settling down.* "The ceremony's starting," I said, hoping that would shush them.

"Did you talk with Bernie's niece?" my mother asked. "She's twenty-six and just graduated from law school."

"She graduated a year ago," my father rebutted.

"Either way, she's a lawyer."

"Mom!" I admonished under my breath.

"What's the matter? You're not related by blood."

"It's a funeral."

"It's a *mitzvah*."

I had no energy to disagree. The combination of heat and ancient incantations was making me woozy. Jewish custom dictates burial within twenty-four hours of death, so I'd been going practically nonstop since I received my grandmother's call as I was leaving the Cornelia Street Café.

It had been a long day. A long year. Well, four months anyway.

It seemed like it was going to be five before the eulogy was over. The rabbi was droning on. He had switched to English, but I found it even harder to focus on his platitudes about sunsets and burning candles. Looking around, I wasn't the only one who seemed to be wilting. My father's eyelids were at half-mast.

Finally, we were reciting the kaddish, the prayer for the dead, and the casket slowly descended into the grave. The rabbi lifted a shovel for the ritual task of throwing dirt onto the coffin. When no one fetched the spade from him, he loudly cleared his throat, cueing us into action.

"Saul!" my mother brayed.

"What?" My father's eyelids flew open and his head jerked like that of a bus driver about to collide with the back of a semi.

"Take the shovel."

"You take the shovel," he said, embracing his inner toddler.

My grandmother flinched but didn't say anything.

"Will one of you please take it?" I begged.

"He's not my father," was *my* father's response.

"He's not my father either," my mother volleyed, eliciting another convulsion from my grandmother.

"Then why's there five pounds of smoked salmon in our refrigerator?"

My mother grabbed the shovel. I'm guessing her intention was to force it into my father's hands. I'm guessing, because I can only assume she had a lucid goal in mind when she thrust it toward him. Unfortunately, he chose that precise moment to sneeze. As he bent over, she whacked his forehead, drawing blood.

"Jesus Christ!" he yelped.

The rabbi's eyes bugged out.

Laurel was right. I lived in mortal fear of becoming my parents. All my protestations about wanting to get married were lies. Marriage terrified me. When I thought of marriage, I thought of two people bickering for eternity and walloping each other with oversized garden tools. Marriage was just legal permission to torture someone with impunity.

I seized the shovel. "I'll take care of it," I said.

"I need a Band-Aid," my father muttered, and a dozen purses zipped open in unison, as if bandages could solve his problems.

Why hadn't someone stopped my parents from mating? Someone should have pointed out that liking the same radio station and brand of ginger ale made them compatible bowling teammates, not life partners. They should never have fallen in love. The fact that they did proved that love was not only blind but heartless. Not to be trusted. Of course I was afraid of marriage. I'd been imprinted from infancy to seek out a long-term dysfunctional relationship with someone who would make me miserable. It was like being a genetic carrier of a disfiguring disease—one that I could potentially pass on to another generation.

I attacked the fresh mound of dirt with ferocity, flicking a shovelful into the open grave. I heard the soft thud of impassive soil hitting wood and skidding scattershot across the coffin. It made me horribly conscious of what I was doing.

I was burying a man beneath the earth, dispatching him to the jurisdiction of invertebrates. Polonius had it wrong; we are all both borrowers *and* lenders. I was returning Bernie for final payment. Or was I hiding him? We bury what we want to forget, and I desperately wanted to forget seeing him in his casket. I pictured him lying there now. Worse, I pictured myself in his place. A body in a box in a hole. Alone. It all became too much. The heat and the dirt. The shovel and the blood. Laurel and Melinda. I dropped to my knees, sobbing.

My grandmother leaned over and kissed the top of my head. "Bernie loved you too."

The guests, mercifully, dispersed quickly. My parents, having regained higher brain function, escorted my grandmother to their car, where condolences could be offered with air-conditioning. I lingered beside Gary, while Leslie waited in their rental car, also air-conditioned.

"That was intense," Gary said. "I didn't know you felt so deeply about Bernie."

I filled him in about Laurel's accusation. "Standing at the graveside, I realized there's something worse than ending up like Mom and Dad, and that's ending up alone." It seemed so obvious, yet I had chosen precisely that. To be alone, and, worse, I hadn't even admitted to myself that I was making the choice.

"I know," Gary said, placing his hand on my shoulder. "I've been thinking the same thing."

"You have?" I wasn't alone. I had Gary. I would always have Gary. I almost welled up again.

"I proposed to Leslie last night."

I knew how my father felt getting ambushed by a family member.

"We were waiting until after the funeral to tell everyone." Gary hugged me. "Congratulate me. I'm getting married."

Chapter Twenty-six

No Day but Today

"I know I shouldn't be calling you," I said while standing in the floor-to-ceiling lavender guest bathroom of my parents' home. I took a deep breath, hoping I didn't sound like an obscene caller. There was so much I wanted to say to Melinda. None of it appropriate for the particular time and place, as bladder-challenged guests jiggled the locked door.

I had snuck away from my assigned duty of greeting the parade of bereaved friends bearing brisket. I could hear my mother's muffled voice calling my name. It was only a matter of minutes before she'd be knocking on the door, demanding I come out or confess to intestinal distress from eating too much smoked salmon.

I was in distress, but it had nothing to do with kippered seafood.

I'd been thinking about calling Melinda ever since the funeral ended. Strike that. I'd been thinking about it since the moment she ran away from me. It had been nonstop since the funeral.

I'd been afraid of her reaction. I didn't want to cause her more pain. And I didn't want to be rejected again. But if Laurel was right, that was all just an excuse.

The phone felt heavy in my hand as I weighed my words. I wanted to apologize. To let her know that I never meant to hurt her. But mostly to tell her I was hopelessly and helplessly in love with her and to find out if there was any chance my feelings could be reciprocated. Of course, I didn't think that was the kind of thing to say on voice mail. So I just asked her to please return my call.

Then I tried to remember why I thought calling would make me feel better.

"Why are you still single?" Matt Lauer asked me with the discretion of a demolition wrecking ball.

It wasn't an interview. It was an interrogation. I thought I'd be sharing amusing anecdotes about bridezillas, not defending my extended bachelorhood on national television.

"Doesn't it bother you going to weddings week after week and not being married?"

For the past several days I'd harbored a secret fantasy of being offered a job as a cohost of the *Today Show*. I imagined Matt and me bonding instantly, one Jewish reporter to another (yes, he's only half-Jewish, but it's a genetic thing). I pictured him telling me (and America) that I'd missed my calling, and asking me to join the *Today* team. Then, for good measure, he'd invite me to the *Vanity Fair* Oscar party.

Okay, I knew Matt Lauer wasn't really Santa Claus and Graydon Carter rolled into one, but if Elisabeth Hasselbeck could be a morning-show host, why not me?

"Do you *want* to get married?" Matt asked with no hint of Semitic kinship.

Of course I wanted to get married. Did being thirty-seven and single make me some kind of freak? "Yes," I answered, sweating under the hot studio lights and regretting, well, everything about my life.

"Why?" he asked.

I smiled blankly.

"Why do you want to get married?"

No one had ever asked me that before. My eyelids swung up and down. My jaw dropped open. It shouldn't have been such a hard question to answer.

I wanted to get married so I'd have someone to watch *The Daily Show* with. I wanted someone to ride with me on an overnight train through the Canadian Rockies and on a hot-air balloon in the Hudson Valley. I wanted to hold someone in my arms and make her feel protected. I wanted to put someone's happiness before my own.

"I want to get married so I don't have to shave my back."

The audience standing outside the *Today* show erupted with laughter. I had no idea why the words of Mike Russo's best man were still occupying cranial real estate, let alone how they had tumbled out of my mouth.

"Well, Gavin,' Matt said, "different *strokes* for different folks."

The audience laughed again. There was an eighth circle of hell reserved for mortals who dared to fly too close to the klieg lights.

"Coming up," Matt said, looking into the camera, "taking the 'maid' out of 'bridesmaid.' After the break."

There was a flurry of activity as the show went to commercial. A production assistant seemed to crawl up from under me as he removed my microphone. Matt gave me a brisk handshake and a consoling pat on the back. His expression said, "Sorry, dude, but you're going to be seeing that clip on YouTube for the rest of your life."

Another assistant with a goatee and headset escorted me back to the green room to gather my belongings and the shreds of my pride. But pride be damned. When I had pictured the woman I wanted to love and protect, it was Melinda, and my top priority was checking my voice mail to see if she had called.

I had left her a half dozen messages and received none in return. Standing in a corner of the waiting room, amid the oversized photos of overexuberant NBC stars, I felt like a junkie getting my fix as I stabbed at my cell phone. If I had refrained from contacting her, the possibility of doing so would have remained an option. Instead, I was left without prerogatives beyond compulsively calling my voice mail.

I had no messages. The morning was a smorgasbord of disappointment.

Roxanne hurtled into the room, looking grim and clearly regretting having booked me on the show. She was accompanied by a tall, wiry guy with a mop of dark hair. They both eyed me like anthropologists examining a specimen from the species *Homo uncommiticus.*

"You really have a way with words," Roxanne said. Translation: It's obvious why you're still single. "This is Liam O'Neill, one of our segment producers."

"You're one funny dude," he said with a distracted glance my direction.

I wasn't sure if he meant "funny" as in "ha-ha" or as in "scary."

"We usually don't comment on a guest's 'performance.'" Roxanne displayed air quotes like she was Richard Nixon with

Tourette's. "However, we try hard to maintain the quality level of the *Today* brand, so we felt obligated to say something to you."

The last thing I needed was a reprimanding. I picked up my shoulder bag and grabbed a bagel for the road. There was nothing they could say I had any interest in hearing.

Liam cracked a smile. "I have a job proposition for you."

Except that.

Chapter Twenty-seven

The Wedding Beat

"No, no, no, no, no!" squawked the exasperated bride-to-be.

I was back to being a wedding reporter, but this time I had a partner in crime. Liam had a video camera slung over the back of his shoulder and a *Today Show* ID hanging round his neck as we stood in the rear of the Abyssinian Baptist Church, a neo-Gothic landmark in Harlem. A gospel choir was practicing thick, joyful harmonies in the amphitheater-shaped sanctuary, and accompanying, or, rather, overriding them were the yawps of Wanda Robinson, a spitfire of a woman in her fifties with café au lait skin and long, painted fingernails that were a miracle of modern cosmetology.

"Do those choir robes look pink to you?" she challenged her wedding coordinator, whose weary expression suggested it had been a long night.

"Honey, if they were any pinker, they'd be illegal south of the Mason-Dixon Line."

"I want pink," said Wanda, her snug green suit creeping up her ample bosom. "Not hot pink. I've got a hundred and fifty people coming next Saturday, and they're not expecting a Victoria's Secret runway show."

"Just because they're not expecting it don't mean they wouldn't enjoy it," said a bemused man with a gray buzz cut, sitting in the last pew.

Wanda turned to us. "You can take him away any time you like."

The "him" in question stood up and extended his hand. He was also in his fifties, with a lineman's build, dark skin and a gentle handshake. "Duane Mackenzie. Everyone calls me Big Mac."

"They most certainly do not," was the immediate, high-pitched rejoinder.

"Everyone but Wanda," he said.

"He's not a cheeseburger," she said with an emphatic shake of her head. "He's a grown man, and occasionally he acts like one."

"I'd do a whole lot more than acting if you wore one of those hot pink robes."

Liam chuckled.

My problem was that there was only one wedding I was interested in, and that one was taking place in a little less than twenty-four hours at a synagogue four miles south. I hadn't heard a word from Melinda, but I kept calling anyway. Listening to her voice on her outgoing message seemed to be as close as I was going to get to her. I knew I should give up, and told myself that every time I checked my voice mail.

"You have a hot date tonight?" asked Liam as he caught me looking at my phone for the umpteenth time.

Bad move. This assignment was my audition. Liam had been amused by what he called my "unpretentious" on-air style and pitched his executive producer the idea of doing a video version of my wedding column. If I aced this trial run, I'd get a staff position at three times my previous salary. If I flubbed, I'd be back on unemployment.

"No date," I assured him. "I'm all yours." We were setting up in the balcony while Wanda held court below. Actually, Liam was setting up. I was fidgeting with my phone and trying to look as if I knew what I was doing.

"So, you're on the wedding beat?" Duane asked me while Liam finished attaching his camera to a tripod.

"That's what they call it," I said.

"I dig it," he said, sounding every bit the jazz musician that he was.

Just my luck. I finally got a musician to interview, and I'd been instructed to stick to questions about why it took him thirty years to marry his college sweetheart.

"Oh, can't say I know the answer to that," he drawled. Never a promising start.

Liam grimaced behind the camera. I prodded Duane. "What was Wanda like in the seventies?"

"Same as she is today. We picked up right where we left off. Of course, she sometimes treats me like one of her fifth-grade students, but I sometimes act like one."

That would make a lovely quote for their twentieth anniversary video, but it was doing *bupkes* for me.

"Duane . . ."

"You can call me Big Mac." I could, but I'd feel like I was interviewing the Hamburglar.

"Guys don't usually let the woman they love marry someone else." Or maybe they did. I peeked at my phone while he ruminated.

"After college, she made it very clear she wanted a ring," he said.

"What about you?"

"I wanted a new horn." His eyes crinkled as he shot me a sheepish grin. Then he became contemplative again. "You know, it *is* kind of like a beat."

"Excuse me?" I asked.

"The wedding beat. It's like a drumbeat. A bass drum. Steady and slow. Getting louder and heavier as more and more people join. On bongos and tom-toms. But not everyone hears it. No, that's not true. Everyone hears it, but some ignore it. Some people think they got a different beat inside them. They want to move to their own rhythm. And if they're lucky, they will. They'll find a groove that's theirs and theirs alone, but one day they'll look up and realize there's no one else ever gonna dance along to that beat."

The wedding beat.

It had been booming in my head for the last five years. Amplified week after week in couple after couple. A thunderous sound, pounding and pulsating. Incessantly. Beating me into admission that I was a failure at love. A failure at finding it. A failure at sharing it.

My phone rang. Melinda's number flashed on the screen. I answered without thinking.

"She doesn't want to talk to you!"

The angry male voice was jarring.

"Stop calling her," Alexander commanded. "Stop calling her, or I promise you'll regret it." That's all he said before clicking off.

I was too shocked to be upset. And I couldn't really blame

Alexander for being angry. He wouldn't have called me if he hadn't felt threatened. And he wouldn't have felt threatened unless . . .

I was already running toward the stairs before I registered the bewildered look on Liam's face or the inquisitive one on Duane's. "I'm sorry," I proffered midstride. "I have to go. Wedding emergency."

I raced down 138th Street. I was endangering a job I couldn't afford to lose. I needed to go back, apologize to Liam, and pull myself together, which was precisely what I was instructing myself to do as I hailed a taxi and recited Melinda's address to the driver.

The cab zipped through the night streets, yet it seemed to be taking forever to reach Melinda's block, which gave me more time to think about what I was doing and the wisdom of doing it. And that was my biggest problem: thinking too much. Every choice was a monumental task for me, because I never wanted to make a decision without having all the facts. What was considered an admirable trait in my work had become a debilitating one in the rest of my life.

I needed to let go. I needed to be the bee.

No, that was too simplistic. I was parroting other people's advice, when I didn't need any advice to know what I wanted. I wanted Melinda. From the moment I met her. Yet I had hesitated, waiting as always to analyze the facts. But there were no facts. There was only a feeling. And I hadn't appreciated what an extraordinarily rare feeling it was until it was too late.

But it wasn't too late. Not yet.

My hands were shaking as I paid the fare. I tried to do deep breathing, counting slowly from one to ten, but I kept losing tally after three. A vivid splash of colored flowers caught my eye at the corner deli, and I quickly bought a bouquet of lilacs along with a roll of mints.

I could see a light in Melinda's window. The last steps to the front door of her building were the hardest. I was gambling everything on a Hail Mary, and if it didn't work, there was no fallback position. I reached for her buzzer.

Then I stopped. If she wouldn't pick up my phone calls, there was no reason to assume she would let me in. It would be easy for her to ignore my buzzing, and she wouldn't have to risk looking at me or listening to me. I had a much better chance of wearing down her resistance if I was standing outside her actual apartment and pleading my case with only a door separating us.

Or a window.

Moments later I was scrambling up the fire escape, glad I'd had a practice run in daylight. I leaned over the railing nearest her apartment and peered inside. The room was barren. I had to double-check I was on the right floor. There were moving boxes piled along the stripped walls. The photographs were gone. The furniture was gone. And there was no sign of Melinda.

Yet the lights were on, so my guess was that she was in the bedroom. How was I going to get her attention? I hadn't really thought this through beyond envisioning her charmed by my Romeo-like appearance at her window, lilacs in hand. I was considering my options when I heard rustling inside the apartment. I didn't have much longer to wait before Melinda appeared from around a corner. Or, more accurately, a large box appeared with well-toned legs beneath it.

I gently tapped on the window. The box descended a few inches, revealing a startled face. But the face belonged to Alexander's mother. She screamed. I screamed. The box fell. The flowers flew. She screamed again. There was the sound of breaking glass. Probably from the box hitting the floor. I can't say for sure, because I was already running down the metal steps, hoping she hadn't recognized me. Knowing full well that she had.

Chapter Twenty-eight

Mayday

Spring sunshine spilled in through my drawn blinds. It only felt like the darkest day of my life.

"Did you call the police?" Hope asked.

I eyed her with disbelief. "To turn myself in?"

"To make sure that woman was okay."

There were many times I admired Hope for being such a conscientious physician. This wasn't one of them.

"She could have gone into cardiac arrest," Hope said. "She could be lying unconscious on the floor of that apartment."

"Well, I'm sure as hell not going back to find out."

"When did you become such an asshole?" Hope was infuriated, but in my defense, it was less my doing than A.J.'s. "Is every man in this city lacking all moral judgment?"

To A.J.'s credit, he finally did call her. To his eternal damnation, it was to inform her he was getting married. When pressed, he admitted he'd been engaged the entire time they'd been dating. I thought he would have been better off going with the traditional "It's not you, it's me."

"How hard is it to pick up a phone and dial nine-one-one?" Hope grumbled while gorging herself on my Frosted Flakes, which were surprisingly effective for self-medicating abrasions of the heart. "You didn't even have to leave your name."

"Why aren't you worried that *she* called the police? There could be an APB out on me as we speak."

"If the police were looking for you, don't you think they would have found you by now?"

Hope had a point. Which meant I could stop wincing every time I heard a siren. The truth was I shouldn't have run away from Genevieve. I should have stayed and held my ground, or railing, and demanded she tell me where Melinda was.

Of course, she would have sooner stabbed me with a hat pin.

"What if she's dead?" Hope badgered.

"What if she's not?" I lashed out. "What if she's at Temple Emanu-El, tying her son's bow tie as we speak? The wedding's in less than two frigging hours." I was caught in a vise that was slowly and inexorably closing.

Hope's expression softened. "I'm sorry," she said. "I didn't realize it was today." Then she socked me in the arm. "What are you still doing here?"

"Where am I supposed to be? Crashing the wedding? That would be insane."

"Didn't stop you yesterday."

"I've done everything I can do."

"Except tell Melinda how you feel."

"She doesn't care how I feel!"

"Because she doesn't know!" Hope's tears came so quickly, I was baffled by what had triggered them. "You owe her the truth."

I had to stop making women cry.

"What kind of person uses an online-dating site when he's engaged to be married?" she blubbered.

"A despicable person," I assured her, wanting to staunch her weeping while also envying it.

"What's wrong with me?" she moaned. "Because there must be something wrong with me. Or am I just doomed?" She was clearly asking the wrong person.

"You're not doomed," I said, thinking friends should really coordinate their emotional crises so they don't overlap.

"Then maybe I'm doing this to myself. Maybe I purposely pick guys who are gong to leave. Or maybe I make them leave. So I can play out some childhood psychodrama over and over." It was the closest she had come to talking about her father in years.

"Or maybe A.J.'s just an asshole," I consoled.

"A.J. is such an asshole." She was still crying. But also smiling.

My buzzer rang.

"Who's that?" Hope asked between sniffles.

I'd been expecting Liam when she arrived. "My producer," I said as I buzzed him in the front door of my walk-up.

"He didn't fire you?" Her confidence in me was underwhelming, but so was Liam's.

"He recently had a bad breakup, so he's taking pity on me." And by "pity" I meant that he had allowed me to beg him for a second chance, which was bestowed on the condition that I agreed to be his personal slave. He was dropping off some video footage. Along with his laundry.

There was a knock at the door, and while Hope continued seeking sugared solace, I wearily went to open it.

"You fucking son of a bitch."

It wasn't Liam.

Alexander was wearing his wedding tuxedo and a murderous look. His face resembled a ripe tomato.

"I told you to stay the fuck away from my fiancée." At least I knew that Genevieve was alive.

"Technically, you told me not to call," I said, flirting with a death wish.

"I'll give you technical, you piece of shit." Spittle flew from his mouth.

I was surprisingly calm for someone about to be pummeled. Until Hope came up behind me. Worse than getting beaten up by the guy marrying the woman I loved was having it happen in front of Hope. She gaped at Alexander.

"A.J.?" she said.

Alexander looked as if he had just been hit by a Mack truck.

"What on earth are you doing here?" Hope asked him.

His eyes darted back and forth between us. "Is this some kind of setup?"

Hope turned to me, accusingly. "How do you know him?" I was no longer sure I did.

"Just stay away from me," muttered Alexander or A.J. or whoever he was. "Both of you stay the hell away from me." He took off down the stairs.

Hope and I stood in the doorway, staring after him in shock. I grabbed my jacket and ran.

"Where are you going?" she called out.

"I have a wedding to stop."

The imposing limestone and stained-glass facade of Temple Emanu-El rose along Fifth Avenue like an ornate fortress wall. A policeman guarded the ten-foot bronze doors. I feared he was stationed there solely to detain me. Keeping my head down, I joined a handful of people standing in line.

"Name?" the officer asked the couple ahead of me without glancing up from his clipboard.

"We're here for the wedding," said a middle-aged woman with "Long Island" stamped on her forehead and in her sinus cavities.

"That's why I'm asking your name. The mayor's attending, and only people on the official list will be allowed inside."

"How exciting."

"Frustrating" was more the word I had in mind. I slipped out of the line to reassess. Coming up with another tactic, I inconspicuously strolled to the street corner, then zipped down the block to the service entrance. There was an officer posted there as well.

Returning to Fifth Avenue, I was lacking options other than making a dash for the doorway and using the element of surprise to get past the cop. I was calculating my odds of finding Melinda before being read my Miranda rights when I almost collided with Melinda's grandfather. He was on a cigar break. Or lookout duty.

He was turned the other way, so he didn't see me do a one-eighty and double back around the corner. Retrieving a newspaper from a sidewalk trash can, I shielded my face before inching my way forward. I glanced above the headlines. Her grandfather was still standing there. He was using a cane, but otherwise seemed to have recovered well. I doubted his doctors would approve of his smoking, but that was probably also true before his attack. Maybe I could appeal to his renegade spirit. Maybe I could kidnap him.

"Does The Paper now pay you to loiter at synagogues?"

There was no mistaking the gravelly voice or the phlegmy cough that followed the query.

"I can explain," I said.

"I seriously doubt that," he grunted. "So, is this what you consider taking care of my granddaughter? Hiding your nose in a newspaper outside her wedding?"

If it wasn't for the sting on my thigh where he rapped me with his cane, I would have thought I was hallucinating.

"You remember asking me to do that?" I had replayed his request in my mind countless times. "I assumed you had mistaken me for Alexander."

"I've got a heart condition, not a brain tumor," he chided. "I saw how you looked at her. I've only seen that look once before in my life. On my son's face, when he looked at Melinda's mother."

I would have teared up if I wasn't afraid he'd hit me again.

"I need to get inside," I said.

"Damn straight."

He rocketed through the growing crowd, swinging his cane like a machete and lurching from side to side with his unsteady gait. "Old fart with bad knees coming through," he said. I barely kept up with him.

"I already passed the entrance exam," he barked at the policeman, breezing by and dragging me behind him by my jacket sleeve.

"Wait a second there, sir," the officer said. "I need this gentleman's name."

"He's with me."

"I need to check everyone's—"

"This is my grandson. My numbskull grandson who showed up at the last minute without letting anyone know he's coming."

The cop looked skeptical.

"Are you going to deprive an old man of his grandson's company?" It was a heartfelt plea, minus the flinty theatrics. The officer waved me in.

As soon as we were inside the travertine marble foyer, Melinda's grandfather pulled me to the far end of the oblong antechamber through a set of brass doors and into a stone stairwell.

"Melinda's in the basement bridal room," he said. I sprang toward the stairs, but he swatted me and pointed to a set of doors on the other side of the stairwell.

"There's a small chapel in there."

As much as I appreciated his help, I didn't think this was the time for a tour.

"It's someplace you can lay low," he said. "I'll tell Melinda I want a private moment with her and ask her to meet me in the chapel." Sounded like a plan. "You're on your own after that, buster."

I didn't know how to thank him, so I said precisely that.

"I called you my grandson back there," he said. "If you want to thank me, don't make me out to be a liar."

He limped down the stairs, and I launched through the doorway, finding myself in a short corridor leading to even more doors. As I pushed them open, I heard male voices singing "For He's a Jolly Good Fellow."

I glimpsed ruddy men in tuxedos and dropped to the floor.

"For he's a jolly good feh-eh-low. The rest will be denied."

There was a chorus of guffaws and the clinking of glasses while I crawled backward through both sets of doors. Loudspeakers in my brain broadcast the emergency alert "Abort plan!" Jumping to my feet, I sprinted down the stairs, but came to a dead halt when I spied a silvery chignon ascending from below. Beneath the chignon was Genevieve, eyes cast downward, watching her step in her slate gray, long-sleeved gown.

"There's simply no time," she said to a bridesmaid accompanying her. "Melinda can speak to her grandfather after the ceremony."

Doing an about-face, I bounded back up two more landings, and through an open doorway, closing the heavy wooden door behind me. Turning round to get my bearings, I was greeted by a blast of Bach from a pipe organ. I was standing in the rear of the temple's balcony, looking out at the ten-story arched basilica of marble mosaics and gilded tiles. There was an elaborate wedding canopy of wisteria vines and orchid blossoms, and guests were already filling the dark-wood pews below. I was running out of time.

I put my ear to the door and listened for footsteps. Not hearing any, I pressed against it. I heard a click. I didn't want to hear a click. A click was not my friend. I pushed again, but it didn't budge. I was locked in. No, I was cursed.

I pictured being trapped on the balcony for the wedding, forced to witness the event against my will. Unless I reenacted the ending of *The Graduate* by screaming out Melinda's name— and then requesting she come upstairs and rescue me.

Sweat trickled from my brow, but I refused to panic. I was going to succeed. I *had* to succeed. Scanning the balcony, I saw an exit on the other side. I crept along the back wall of the synagogue, past a bank of glowing, jewel-stained windows. Then I made a quick turn into another stairwell.

And down.

I half ran, half leaped, sliding along each landing and pivoting to the next set of steps until I was on the ground floor, dashing through a set of doors and into the foyer. I was in full gallop when Alexander emerged from the opposite end. I reversed course and propelled myself back into the stairwell.

I was panting as I paced the small vestibule. Back and forth.

Occasionally banging my head against the stone wall. I heard the muffled sound of the organ playing Mendelssohn's "Wedding March." It might as well have been "Taps." I peeked through a small window in the door and could see the bridal party lined up two by two in the foyer: the men in deep gray tuxedos and the women in lighter gray, cap-sleeved gowns, carrying bouquets of white orchids. The sheer inevitability of it all was overwhelming. It occurred to me I should step aside. Make an unobtrusive exit after the ceremony began.

Then I saw her.

A fairy-tale princess in cascading white tulle floating across the polished floor. Her bare, slender arms hovering around her embroidered silk corset. Her face framed with soft curls.

I don't know how long I stood there transfixed, but before I knew it, the maid of honor was entering the sanctuary, and the antique walnut doors closed shut behind her. Melinda was alone. I took a deep breath. Everything in life is a choice, and I was choosing to be happy.

I opened the door. "Melinda," I said, moving toward her.

She recoiled in surprise.

"There's no excuse for what I'm doing." I searched her eyes for encouragement, but all I found was disoriented distress. "Except I'm in love with you, and I think I have been since New Year's. Since I saw you at that party." I was finding language to be a terribly inefficient way of communicating. "Of course I remember meeting you there. I remember the first thing you ever said to me. You were standing on the terrace and asked if I had a bungee cord. You said you wanted to make a quick escape. Well, I'm your bungee cord. Or I want to be. I want to be the one who lets you fly and keeps you safe."

She didn't say anything. Not at first. But that didn't last long.

"*Now?*" she said. "You're telling me this *now?*" She hurled the words at me.

"Better late than never?"

She looked at me like I had two heads, and then she slapped me. Hard. I didn't expect that.

The doors to the sanctuary burst open, and as I turned to see more than four hundred faces staring at me, Alexander cold-cocked me.

Now, *that* I should have expected.

As I staggered around, I thought to myself, *He's entitled.* After all, I was intruding at his wedding. Embarrassing him in front of family, friends and the mayor of New York City. I realized that my behavior was abominable.

Then I lunged at him, headfirst into his solar plexus. Or something bony in that vicinity.

Guests shrieked and scattered as he fell backward onto the white aisle runner. I was on top of him. Briefly. Before the groomsmen pulled me off of him. I'd like to say I gave as good as I got, but I'd be lying. They were beating the crap out of me.

"Stop it!" Melinda screamed.

I saw stars. I heard sirens. Well, one siren. Getting louder. Coming closer. Then I felt my body rising. Was this it? Is this what it felt like to have sacrificed everything for love? If so, I wondered why my arms hurt. Then I realized two groomsmen were lifting me by my armpits for Alexander to have one last go at me.

"You have some nerve showing up here," he spat. He was pulling back his arm to do maximum damage when someone's fist caught his chin.

Hope's fist, to be precise. The ambulance siren was still wailing as she stood there with a gurney, two paramedics and Liam, video camera glued to his eye.

Alexander was still rubbing his jaw when Hope came back for seconds, socking him full force in the stomach. He doubled over.

"That's for Doctors Without Borders," she said, shaking out her hand.

"Who the hell are you?" Melinda was bewildered.

Hope looked at her as if she was mentally challenged. "I'm your freakin' fairy godmother."

"Don't listen to anything she says," Alexander coughed out. "She's a stupid whore."

I pounced on him. My hands reached for his neck. It was too thick, which just added insult to injury. I pressed my thumbs into his trachea as we both tumbled to the ground.

"Don't ever say that again," I snarled. I didn't know what had come over me, but I kind of liked it, assuming I didn't end up dead or in jail. "Do you hear me?"

There was no response. I pushed harder.

"Yes," he gurgled. I released him. A feeling of infinite power swept through me as I rose to my feet. I was king of the world, or at least a few square inches of it. Until I saw the stricken expression on Melinda's face, and my knees buckled.

The paramedics were quickly at my side, carrying me to the gurney. There was blood—I wasn't sure whose—on my hands. I wiped my arm across my mouth and it came away with more blood. That pretty much answered the question.

"Melinda," I called out as I was wheeled away. There was so much I wanted to say. So many things I wanted to explain. "I'm sorry for messing up your wedding."

Chapter Twenty-nine

Sanity Is in the Eye of the Beholder

The siren continued to blare as we careened through the streets of the city. I lay on the gurney, painfully aware of each bump in the road. Hope stabbed me with the third needle in as many minutes, and Liam moved his camera in for a close-up.

"Will you turn that thing off?" I grunted.

He shook his head.

"Why the hell not?"

"That's good," he said. "Show some emotion. The lying-inert stuff's kind of lame."

Hope shushed him. He turned the camera on her, and she blushed. "Don't get Gavin riled up," she said, talking like I wasn't there. "I just gave him a sedative."

"I don't need a sedative," I said, "and I don't need to go to the hospital." I tried to sit up, but a crippling pain in my side convinced me to abandon that plan of action.

"Hulk Hogan here's ready to go another round," said Liam.

My phone rang, and I fumbled with it. My fingers were moving in slow motion, but I was determined to answer in anticipation of hearing Melinda's voice.

"Gavin, why didn't you return your brother's calls?" It wasn't Melinda. "He said he left you three messages about potential wedding venues." Ever since Gary and Leslie announced their engagement, my mother had become their unofficial event coordinator. The surprising part was that Leslie claimed to be enjoying her help.

"They're thinking about getting married in New York, and you're the expert. Why do I hear a siren?"

"I'm kind of in an ambulance." I braced myself for a shriek that didn't come.

"Did you have an accident?"

The simplest answer was "Yes." Still no shriek. "I'm fine," I added.

"Make sure the doctors know you're allergic to chlorine."

"I don't think they'll be taking me swimming."

I thought I heard her laugh, but it could have been the drugs.

"Will you call me from the hospital?" Her voice was calm. And soothing. I'd forgotten how good she always was at dealing with emergencies. When I was a kid, I had broken arms and I had totaled cars, one time simultaneously, and she was Supermom, riding to the rescue without question or complaint.

"I'll call," I heard myself promising.

"I love you, Gavin," she said before hanging up. Those were precisely the words I wanted to hear. I just wished there was someone other than my mother saying them to me.

I turned to Hope as a dark thought percolated in my groggy

mind. "You don't think Melinda will go through with the wedding, do you?"

I could hear Alexander begging for forgiveness. Worse, Melinda offering it. I watched them walk down the bloodstained aisle. Then I opened my eyes.

There were fluorescent lights overhead, and daylight streamed in through a small window. I was in a hospital bed, attached to an IV. I had a throbbing headache. I went to rub behind my ear and found gauze wrapped around my head. There was more wrapped around my rib cage.

A young nursing student stood at the foot of my bed, holding my chart. She smiled at me and said, "You just missed your girlfriend."

I saw Hope's writing on a Post-it note beside the bed. "She's not my girlfriend."

The note said "Good morning, Hulk. I'll come by again on my break."

I noticed she had also left me a get-well-soon card. I opened it up. "They don't really make an appropriate greeting for this kind of situation, but I hope you feel better." It was signed "Melinda."

I bolted up in the bed, ignoring my body's protestations. "When did she leave?" I asked the nursing student.

"Who?"

"Melinda," I nearly shouted. No response. "My girlfriend."

"You said she wasn't your girlfriend."

"Did you see someone leave this card?" I waved it spastically.

"I just told you, she walked out about a minute before you woke up."

I swung my legs out of the bed.

"What are you doing?" she asked me.

I grabbed the IV stand and headed for the door.

"Get back in bed."

That wasn't about to happen. But neither was running down the hallway. A piercing pain made me grab hold of my right side.

"You have two broken ribs and cranial contusions," she scolded while nervously shadowing me. "Where are you going?"

I wished I knew. I half shuffled, half stumbled down the hallway. Until I came to a crossroads. Well, cross corridors. Melinda could have gone any of three directions.

"I'm going to call security," the nurse threatened.

Melinda had a head start on me, and she wasn't tethered to a medical apparatus. Two orderlies approached, looking ready to tackle me. It was time to turn around.

And there she was. In the doorway of my room.

If I couldn't run, I could at least hobble at an accelerated pace. Melinda didn't back away at the sight of a rampaging bandaged man dragging an IV stand. She was smiling the way I remembered when I first saw her. And then she was in my arms.

It was the moment I'd been dreaming of for months, the kind I'd seen in cheesy films where a camera pirouettes around a couple as violins swell. Our lips eagerly met and our bodies melded together as I held her to me. Aside from the hospital gown and abdominal pain, it was everything I could have wished for.

Minutes passed. Maybe millennia. My fingers massaged a soft spot between her shoulder blades as we momentarily paused to catch our breath.

"I haven't forgiven you," she said quietly. "I don't know if I ever can."

The violins squealed to a halt.

"It's not that I don't appreciate knowing Alexander is a lying bastard. I just find it hard to believe that an experienced reporter couldn't have found a better time and place to inform me."

I nodded my head. Though the movement came with a sharp pain. I couldn't really dispute her point.

"I'm sorry," I said, moving in to kiss her again. Things were going much better when we were kissing.

"Why weren't you attracted to me before my wedding?" she said, pulling away.

"I was attracted to you from the moment we met."

"That's what you say now."

"I wanted to say it to you then."

"But you didn't."

I was going to regret that for the rest of my life.

"I'm sorry about that too." I took her hand in both of mine and traced the contours of her palm. When I looked up there were tears in her eyes.

She withdrew her hand and wiped at her eyes. "I came here to say good-bye." That's when I noticed the large rucksack propped against the door. "I have a nonrefundable ticket to Thailand, and I decided to still use it."

I didn't know how I was going to convince her of my sincerity if she was on the other side of the planet, but I was going to be supportive if it killed me. And it felt like it might, given how much my body was aching. "Getting some time to yourself sounds like a good thing."

"Jamie's going with me," she said, looking away. "Then we're heading back to Nepal. Going to volunteer at the same orphanage I worked at a year ago. Also do some more research for my book. Might also spend some time in India. We're going to play things by ear."

My headache was getting worse, and I wasn't entirely following what she was saying.

"I don't know when I'll be coming back."

That part I understood.

"I'm sorry, Gavin, but I just don't want to deal with . . ."

"Me?" I asked. My head and ribs pulsated in syncopated spasms, and I had to sit down on the bed.

"What you did last night was the most humiliating thing anyone's ever done to me." She came toward me, and I anticipated getting slapped again. Instead, she kissed me. On the lips. "And maybe the most wonderful."

She picked her pack off the floor as she ran out of the room, and, once again, she was gone.

Another Week, Another Wedding

The downtown skyline glistened across the harbor as I waited alone at a sun-bleached driftwood bar in the August heat.

"Gin and tonic," said the bartender, handing me the filled-to-the-brim glass.

I focused on keeping my hands steady and making it back to my table with the contents of the tumbler intact. Walking barefoot in the warm sand, it didn't feel like I was at a wedding, which was precisely what Gary and Leslie had in mind.

Leslie, a New York native, had wanted a city wedding but without the expense or formality. So it was lobster rolls and fried clams at the Water Taxi Beach, an urban oasis on an island off the tip of Manhattan reached by canary yellow speedboat taxis.

"Gavin," Hope called to me, with Liam by her side. "I was so touched when your parents said they considered me part of your family."

"As opposed to scared?" I asked.

She ignored me. "It was very nice of them to include me, and thanks for getting Liam an invite."

"Does this mean I now have to do *your* laundry?" he asked me.

He owed me a lot more than laundry. My life had become a public Rorschach test since his video of Melinda's wedding went viral. Everyone from *The Huffington Post* to *The Daily Show* had weighed in on my antics. The notoriety killed my short-lived career at *Today*. They dropped me before they even aired my first piece.

Fortunately, there's a place that welcomes the radioactive casualties of tabloid fame. They call that place Fox Broadcasting Company. Within a week, Liam and I were asked to be co-producers of a new reality show, *Brides Gone Bad*.

I was only a little jealous that he also got a girlfriend out of the deal, but he seemed to be a good match for Hope. Before they headed toward the bar, she asked, "Did you know he used to work for Reporters Without Borders?"

They strolled off arm in arm, and I quickened my pace, smiling at distant relatives and trying not to seem agitated.

"Could I have everyone's attention?" It was Gary, holding the DJ's microphone while standing on the beachfront dance floor. I felt obligated to stop where I was.

"We're obviously not big on tradition," said my brother. With his open-collared shirt and linen pants rolled to his knees, he looked more like a J.Crew ad than a bridegroom. "But I wanted to say a few words about this amazing woman I just married." Leslie blushed, her white sundress billowing in the light breeze. "As Adam Sandler said in *50 First Dates*, 'Love is not a feeling. It's an ability.'"

"It wasn't Adam Sandler," Leslie interjected. "It was Steve Carell in *Dan in Real Life*."

"No, it wasn't Steve Carell," said Gary. "It was the girl who played his daughter."

"It wasn't the daughter. It was the daughter's boyfriend."

"To hell with the speech," he said. As he swept her into his sunburned arms, the Beach Boys crooned in recorded harmony, "God only knows what I'd be without you."

Watching them together, I felt a familiar yearning. I hurried toward the picnic table where my family was seated, putting the dripping drink down on a napkin.

Melinda looked up at me with a grateful smile.

I wanted to remember forever the way she looked with the late-day light bathing her face in golden shadows. But I wanted to remember every moment with her. Spending even a few minutes away from her, getting a drink, made me eager to return to her side.

She was wearing a coral-colored sarong she had brought back from Nepal, and as I sat down, I let my fingers linger along the curve of her bare arm. Her grandfather winked at me. Or I should say Max. Since that's what he insisted I call him. Gary had invited him as a favor to me and as potential company for our grandmother, but she had barely spoken to him.

"How about we trip the light fantastic?" Max asked her, rising to his feet.

"I don't think that would be appropriate," she replied, smoothing her black cotton dress.

"Mom, who cares what's appropriate?" my mother said. "It's a beautiful summer day."

"Enjoy it," my father added as he helped my mother up from the table.

My parents had turned into aliens. Friendly, cuddly aliens. All weekend they'd been holding hands and giggling. It was freaking me out.

"I don't know." My grandmother was wavering.

"I'm asking for a dance, not a date," Max teased.

"Well, then, you're not very ambitious," she shot back, gingerly taking his arm.

"Is there a reason we're the only ones still sitting?" Melinda asked.

"Yes," I said. "I'm a terrible dancer."

"That's a terrible excuse." She got up and led me to the dance floor. Watching the sway of her shoulders and the swish of her hips, I was a happy man.

"Wouldn't it be nice to live together?" sang the Beach Boys, and as the medley continued I took Melinda's hand in mine, the way I had done so briefly the day we had met.

"Your parents are sweet," she said.

"Those aren't my parents."

"Well, whoever they are, I like them."

I pulled her close, trying to hide my lack of any discernible sense of rhythm.

"And I like this song."

I murmured my agreement, whispering in her ear, "Anything else you like?"

"A little more each day."

Kissing her was easy. The hard part was not stepping on her toes. There were so many couples around us. Moving to the same music. Melinda pressed against me, and I could feel the beat.

Acknowledgments

I want to thank everyone who ever said yes.

There is so much opportunity for rejection in life. Especially as a writer. So I can't overemphasize the debt I feel toward every person who has ever offered me encouragement.

High on that list is Danielle Perez at Penguin, who took a chance on a first-time novelist. As did my agent, Deborah Schneider, who has been my wise and steadfast companion on this journey.

I want to thank my parents for having faith in me and supporting my choices. My brother for telling me to write whatever I want and for meaning it. And my grandmother for being an inspiration (in real life she's ninety-five and does indeed run every morning).

I dislike when authors thank long lists of people most readers have never heard of, so please forgive what follows. But these are some wonderful writers whose names may soon be on your bookshelves or electronic devices—if they're not already. They've shared their talent, taste and patience through my countless rewrites and kept their sense of humor every time I asked, "Is this better, worse or exactly the same?" (It's amazing how many ways you can make something "exactly the same.")

So thank you to Stacey Luftig, Badria Jazairi, Jami Bernard, Stephen Gaydos, Kimberlee Auerbach Berlin, Andrea York, Frank Basloe, Nina Dec, Wendy Shanker, Amy Welsh-Hanning, Adam Szymkowicz, Janis Brody, Amy Klein, Anne Newgarden, and the entire Sunday writing group. And special thanks to

Susan Shapiro (who will turn to this page before reading the rest of the book) for pushing and prodding and being the big sister I never had (and didn't always want).

There's an additional list of people, without whom this book simply wouldn't exist, starting with Robert Woletz at the *Times*, whose generosity as an editor and a person is matched only by his impeccable judgment. Thanks to Heidi Giovine and Erika Sommer, without whom I never would have worked at the *Times* in the first place, and to Lois Smith Brady for setting an impossibly high standard in the art of writing wedding columns.

To the extraordinary Elizabeth Hayes for believing I had this book in me long before I did. To Rich Green for believing it could be a movie. To Ken Sandler, the Medici of the medical advertising world, and Jean Banks at BMI for supporting me all these years (and to the late Allan Becker for championing a twenty-three-year-old kid with a big dream).

To Julia Fleischaker, Erin Galloway, Katie McGowan, Cathy Gleason, Victoria Marini, Rosalind Parry and Adrian Garcia for all their effort on my behalf.

To Ruth Andrew Ellenson, Julie Doughty, Nicki Wheir and Kelly Macmanus for not only offering but coming through with vital help when it was needed most.

To June Cuddy, Vincent Mallozzi, LeAnn Wilcox and Nadine Brozan for welcoming me into the fraternity at 229 West Forty-third Street and educating me in its ways.

To Dr. Bruce Yaffe, Dr. Craig Antell and Dr. Sandra Engelson for keeping me healthy.

And to Stacey Luftig and Badria Jazairi for keeping me sane.

There are so many more people in my life, both personal and professional, who have offered crucial support and made me the writer (and person) I am today. However, as Gavin says in the book, "Everything in life is a choice." And I'm choosing to stop.

the wedding beat

devan sipher

Questions for Discussion

1. *The Wedding Beat* begins with a cry of "Help!" as Gavin Greene contends he's being held captive at a black-tie wedding. However, Gavin is both a skeptic and a romantic—sometimes in the same paragraph—and his romantic nature wins out time and again. What was it like reading a male's perspective on romance? Can you think of other fictional male protagonists who are romantics? Is this a trait you expect more from a female character? How did you feel about a man sharing his inner feelings and vulnerabilities about dating?

2. Gavin says that being alone is like having a scarlet letter, and it's the first thing people notice. Is he right about that? How hard is it to be single at a social event where everyone is married? Is that something that gets easier or more difficult with age?

3.   Mike Russo, the dating coach, compares dating to pollination and suggests that Gavin needs to "Be the bee." Is this good advice? Does Mike's bee theory reinforce old-fashioned stereotypes or does it acknowledge innate sex roles? Do you think this advice can be inverted for women? Is being "the flower" the way for women to attract the best mate? If a guy's not willing to be the bee, does it mean "he's just not that into you"?

4.   Even when Gavin's love life is a mess, he sustains an intimate relationship with Hope. Does their relationship help or hinder them when it comes to finding love? Though Gavin and Hope aren't physically attracted to each other, should they have tried dating each other?

5.   Laurel says the reason Gavin's alone is his fear of ending up like his parents. Is that a reasonable fear for him to have? Do you think Gavin is being accurate and fair in his description of his parents? At Bernie's funeral their behavior is particularly over-the-top. Does dealing with death bring that out in families? Are there any examples you've witnessed?

6.   Why does Gavin have less conflict with his grandmother than with his parents? Why does her devotion to Bernie seem to frighten him? What does Gavin mean when he says he feels like he's mourning the younger version of his grandmother? Have you ever felt that way about an elderly family member while they were still alive?

7.   Melinda says she believes in doing one thing every day that scares her. Is that a healthy approach to life or a good way to get yourself killed? Over the course of the book, Melinda's

adventurousness seems to rub off on Gavin. As he climbs her fire escape he says, "Something about Melinda made me want to be better than I was. Braver. And a little stupider." Is that how love should feel or is that a romanticized ideal?

8. Does Gavin romanticize love because he writes about weddings, or does he write about weddings because of his romantic nature? Halfway through the book, Gavin gets accosted by Mike Russo's best man, Brody, who accuses Gavin of writing fairy tales. Is Gavin contributing to the fantasy version of weddings that proliferates in movies, magazines and Web sites? How do such fantasies affect the expectations of married and single people?

9. At the Malibu wedding of Roxanne and Ari, Gavin describes "a petting zoo, where bleating sheep wore pink ribbons round their necks. It was a cross between wedding kitsch and animal cruelty." Which do you think it is? What's the most outlandish thing you ever saw at a wedding? Would you have liked to attend any of the weddings described in this book? If so, which? Would you like to have Gavin's job? Would you enjoy attending weekly galas, or would you find it frustrating having to work at lavish parties where you can't eat or drink?

10. What did you think of the strict professional and ethical standards at The Paper? Did it surprise you that those standards would apply to articles about weddings? How long do you think those standards will last in the world of continuous online news as old-school journalists like Renée retire or get laid off?

11. Do you feel Gavin and his peers were too submissive about the layoffs? How much should one put up with to keep a job? Do you believe Renée when she says it's the best job on the planet? Why do you think she feels that way even after how she's treated?

12. Throughout the book Gavin has a hard time making choices unless he's able to fact-check first. But when he sees Melinda in her wedding dress, he says, "Everything in life is a choice, and I was choosing to be happy." What do you think he means by that? How does a person choose to be happy? Do you think Gavin and Melinda will be happy together?

PHOTO BY STACEY LUFTIG

Devan Sipher has been writing about weddings for the *New York Times*'s "Vows" column for more than five years. He received a master of fine arts from the Tisch School of the Arts at New York University, and he lives in New York City.